HIS ONLY WIFE

HIS
ONLY
WIFE

a novel by

PEACE ADZO MEDIE

ALGONQUIN BOOKS
OF CHAPEL HILL
2020

388 0418

Published by
ALGONQUIN BOOKS OF CHAPEL HILL
Post Office Box 2225
Chapel Hill, North Carolina 27515-2225

a division of
WORKMAN PUBLISHING
225 Varick Street
New York, New York 10014

LIBRARY OF CONGRESS CATALOGING-IN-PUBLICATION DATA

Names: Medie, Peace A., author.
Title: His only wife : a novel / by Peace Adzo Medie.
Description: First edition. | Chapel Hill : Algonquin Books of
Chapel Hill, 2020. | Summary: "An intelligent and funny debut
about a relatable, indomitable heroine: a young seamstress in
Ghana who agrees to an arranged marriage, only to realize that some
compromises are too extreme to accept, illuminating what it means
to be a woman in a rapidly changing world"— Provided by publisher.
Identifiers: LCCN 2020009732 | ISBN 9781616209155 (hardcover) |
ISBN 9781643751115 (e-book)
Subjects: LCSH: Marriage—Ghana—Fiction. |
Women—Ghana—Social conditions—Fiction.
Classification: LCC PR9379.9.M39 H57 2020 | DDC 823.92—dc23
LC record available at https://lccn.loc.gov/2020009732]

10 9 8 7 6 5 4 3 2 1
First Edition

For my grandmother,
Madam Juliana Mansa Tsekumah

HIS ONLY WIFE

ONE

Elikem married me in absentia; he did not come to our wedding. The ceremony was held on the third Saturday in January in the rectangular courtyard of my Uncle Pious's house, which was bordered by two-roomed apartments and a wooden gate that opened onto a busy footpath. Our relatives, stirring with equal measures of happiness, but for different reasons, sat opposite one another on rented plastic chairs that were neatly arranged in rows that filled the courtyard. The partly walled kitchen had been scrubbed and cleared of the cast-iron coal pots, on which my uncle's wives prepared the evening meal, and of the enamel basins that they used for washing and storing dishes. My uncle's sitting-room chairs, upholstered with a carpet-like fabric and polished so that the chocolate-brown wooden frames glistened, were also brought outdoors and comprised the front row where the elders of each family would sit.

Before the guests arrived, my Uncle Pious, who was my *togã*, my late father's oldest brother, deposited his bulk into a chair, beaming, as though he was the one to be married. He was flanked by his two younger brothers, my uncles Bright and Excellent. Togã Pious's chiseled face, with bushy eyebrows that grew in every direction, did not match his soft body. His smile resembled a grimace. That morning as he sat in his itchy armchair, his blue *kente* cloth had come loose, slid down his arm, and pooled around the elastic waistband of his culottes so that his fleshy chest was on display. He didn't bother to pull the cloth back up. Other uncles and older male cousins, about fifteen of them, shoulders high with unearned authority, settled into three rows of plastic chairs behind Togã Pious. They all longed to be in his position so much that they had begun to imitate him. They copied his guffaw, which was usually accompanied by several thigh slaps and followed by a loud, drawn out, woooohoooo; they snapped their fingers like him when they wanted attention, and when that didn't work, they whistled. Today, they were ready to support him in executing his head-of-family duties, as though he would need help in stretching out his hands to receive the bottles of schnapps, cash-stuffed envelopes, and gaily wrapped parcels that my soon-to-be in-laws would present. The youngest and most inconsequential among the cousins would, of course, be displaced by my older aunties when the ceremony began.

But for now, most of the women were in my grand-aunt's house, which sat opposite Togã Pious's. They were bustling around in her roofless kitchen, preparing the food that would be served after the ceremony. When I had visited earlier, there had been okro soup, reddened with palm oil, bubbling in a cavernous pot on a clay stove. My father's sister, Sylvia, who lived in Togo and only visited on special occasions, shoved several twigs into the clay stove to turn up the heat and then scooted away with a yelp when sparks began to fly. The sparks still dotted the air when someone broke out in song, which the others picked up and sang, repeating verses until the soup began to boil over into the wood fire, the smoke sending everyone into a coughing fit. Despite the smoke, the air in the kitchen was thick with the aroma of spices and herbs that tickled my nose. The women shooed me out of the kitchen when I began to sneeze repeatedly, and I reluctantly returned to Tɔgā Pious's house where the others were also hard at work.

A few of them meandered among the chairs, their hands heavy with branded handkerchiefs, bottle openers, mugs, and picture frames that had been stuffed into small, multicolored gift bags and were being lined up on a table draped in a white tablecloth. These were gifts intended as souvenirs for the wedding guests. My mother had selected Nancy, my ferocious cousin who had just completed secondary school, to oversee the souvenirs table. She could be trusted to drive away those guests who would tuck their gift bags into the folds of their cloths and come back for second, third, or even fourth helpings. It was also especially good that she could control the children who were always underfoot, no matter how many times they were shooed away.

I watched Nancy through the black window bars of Tɔgā Pious's sitting room, her face a frown of concentration, as she carefully counted each colorful bag that was placed on the table. I'd never seen her so focused on anything, but then, this was the first time that something of this magnitude had happened to us. Mawusi, one of Tɔga Pious's daughters and the cousin to whom I was closest, strode out of the bedroom and began dabbing my face. My eyelids fluttered closed as the white handkerchief, which she wielded like a surgical tool, migrated from the bridge of my nose to my forehead. It was immediately replaced by a sponge from a compact that she had fished out of a small rhine-stone-encrusted clutch tucked into her armpit.

"It's enough," I said in protest as she lightly brushed my checks. This was the fifth time that she had touched up my makeup in the last hour. I couldn't have been sweating that much; I wasn't nervous, not then anyway. I was mostly weary. Since my mother told me that I would be marrying Eli, I had felt as though I was balancing our two families like a basin of water, which was full to the brim, on my head. It wasn't easy being the key to other people's happiness, their victory, and their vindication. I desperately wanted the wedding to be over because then I would have done my part. Or, rather, I would have begun to do my part.

"Ah, it's okay, you're only adding to my stress with all this makeup," I protested when Mawusi's hand and the makeup sponge continued to hover in my face.

"Stress? Haven't I told you to relax? There's nothing to be stressed about. You should be happy and smiling." She was glaring at a small pimple on my chin as she spoke.

"You make everything sound so simple. I barely know the man. And what if things don't work out, what if this marriage doesn't make him leave the woman, what if it doesn't bring him closer to his family, what if I let everyone down? His family? My mother? This whole town? I couldn't sleep last night just thinking about this," I said in a whisper, because we weren't alone.

"Everybody says he's a good man so there's no need to be afraid."

I sighed heavily, not caring that she was standing so close that I was exhaling into her face. My cousin was obviously too overcome with excitement to have a proper conversation. In fact, it was as if she wasn't even listening to me. As soon as she freed me, I lowered myself onto a coffee table to give some relief to my feet, which were crammed into cream, pointed-toe pencil heels.

"Is it clean?" I heard my mother call out from across the room. She was overseeing the stacking of plates onto the dining table. The plates would be used to serve Eli's mother, his uncles, his siblings, and their special guests from Accra. They would eat plates of fried rice, grilled chicken and pork, and vegetable salad, inside the house at the table, unlike the others, who would eat their *akple* and goat-meat okro soup outside, where they had watched the ceremony. The caterer would soon return with the chafing dishes; my mother had placed the fried rice order herself, reluctant to leave this task to my aunties who were in charge of the food.

I sprang to my feet as she bustled over to us in her floor-length, fitted skirt.

"Give me the handkerchief," she snapped at Mawusi, who was still shadowing me and now appeared to be stricken with guilt; she had failed in her duties as my attendant. My mother folded the handkerchief to hide the side that was covered with brown face powder and began carefully dabbing at my lace-covered backside. She couldn't risk any of the sequins coming loose.

"Afinɔ, let me do it," Mawusi offered, but my mother swatted her hand away.

Mawusi flinched and looked at me with a mix of exasperation and pain. "Don't mind her," I mouthed. Three months before, I wouldn't have been afraid to give sound to my words but now I dared not. This wedding was so important and my mother so anxious that all go according to plan that I expected her to throw a fit at any moment.

She wanted everything to work out perfectly: for Eli to be satisfied with me; for Eli's mother, Aunty Faustina Ganyo, to get back her son; for us to enjoy the status that would surely come with being tied, by marriage, to the Ganyos. Aunty had done so much for us. When my father died ten years before, in 2004, we were forced out of the government bungalow and most of our valuables seized by those who claimed, without showing any proof, that my father owed them money. It was Aunty who offered us one of her properties, a two-bedroom house with an indoor bathroom and kitchen. Meanwhile, Tɔgã Pious had sat back, his gut resting on his thighs, lamenting the lack of rooms in our family's compound and the tenants' refusal to move out after their leases expired. It was also Aunty who gave my mother a job as a saleswoman in her flour-distribution depot, without my mother even asking. And the woman wasn't even a relative or a friend! We, of course, knew of her like everyone else in Ho. We knew that she wasn't the only rich businesswoman in town but was the most generous and never hesitated to help those in need. We were used to seeing her white Pajero drive down the main road, the driver in the front with her nestled near the door in the back. I had attended the Christmas parties she threw every year for the town's children. The ones—initially held on the lawn of Parks and Gardens but later moved to the stadium when the regional minister timidly lamented the bald patches that our feet left behind in the grass—where you could drink as many cups of chilled *leha*, the sugary corn drink, as you wanted, and each child was sent home with a small transparent plastic bag of doughnuts, chips, and toffees. And my mother was a member of the Women's Guild, of which Aunty had been president for so many years that no one remembered her predecessor or cared to schedule new elections.

"God bless her!" my mother would say as she admired a sack of maize or some other gift that Aunty's driver had dropped off. Half of our morning devotion was spent entrusting Aunty into God's hands and praying for her cup to overflow. When I was younger I would imagine, with great concern, Aunty neck-deep in supernatural water as a hovering golden chalice rained even more water down on her head.

"Father, let your blessings flow, overwhelm her with your love, overtake her with your grace," my mother would plead, a tremor in her voice.

But my mother had never imagined that she, Afinɔ, Afi's mother, would ever be able to repay Aunty's kindness, until Aunty proposed marriage between our families. So now she carefully smoothed the sleeves of my shimmery boat-neck top, and directed Mawusi to hold up the slippery, cream fabric of my slit so that the hemline wouldn't drag on the linoleum.

THE CRIES OF *"mia woezor"* rang out, an enthusiastic welcome that couldn't have been for anyone other than Aunty. She and her entourage had arrived.

My mother shooed me into the bedroom before breezing out the door. "Don't let anyone see you," she warned before she shut the door.

I thought for a moment about my mother's transformation. It was like she was a different woman. She had on a shiny black wig, styled into a bob, which she had bought on her shopping trip to Accra, her first since my father's death. Her off-shoulder *kaba* and the fish-tailed slit were made of a white-and-blue wax-print fabric, which marked her as the mother of the bride. Blue clay beads, which had once belonged to my maternal grandmother, adorned her neck and wrists, and her kitten-heel slip-ons matched the white satin of her purse. It had been a long time since she had looked so elegant.

I could hear everything going on in the courtyard because Eli's younger brother, Richard, had insisted on microphones. He's also the one who hired the *tsiami*, the spokesman who came from Accra, along with the videographer and photographers who thrust their cameras in my face throughout the day to capture my every expression for Eli's viewing.

The ceremony began with greetings; Eli's older brother, Fred, who tirelessly campaigned with the president during the last presidential election and was now a deputy minister of transport and a real-estate mogul, sought permission to greet my relatives. After the greeting, he announced their mission.

"We have seen a beautiful flower in this house, a bright and fragrant flower that we have come to pluck," he said to cheers. Of course, the guests would have cheered at any word that came out of Fred's mouth. He was an important man, after all, and regardless of what he said, they knew they would be celebrating my marriage to his brother. The *tsiami* had to shush them.

"*Yoo*, welcome to our house," Tↄgā Pious responded to the mission statement, his voice shaking with giddiness. It wasn't a small thing to have a minister in your house, a minister who often appeared at the president's side on the evening news. Now here he was asking something of us. The *tsiami* joked that prayers would have to be said before any flowers were plucked. One of the men from our clan, a calabash of palm wine in hand and his cloth knotted around his waist, poured libation to the gods. Father Wisdom, ever efficient, immediately followed with a short prayer. I'm sure the guests were grateful for the brevity. After the prayers, Fred presented two bottles of schnapps to Tɔgã Pious. Next, he gave gifts to my relatives, Tɔgã Pious first.

"*Agoo,*" the *tsiami* began, demanding everyone's attention; we all wanted to see what the Ganyos, with all their money, would bring. We had given them a modest list of the gifts we wanted but there had been talk that instead of two bottles of schnapps they would give ten boxes of Black Label whiskey, and instead of a gift-wrapped suitcase stuffed with panties, bras, yards of cloth, nightgowns, necklaces and earrings, and the other basics that every woman needs when starting a new life, they would come with a gift-wrapped 4x4 vehicle, the interior of which would be a mini-boutique. I will confess that I broke into a wide smile at that bit of gossip.

"First, here are the drinks. Five more bottles of schnapps! Five crates of soft drinks! Five crates of beer! Five crates of Guinness! Two gallons of palm wine!" the *tsiami* boomed, as though he were announcing the prizes on a game show. He then invited my relatives to inspect the bride price that my soon-to-be husband, through his siblings, had brought and placed in another room in the house. My aunty Sylvia, who was my father's only sister, and other women from my father's side,

went in to inspect the items. They came out about five minutes later and told the *tsiami* that all was in order, the Ganyos
had not disappointed. In fact, they had done way more than
requested.

"Papa, we know how you have suffered for your daughter,
so we are not simply going to take her away like that. No, not at
all," the *tsiami* intoned. "We know that it is not a small thing to
raise a good daughter in today's Ghana. One who is respectful
and humble, despite her looks," he continued, to murmurs of
agreement. "A daughter who has both school education and
home education, a daughter who can read a book and cook
a tasty pot of soup." He paused for dramatic effect. "That is
why we did not come with small gifts. We came with gifts that
match the work you have done!" The *tsiami*'s voice rose to
cries of "*Yueh!*" from the eager guests. "We came with spec-
tacular gifts, magnificent gifts, gargantuan gifts," he cried to
fervid applause and ululation. "Shhhhhh," he whispered half-
heartedly. After the noise died down, there was the rustling of
paper as the gifts changed hands and then Tɔgã Pious's breathy
"*akpe, akpe, akpe*" repeated until the *tsiami* interrupted him.
I'm sure he would have continued thanking the Ganyos all day
if the *tsiami* hadn't stopped him. I wouldn't have been surprised
if my dear uncle collapsed into a quivering mound of joy. Of
course he was happy to receive a reward for work he had never
bothered to do.

It was then my mother's turn.

"We know it's not easy being a mother; carrying your
daughter for nine months, feeding her, running to the hospital
when malaria struck, soothing her when she cried, traveling to

Kpando to visit her in boarding school. We know it's a difficult job and you have done it well; that is why we have brought these things for you. We thank you for taking care of her for us," the *tsiami* said, his voice less playful; someone must have told him our story of hardship. My mother's thank you was as effusive as Tɔgã Pious's but the *tsiami* didn't interrupt her. I didn't have to see her face to know the joy she was feeling; her sacrifice was being acknowledged by important people in front of those who had once thought nothing of her.

Fred, through the *tsiami*, presented more gifts. White envelopes to the other uncles for helping Tɔgã Pious raise me and to the aunts for minding me when my mother was away. There were gifts to the older cousins for holding my hand on the way to school and to the younger cousins for playing with me after school. It was only after this that Aunty Sylvia ushered Mawusi into the gathering.

"Here she is," I heard Aunty Sylvia declare playfully, a minute later, before adding, "Are you saying she's not the one?" There was laughter and then a chorus of "No." "Okay, I will go fetch her, but you have to give me something small. I have to cross a bridge to get to where she is and there is a tollbooth," Aunty Sylvia said slyly. There was more laughter and a long pause—during which I imagined one of the Ganyos handing a few notes to Aunty Sylvia. This time she and my mother came into the room in which I was waiting.

"Are you ready?" my mother asked as Aunty Sylvia waited in the doorway.

I nodded and then swallowed loudly.

"Don't be afraid," my mother said, reaching for my hand.

I nodded again and squeezed her hand until mine hurt. We both flinched. I was afraid.

"Afi, there's no reason to worry, no reason to be afraid. You have made me so proud. You have wiped away my tears, you have removed my shame. Because of you, those who laughed at me are now laughing with me. May God bless you, my daughter," she said, a hitch in her breath.

"Yes," Aunty Sylvia said under her breath, reluctant to interrupt the moment but impatient to move things along.

I hugged my mother tightly.

"Your makeup," she said and pulled away when my face touched her hair.

"The people are waiting," Aunty Sylvia reminded us softly when it seemed like I would not let go of my mother.

She and my mother, each holding a freshly manicured hand, then led me outside to ululation, applause, and somewhere in the back, the rhythmic rattles of an *axatse*.

They deposited me in front of our two families. I was acutely aware of every eye inspecting me for flaws. I searched for Aunty. She sat plump and dignified in the front row, her *kaba* and slit made of a fabric too unremarkable to recall, a thin gold chain culminating in a small, unshaped nugget at the base of her throat. She was flanked by her sons; Fred, big with muscles, sat at her right, and Richard, smaller and rounder, the stand-in for Eli, was comfortably tucked into the chair to her left. An almost-blind paternal uncle, representing Eli's late father's side of the family, also occupied the front row. Aunty's only daughter, Yaya, dressed in lace that rivaled mine and a glittering head-tie modeled after a hexagon, sat in the second row with other relatives. Fred's wife, Cecelia, sat beside her in a less eye-catching ensemble. I followed my mother's lead and shook their hands before greeting my relatives. My heart began to beat faster when I took my seat beside Richard. I think I would have been less apprehensive if Eli himself had been present. Then I would have known what he really thought of me. Aunty had told me that Eli was happy to be marrying me. Indeed, when he called my phone from Hong Kong, he had said that he looked forward to spending time with me. He had apologized for having to miss our wedding, a last-minute change of plans. There was pressing overseas business that required his attention. But that had been such a short conversation and there had been so much static on the line that he sounded like a robot.

Eli had always been a distant figure. He was the son who lived overseas; the most successful of the three brothers but the least visible. He had attended senior secondary school thirteen years before I did and had graduated from the university while my hair was still cropped short in the style of a schoolgirl. I saw him once during the long vacation when he visited the flour depot where I would go to help my mother. I remember him smiling kindly at me, or in my direction, and sending one of the shop boys to buy a bottle of Coke for every worker. I had been in awe of him; after all, he was Aunty's son. The son who wore starched khaki shorts that revealed the length of his sturdy legs and a Lacoste shirt that hugged the muscles of his chest and biceps; who drove a Peugeot 504, which had once been used to ferry his mother around town; who was about to graduate from the university. The man who might one day own the house we lived in and the store that employed my mother. How could I not be in awe? And now, how could he not be at our wedding? I knew that men were sometimes unable to attend, but it was usually because of issues beyond their control: expired visas and resident permits, insufficient funds to afford plane tickets for themselves and their new brides, poor health. But I had never heard of a man missing his wedding because of a business trip. What kind of business keeps a man away from his own wedding?

This question had been bouncing around in my head since the Hong Kong call. Now as Father Wisdom blessed the Bible and the gold band that Richard had brought, the crushing doubt seeped back into my chest. What had I gotten myself into? Would I be able to do what had been requested of me? Requested by Aunty, by my mother, by every guest here? To my right, my mother smiled widely. That unfettered smile, which I hadn't seen in almost a decade, was the embodiment of years of hope, previously buried by death, by the stresses of life. Across from me, Aunty's round face was reposed, at rest; the face of a woman satisfied at having solved her greatest problem. Around me her people buzzed with excitement; thanks to me, their man would soon be theirs again.

If Eli had been there, I would have known with certainty from the pride on his face as his sister presented me with two large rolling suitcases wrapped in sparkly gift paper, extras packed with clothes and shoes. I would have known from his satisfied smile when I answered "Yes" to Tɔgã Pious's question: "Afi, should we accept the schnapps they brought?" I would have known from how tightly he hugged me after he gave me the Bible and slid the ring on my finger and how hearty his "Amen" was when Father Wisdom blessed our marriage and reminded me to be a respectful and loving wife. Instead I had to make do with Richard. And I had to continue to wonder.

Four hours later and it was over. The guests had eaten and drunk, after which some protested that they hadn't had enough food, or enough drinks, or enough gifts. They wanted some of the restaurant food that was being eaten inside, by the chosen few, at a table with forks and knives. They wanted take-away packs that would feed them for supper. This was a Ganyo wedding after all. Nancy's scowl eventually sent them on their way but not before they grabbed what they could: one grilled tilapia wrapped in a paper towel and then in a headscarf, a glass shoved into a purse, a set of cutlery slipped into a gift bag, two plastic chairs hidden behind a water drum from where they would later be retrieved and placed in Tɔgã Pious's bedroom. Everyone had to get something out of this union.

We left Tɔgã Pious's house in Aunty's car. I was tired and my feet were sore; I wanted nothing more than to ease into bed and stay there for a long time, but my mother and my in-laws wouldn't allow it. We were on our way to Aunty's where the family would call Eli and share the details of the day. They would send him the pictures and video later. After that, the driver would take Aunty, my mother, and me to the parish where we would meet with Father Wisdom to ensure that all was set for Sunday mass where our union would be blessed. My mother and I would begin packing after mass; Aunty wanted us to leave for Accra as soon as possible.

"You are his wife now, you have to live in his house," she said in her calm but firm way when I climbed into the back seat between her and my mother. Children waved and cheered as we set off, gift bags from the wedding littered the ground around them. Aunty waved back. "You have to claim your rightful place," she added when she turned away from the window. She didn't have to say that at present my place was being occupied by the Liberian woman, a woman who wasn't Eli's wife, who despised his family, who looked down on our ways. She didn't have to say it because we all knew. It was what kept us up at night, what woke us up with a start at dawn. It was the problem I had been chosen to solve.

TWO

On Monday, I slept past midday. I had never slept past midday. My mother would never allow it. I had heard her sweeping at dawn when I woke up to empty my bladder, which pulsed with the Malta Guinness I had downed at the reception held after the church service the day before. It had always been my job to sweep up the brown, withered leaves of the almond trees in our small, unfenced dirt yard while the morning coolness still buffeted us from the approaching heat. Only three years at a public boarding school, several towns away, had gotten me out of this chore in the past, and now marriage, marriage to Eli Ganyo. I realized, then, that I didn't know my name. Was I now Mrs. Afi Ganyo or still Afi Tekple? Did the "Mrs." and the new last name only come with a church wedding or could a traditional wedding, like what we held in Tɔgã Pious's house, confer these changes? I don't think anyone in either of our families had thought of this. To them what mattered was that I was recognized as his wife before our people and before God. But my father, if he were alive, would have insisted on me getting a marriage certificate.

My father, Illustrious Tekple, had been a stickler for legitimacy, for doing things the way they should be done. He had married my mother at the registrar's office, when many people didn't mind not having their marriage officially recognized by the state, and had proudly displayed their marriage certificate in our bungalow, assigned to us by the Ministry of Roads and Highways where he had worked as a road engineer. He had allowed only one of his nephews, Mawusi's oldest half-brother, Dodzi, to live with us because it wasn't right to cram too many people into a small house, and because my mother had insisted.

"But your sitting room is there, your kitchen floor is there," Tɔgã Pious, his most demanding brother, had declared in protest, his face scrunched up until it resembled the wrinkled, toffee-colored exterior of a tiger nut. "Even your verandah is there, it has a roof," he had added, leaving my father to wonder if that last part was meant as a joke. They were in the sitting room and I was hiding behind the doorway curtain, eavesdropping at the behest of my mother, but also because I was a nosy eight-year-old and knew that my uncle walked hand-in-hand with drama.

"*Fo* Pious, first of all, having too many people in such a small house is a health hazard. And also think about my wife, my daughter—I can't force them to share our small house with so many people. You know how women are. My wife needs to move freely in the house. How is she supposed to cook in the kitchen when my relatives are sleeping in there?"

Tɔgã Pious had shaken his head slowly in disbelief at the foolishness of his brother, the kind of foolishness that plagued Ghanaians who spent too much time in school. "What is health hazard? And why will my children living in their uncle's house bother his wife? Are you not their uncle? Is your house not also their house? How much space does Afinɔ need? And Afi, small like that, how much space does she need?" He bounced his upturned palms in front of his chest in a motion that straddled a plea and an interrogation. At that time he had eleven children by his three wives and operated a small poultry farm, which was mostly worked by the women and children. He had taken over my grandfather's compound house years before, while the old man was still alive, and had since divided the rooms among his wives and children. He would later rent out two of the chamber and hall apartments when the older children moved out, and he kept the proceeds, even though those apartments rightfully belonged to his four younger siblings, including my father and his sister, Sylvia.

"That brother of yours! Even if we gave him half of everything we have, he wouldn't be satisfied," my mother had complained to my father when she returned from the market one day to find a second cousin, his meager belongings in a jute bag, awaiting her on the porch. "What kind of man expects other people to raise his children for him when he is perfectly able to do so himself? Are you supposed to carry everybody's burden because you receive a salary? Isn't the money that he gets from selling his chickens the same color as the money the government pays you?" she had shouted in the bedroom I shared with them, not caring that my two cousins, pretending to watch TV in the sitting room, could hear her.

"Olivia, don't forget that *Fo* Pious paid my school fees in the university."

"And so what? Is he the first person to look after a sibling? Which older brother or sister has not sacrificed something for the younger ones? Do you have to spend the rest of your life repaying him? Do you now have to shoulder all of his responsibilities?"

"It's okay," my father said in an effort to quiet her.

"It's okay that your brother is turning my house into a boarding school?"

"Olivia, remember that he's my older brother," my father said gravely. Even at that age I knew that he agreed with my mother but was reluctant to speak out against his brother.

"And remember that I'm your wife!"

After this exchange, my father drove one of my cousins back to Tɔgã Pious's, on the other side of town; he would pay his school fees but the boy would have to live with his father. Tɔgã Pious had angrily accepted this offer and then proceeded to tell every person who cared to listen—and that was everyone we knew—about how his brother's wife had driven the boy out of his uncle's house. So when my father died and the ministry people gave us one week to vacate the bungalow, Tɔgã Pious and all who had listened to his story stood with hands on their hips, rocking from side to side and whispering to one another: "Let's see where she will go."

When the ministry people heaped our belongings in front of the brown metal gates of the house, it was Mawusi and her mother, *Daavi* Christy, who came to help us cart them to Tɔgã Pious's house. My mother placed a plastic tub full of dishes on each of our heads and we set off down the road, doing our best to ignore the stares of those who had come to witness our misfortune, and chatting about what my new life in our family house would look like. We made two trips back and forth that day and would have done more if some members of the Women's Guild hadn't rented a truck to move the rest of the things. Tɔgã Pious hadn't lifted a finger to help us, and he was supposed to be my father, now that my father was no more.

My mother didn't have people she could turn to. She had family, of course. Everyone has relatives somewhere. But she didn't have immediate family. Both her parents were long gone and her two sisters had died of something mysterious many years before. The aunt who had raised her now lived in the north with her son. I knew that even though we were surrounded by a large family, we had nobody.

IT WAS MAWUSI's mother, *Daavi* Christy, who stepped in and offered to take us in. For close to a year, my mother and I shared a room with *Daavi* Christy, Mawusi, and her two younger brothers, Godsway and Godfred. Our mothers shared the only bed in the room while the rest of us slept on mattresses on the floor. The boys, already unhappy about having to share the room with their mother and sister, had stuck out their lips for the first few days and when that hadn't made us move out, they had repeatedly crisscrossed the room and stepped on me each time they did. Simultaneous knocks on their heads, delivered by *Daavi* Christy, had put an end to their protest.

It was during that time that Mawusi and I became best friends. We would place our mattresses side by side in the center of the room, in line with the open shutters where there was some hope of a breeze, and talk deep into the night, after our mothers and her brothers had fallen asleep. We came up with answers to questions that we didn't dare ask any adult: Mawusi's newest half-brother was born with a crooked leg because his mother kicked a goat when she was pregnant. Tɔgã Pious had slapped one of Mawusi's teenage half-sisters and then sent her away to live with our relatives in Kpando because she had been caught grinding a Guinness bottle with the intention of drinking the glassy solution to force out the baby in her belly. Tɔgã Pious was planning to build a bathroom with a flush toilet for himself; the rest of us would have to keep queuing at the public latrine at the bottom of our street. The woman who sold neatly cut squares of newspaper at the public latrine was a witch. In fact, she was queen of the witches. She had an open sore on her upper arm that wouldn't heal because her witch friends licked it in homage when they had their evil meetings in the highest treetops at midnight. "Make sure you don't touch her hand when you pay for your paper," we warned each other worriedly. We both suffered from severe stomach pains that year due to our attempts to defy nature and avoid going to the public latrine.

We had even more to talk about when my mother transferred me to the public primary school that Mawusi attended. I was fortunate to get a spot in her class and in the morning stream for that first term. Mawusi made the move easier. Still, it took me a while to adjust to the challenges of state-funded education: sitting three to a desk meant for two; teachers who mangled their tenses and articles so badly that the headmaster didn't complain when lessons were delivered in Eʋe instead of English; hours spent weeding teachers' yards and cultivating their farms and gardens in lieu of class; and the abandon with which the teachers wielded their canes. The slightest infraction, and a cane would land on my back with a force and speed that would leave my eyes smarting and finger-sized red welts on my pale skin. It was a far cry from the private school my father had paid for when he was alive. But I didn't complain because I knew to do so would only remind my mother of what we had lost.

Although we had never been rich, we had always been comfortable, definitely more comfortable than most of our relatives, neighbors, and friends. This is why the reversal in our fortunes was so hard on my mother. Indeed, she had become increasingly despondent as a result of the change in our circumstances. Although grateful to *Daavi* Christy for taking us in, she disliked having to depend on her because it reminded her of how far we had fallen. Just a few weeks before, we had been in the middle class but now poverty was aggressively nipping at our heels. No one could have predicted this!

"I should have paid more attention to what your father was doing with our money," my mother had lamented to me during a trip to Asigãme, the Big Market, where she had been unable to afford most of what we needed: beef, rice, milk, margarine, milo. She had always known that my father spent a great deal of money on his brothers and their families. But because we were always well provided for, she had never harped on the issue. She had only demanded that he begin building a house on a piece of land that had belonged to her parents and was now hers. But all my father had done was pay for one hundred cement blocks to be deposited on the land. If only she had pressured him to build that house. If only she had insisted that he save a portion of his salary. If only she had treated her cake and meat pie business as more than a hobby, she wouldn't be sharing a bed with *Daavi* Christy and I wouldn't be sleeping on a mattress on the floor. She repeated these regrets to me like a children's story so that I too began to share them, to wish that I had not participated in the squandering of this money with trips to Accra to buy patent leather shoes with shiny buckles, and poufy dresses trimmed with lace. I regretted my packed lunches that could feed me and two other classmates and the superfluous pocket money that had accompanied those lunches. So much wasted, and now my poor mother had been reduced to eating from another woman's pot.

MAWUSI, ALSO EXHAUSTED from the wedding planning and execution, came by the Monday after my wedding and squeezed in beside me on my twin bed. It reminded me of the nights we spent on student mattresses on her mother's bedroom floor. How things had changed! I think we were both still in disbelief at my new position: wife of Elikem Ganyo. Nonetheless, my worries and fears were never far away and spilled out as soon as she made herself comfortable.

"I know I've said it many times before but it's strange being married to a man I don't know. What if we don't get along? What if we are wrong for each other? What will I do then?"

"But you know him, we all know him."

"Not the way a wife knows her husband. He could be nice in public and a monster in private. A lot of people are like that!"

"That's true, but if you think about it, every marriage is a gamble, even if you've known the person your entire life. That's why there are so many divorces. But I really don't think you should worry about this. I've never heard anyone in this town speak ill of your husband, people have only nice things to say about him. Even my father who doesn't say anything nice about anyone!"

"Hmmm. My husband?"

"Ah, why are you saying it like that? Isn't he your husband?"

"We don't have a marriage certificate. I don't even know if I'm a 'Mrs.'"

"But you don't need a marriage certificate to be married. Many people only do the traditional wedding, they don't bother to register it. Yet they live together as husband and wife and everyone knows that they are husband and wife."

"Everyone minus the law."

"If it bothers you so much then go and register your marriage when your husband returns."

"Look, I'm already tired with all this marriage business—church marriage, marriage in the registrar's office, traditional marriage. I feel like I need to read a book to understand it all. In fact, there's something I was thinking about before you came. Is there a limit to how many wives a man is allowed in a traditional marriage?"

"Limit? I don't think so. Actually, I don't know. But that is irrelevant here."

"Why?"

"Because it's clear that your husband isn't the type of man to go around accumulating wives. Didn't his mother herself have to find you for him and arrange this whole thing? Don't waste your time imagining problems for yourself. Tell me, what are you going to do when you get to Accra?" She was so close that I could count the tiny bumps that had formed around her hairline when the hairdresser braided her hair too tightly. We even looked alike; she was a browner version of me, dimples and all.

"What do you mean?"

"You're not just going to sit in a house in Accra."

"Me? Sit in a house?" I wanted to attend a fashion school in Accra and learn to design and sew the kind of outfits that my new sister-in-law, Yaya, wore. I wanted to have my own store, built with cement—not a wooden kiosk—with a huge display window in the front and apprentices who worked for me. I wanted to experience a world outside of Ho, a world away from sewing the same three styles (for people who never remembered to bring money when they picked up their items) on our verandah, because I was still saving up to buy a kiosk, which, before Eli came into the picture, I had intended to mount on cement blocks beside our house.

Mawusi smiled when she heard my plans. "I can be your PR person," she said. We both had the same gap in our front teeth.

I laughed. "A seamstress with a PR person?"

"Not a seamstress, a designer! Don't you know that all those big designers in Accra have publicists?"

We interlinked our arms like we used to when we whispered about the boys we liked in school. This was all so exciting! Exciting and nerve-wracking. But we couldn't spend the entire day in bed giggling like children. I had to visit my uncle's houses, and the houses of several elders, to inform them that I was about to leave for Accra. I also had to pack for the trip. I managed to get out of bed and into the bathroom while Mawusi waited in my room. I heard my mother speaking to someone when I walked out of the bathroom; it was Yaya. The youngest of the Ganyo children, Yaya was slightly older than me, and had come to pay me a visit.

"Your sister is here," my mother called from the verandah before ushering the glamorous woman into my room. She held aside the doorway curtain for Yaya to enter, all the while disregarding my nakedness, which I was awkwardly covering with a cloth. Mawusi immediately excused herself and went to the sitting room. I had never had a problem being naked around other women, especially after three years of bathing in doorless bathroom stalls and changing in a dorm room with fourteen other girls. But there was something about Yaya that made me deeply aware of myself, of my words, my movements, my appearance. Maybe it was simply because she was Aunty's daughter. Or because of how she carefully chose her words. Or maybe it was because she had a degree from a South African university and had her clothes made by the First Lady's seamstress (this last bit of information came courtesy of Mawusi). Whatever it was, it made me feel like a child standing before a woman. A woman clad in a hip-hugging jean skirt and a red blouse that dipped low enough to show the top halves of her breasts.

"How are you feeling?" she asked kindly while seating herself on the edge of my unmade bed. I immediately felt that light but forceful thing inside me—I liked to believe that it was my spirit—shrink in embarrassment.

"I'm fine," I said, clutching both ends of my cloth, which I had knotted above my right breast. I didn't want to sit beside her so I propped my hip against a table, which held most of what I owned, including my chop box and trunk from boarding school. "You are the ones who worked yesterday," I said in Eυe, not knowing a comparable English greeting that would suitably express what I was required to say to her.

"It was nothing," she said in English, "besides, it was all you."

"Thank you," I said, not sure if that was the right response or if a response was even required. I pulled my cloth higher and she tried to take in my small room without moving her head, so that her eyes looked like they were slow-marching. I didn't even want to imagine what she was thinking about it all: the almost-transparent gecko frozen in a corner of the ceiling; the gray cement of the floor; the mismatched and faded curtains; the piece of tie-and-dye fabric that served as my bed sheet; my manual sewing machine on a low table behind the door; the odds and ends, including a portmanteau from the sixties and a new set of aluminum cooking pots, which my mother had stacked on the large table; my shoes, most of them secondhand, proudly lined up in three rows at the foot of my bed.

"You know," she began carefully, "*Fo* Eli has several houses in Accra."

I nodded even though I didn't fully comprehend. I knew that she was speaking about more than the number of houses that her brother owned. I wanted to ask her which one of them I would be living in but couldn't bring myself to speak up.

"That woman," she said, speaking hesitantly, and then stopped to inspect the rhinestones on my wedding shoes, which I had placed at my bedside. "That woman," she continued, finally lifting up her eyes to meet mine "has caused my mother so much pain. She has tried to rip our family apart. For what? What have we done to her? Do you know she prevented Eli from attending my mother's seventieth birthday party?" Her voice was hard but her eyes were moist. She swiped a manicured hand across her eyes and stood up abruptly. "I will see you in Accra," she said with a wide smile, before stretching out her arms to hug me. I stepped into her embrace with one hand still clutching the knot in my cloth. I spread myself out on the bed when she left, instantly tired all over again.

"What did she say?" Mawusi asked. She had come back into my room as soon as Yaya left.

"To be honest, I'm not even sure. I think she wanted to talk about her brother and the woman, but she didn't say much."

"That woman!" my cousin said, shaking her head.

"That woman," I repeated.

"Don't worry, you will free your husband from her."

"Amen."

Mawusi made me feel confident, at least temporarily, that I would succeed in extracting Eli from the woman's clutches. She'd always been able to reassure me, and it seemed like she had become wiser since she went to the university, so that now I valued her opinion even more than I had before. She was in her third year at the University of Cape Coast where she was studying for a degree in communications. I had envied her when she first began the university and I was stuck in Ho, apprenticing in Sister Lizzie's sewing shop. But here I was now, married to Aunty's son, Elikem Ganyo! She was helping me to comb the tangles out of my flowing hair, a product of a factory in Guangzhou, China. Our mothers' experiences had taught us a lot about marriage. She and I liked to argue about which of our mothers despised Tɔgā Pious more. I've lost count of the number of times I've heard *Daavi* Christy, Mawusi's mother, and the youngest of my uncle's wives, complain about him.

"I have never seen a man like this in my life! A man who is so stingy and heartless," she had told my mother when Tɔgā Pious refused to let us move into my father's apartment in our family house after my father died.

"All men are the same, they only know how to love themselves and to sit on women," she'd told us when Tɔgā Pious had refused to pay Mawusi's university tuition so that *Daavi* Christy was forced to sell all of her good cloths and beads for Mawusi to go to school. My mother had looked on disapprovingly as *Daavi*

Christy gave us her opinion of men. Even though she detested Tɔgã Pious, she knew that every man was not like my uncle. She had been married to one such man. More than anything, I wanted to be as fortunate as she had been.

I KNEW ABOUT the other woman when I accepted Aunty's marriage proposal. It was just another day in October and I had been at Tɔgã Pious's house with Mawusi when my mother called and told me to come home. I immediately knew it was important. She was stingy with her phone credits and usually only texted me. I returned to find her sitting on a low stool on the verandah with her legs stretched out in front of her.

"Sit down," she said, pointing to a stool beside her.

"What is wrong?"

"I said sit down."

I sat.

"What I'm going to tell you will not leave this house," she said, looking down at her feet.

"What?" I asked, alarmed.

"Nobody should hear what I'm going to tell you, not even Mawusi."

"Okay, nobody will hear."

She pulled my hand into her lap, held it there, and told me about a conversation she had had with Aunty less than an hour before. There was a long silence when she finished talking. I could tell she was waiting for me to speak.

"Did you hear me?" she snapped, clearly irritated at my silence.

"He wants to marry me?"

"He will want to marry you. His mother is sending her driver over this evening to come for some of your photos. He will want to marry you."

"How about his wife?"

"That woman, that terror, is not his wife."

"Fine. But he doesn't even know me."

"He will get to know you."

"When, before or after he marries me?"

She sucked her teeth and flung my hand out of her lap. "You are not a child so stop talking like a child. This is Elikem Ganyo we are talking about. The man whose verandah we are sitting on, whose store I work in. The man whose mother bought you an electric sewing machine. It doesn't matter whether he knows you or not, he will treat you well. I am your mother; why would I send you somewhere to suffer? I only want what is best for you," she said while wagging a finger in my face.

I eyed her, surprised at the force with which she spoke. Over the years, she and I had become more like friends than mother and daughter. There was nothing in her life that she didn't share with me and there was almost nothing that I didn't tell her. I found the finger-wagging and sternness to be annoying and a bit hurtful. I stood up and leaned on a column in a corner of the verandah, my arms folded.

"Ma, I don't know him; what if I don't like him?" I said in a low voice.

She sighed with her whole torso and then locked eyes with me. "Afi, don't forget who you are. You are not an actress and this is not a romance film. This is not one of those telenovelas you and Mawusi have been watching. This is real life. This is our life. You will get to know him and like him. That is how it is.

If you don't believe me you can go and ask any married woman you know. Ask any woman if she loved her husband before she got married, or even if she loves him now." She stood up slowly, as though in pain. "We are not ingrates and we are not foolish people. And remember what I told you, no one should hear about this until everything is finalized; not everyone who smiles with you wishes you well," she said before sliding her feet out of her slippers at the doorway and entering the house.

I remained on the verandah, seated on the banister, long after she had retired. The last thing I expected was a marriage proposal. It had been four months since my boyfriend had decided that he could only be happy with two women in his life and I just didn't want that. To be honest, it wasn't the cheating that drove me away; I didn't like him enough to care. But then the other girl had threatened to come to my house and cause a scene if I didn't leave her man alone, even though I started seeing the fool well before she came along. The last thing I needed was some idiot coming to reveal to my mother that I had a boyfriend.

Even though we shared a lot, I did not discuss my love life with my mother. I knew that she would disapprove. Despite my age (twenty-one), my mother would find it disrespectful for me to openly have a romantic relationship when I wasn't sure that it was going to lead to marriage. She wasn't like *Daavi* Christy who had, on more than one occasion, invited Mawusi's boyfriend, Yao, to their house to eat. My mother was old-fashioned and her place in the Women's Guild made it worse. She worried about what other women in the association would say about her. She never learned about Michael (or so I chose to believe), the man I had dated since my first year of secondary school. I was sixteen and he twenty-four when we first met in Kpando.

It was my first time away from home, and in a boarding school. The government had recently posted him to the local health center where he was an accountant. He was not the first man to want me, there was a long list, but he wasn't like the idiots who would follow me and make up poems about my buttocks as they walked behind me down the street. The age difference did not bother me. It was not unusual for some girls, especially when in boarding school and away from the policing of parents, to date older men who would drive to the school during weekend visiting hours and claim to be uncles and older brothers. At least it was better than dating the teachers, especially the national service personnel, who relentlessly pursued us with the promise of good grades. Anyway, I quickly fell in love with Michael and looked forward to his visits. I had become more daring in my final year and would scale the school's fence after lights-out to spend the night at his house and would return in the morning and join the stream of day students entering the campus gates. Michael had been very generous. School would have been so much more difficult without him. He had supplemented the meager *gari* and *shito* that my mother packed in my chop box so that even on the last day of the semester, one could still find powdered milk, milo, cornflakes, and cream crackers in my box. I'd ended things with him after I graduated. My failure to pass the mathematics and science portions of the West African Senior Secondary School Certificate Examination, twice, and to make the grades to enter one of the public universities had taken a toll on our relationship.

But as I sat on the banister that evening, long after my mother had gone inside, I knew that marriage to Eli would be nothing like what I had with Michael; in fact, one can't compare a secondary school boyfriend to a husband. But one of the things that worried me was that Aunty had proposed an arranged marriage. Although I knew little about arranged marriages, I knew that I didn't want one. I didn't know of any young woman who had gotten married this way. Even my parents didn't have an arranged marriage. The thought of marrying a man whom I barely knew, even if he was Eli Ganyo, was frightening. How would I fit into his jet-setting life? What could I possibly have in common with such a man? What would we talk about? How would I fit in with his family and rich friends? What would it be like to live in his house? What would it feel like to undress in front of him, to have his hands on my body? As I sat on the verandah, slapping at the mosquitoes that were landing on my legs, I thought of a hundred things that could go wrong. But the longer I sat there, the more I also realized that many things could go right. I could fall in love with him and he with me. We could have children and build a home like that in which I had spent my earliest childhood. He could take care of my mother and give her the kind of life that she had had with my father. I could have a future that many women in Ho couldn't even dream of: fashion school, a proper boutique. And on top of all of this, I could repay Aunty for everything she had done for us.

She had given me a new electric sewing machine on the day of my graduation from Sister Lizzie's sewing shop. She had also attended the celebration and had been there when my mother, aunts, and cousins spilled powder on me—from head to toe so that I looked like a careless baker—and formed a singing and white-handkerchief-waving procession that followed me from Sister Lizzie's shop to our house where my mother served some finger food and drinks. Aunty had promised me an overlock machine and a button-making machine once I set up the kiosk. The gesture had brought me to tears. How many people would do such a thing for someone they weren't even related to? This last thought had propelled me to my feet. I joined my mother indoors. What kind of person was I for even second-guessing Aunty, for thinking that anything she planned could go badly for me, for putting myself before her, before my mother? How could I throw away the opportunity to give my mother a better life after all that she had suffered?

The traditional wedding happened three months after my mother told me about Aunty's proposal. And now, maybe, my name was Afi Ganyo.

THREE

When we arrived in Accra, Richard came to welcome my mother and me and show us where we would be living. I hadn't known what to expect when Aunty's driver told us we were close. No one had told me where I would be staying or how Eli and the woman would fit into my living arrangements. Mawusi and I had speculated most of the previous evening when I went over to Tɔgã Pious's to say goodbye. She was grinding pepper in a cast-iron *kole* that was held in place by her feet as we perched on low stools in her mother's corner of the kitchen, away from the ears of her father's wives and their children who were busy lighting coal-pot fires to begin the evening meal.

Mawusi was a believer in true love; she watched telenovelas way more than I did. She had started a Mills & Boon and

Harlequin Romance book exchange club when we were in senior secondary school and believed that God created Yao—whom she had started dating in our first year of senior secondary school—to be her husband. My story—the marriage of a poor girl to a rich man whom she barely knew—was better than any telenovela or romance novel.

"I'm sure you'll be in whichever house he's in," she said with confidence.

"THEY ARE NOT going to throw you into a bush," my mother had said when I wondered aloud about where I would call home in Accra. I rolled my eyes at her response when her back was turned. My concerns temporarily receded the next day in Accra when the car drove through high metal gates, manned by two uniformed security guards, and stopped in a parking space in front of an eight-story apartment building. Seated in the back seat with my mother, I gasped at the sight of the white structure with its sliding windows and doors on each floor, which reflected the sunlight and caused the building to sparkle. I could see identical lawn furniture and potted plants neatly arranged on the covered balconies of the lower level flats. Beside us in the parking lot were an assortment of gleaming cars. A generator, which I would later discover was the size of a small house, hummed behind the building. Two men watered a lawn so green that I doubted its naturalness. The leaves of young palm trees, planted in the grass and perfectly spaced so that they looked like soldiers with elaborate headdresses on guard duty, rustled in the gentle breeze.

"Welcome, Madam," someone said, breaking my trance and causing me to shut my mouth, which had been hanging open. It was a young man in a brown-and-yellow uniform.

"Thank you," I mumbled, still enthralled by what I was seeing. I remembered that my mother was with me and turned to check on her. She had stuck her head out of the car window and craned her neck to look up at the structure in front of us. I left her to gawk and climbed out of the car. The driver had already opened the trunk and was removing our bags, which our greeter stood at the ready to collect. I picked my handbag off the seat and hung it on my shoulder and moved to help them with the bigger bags.

"No, Madam," the man exclaimed, and grabbed the nearest suitcase to keep me from taking it.

"He will carry them," the driver said.

The man nodded vigorously and reached for a second bag. I backed away.

"*Fo* Driver!" my mother called, she had climbed out of the car and was now standing beside us. "Is this where we are going to stay?" she asked the man who everyone, except the Ganyos, called Brother Driver. His name was Charles and his family's house was less than a ten-minute walk away from ours in Ho. Charles nodded, his lips quivering in an effort to avoid breaking into a broad smile and his eyes purposely not connecting with ours. He obviously noticed and was amused by our reactions; he had probably come here many times before. Besides, he spent most of his day in Aunty's house in Ho, which was quite majestic though it did not reach as high up in the sky as this one.

"He will show you the way," Charles said to me, pointing to the man who had begun rolling away one of my suitcases while balancing a second on his head. A second man had appeared and was rolling away a third suitcase.

"Are you not coming?" I asked Charles, suddenly alarmed. Was he planning on simply leaving us here and driving away?

"I have to go back, Aunty is waiting, but *Fo* Richard is coming," he told me. He had set the last of our belongings on the pavement that ran the perimeter of the building.

"Okay, thank you," I said as he shut the trunk.

"May God go with you," my mother said to him.

"Stay well," he replied.

CHARLES BEGAN TO drive away just as Richard's white Range Rover entered the compound and pulled into the parking space that Charles had vacated.

"*Mia woezor,*" Richard called as he came toward us, his arms opened wide. He wore dark blue jeans and white leather loafers, which I imagined would feel like a baby's skin to the touch, and an unnecessarily tight polo shirt that revealed everything, including his obscenely protruding bellybutton. He hugged my mother and then me.

"How was the trip?" he asked as he picked up my mother's traveling bag.

"Oh no, please leave it, *Fo* Richard," my mother protested, too rattled to answer his question.

"Let me carry it," he said, brushing aside her protest and walking in the direction in which the men had taken the other luggage. We began to follow him. Behind his back my mother turned to me and formed a silent "Hehn?" with her mouth. Like me, she was in awe of it all, including Richard Ganyo carrying our bag. I broke into a grin and grabbed her arm. I was excited.

We entered the foyer and the girl behind the curved security desk rose and greeted Richard. He responded in a way that told me he came here often, and then he poked one of the buttons on the wall beside the silver lift doors. My heart skipped a beat; I had never been on a lift before. I hoped that I wouldn't embarrass myself in front of Richard and this girl who had a wide smile on her face though I suspected she was laughing on the inside at our awkwardness. I got the feeling that my arrival had been extensively discussed by the staff. When the lift doors opened, I held my mother's hand and pulled her inside to stand behind Richard. We both held on to a hip-level iron bar on the wall, expecting the movement of the machine to rock us. The opposite wall had a mirror so that we could see our reflections. I still had on the weave from the wedding but had tied it back in a ponytail. I had wanted to wear jeans and a flowery off-shoulder top for the trip but had decided against it. I was not sure about where we would be going and who would be meeting us. So instead I had worn a simple pleated dress that I had sewn with batik my mother had bought me last Christmas, and flat sandals with crystal-like baubles on the straps; they had been in one of the suitcases the Ganyos gave me. My mother had on one of her good *kabas* and her wig from the wedding. Just as the lift pinged, I met Richard's eyes in the mirror and we both smiled; me because I had successfully ridden in my first lift, and him, I assume, because he was happy to be showing me my new home.

"This is your home for now," he said as we stepped into an air-conditioned landing on the fifth floor with rose-colored walls and ceiling-high canvasses depicting men clad in *batakaris* and knee-high leather boots, drumming and twirling so that their *batakaris* lifted off their bodies and encircled them. Empty gold-painted clay pots sat on black wrought-iron stands in all corners and two large windows at both ends gave us views of the traffic and streets outside but kept out the noise. There were three doors on the floor. The one closest to us had a brass number fifteen on it. Richard opened it and we followed him inside.

My mother and I paused in the doorway as our feet sank into the soft, cream-colored carpet beneath us. Was this a luxury hotel or my home? The brightly lit entryway led into a sitting room, a dining room, and a kitchen. To my left was the kitchen with its stainless-steel fixtures: a fridge, a stove and extractor, and a dishwasher. A silver toaster and an electric kettle sat on a marble-topped island and the deep brown of the cabinets matched the floor tiles in the kitchen. Between the kitchen and the sitting room was the dining room, bordered by the back of the sofa on one side and the high stools placed against the island on the other. It held a polished glass table and six dining chairs in the same brown of the table legs and the kitchen cabinets. There were many other pieces of furniture, all of them sleek and modern. A coffee table held books that were stacked to form a small pyramid, and a widescreen TV was mounted on the white wall without a wire in sight. Beyond the sitting room was a corridor that I knew would lead to the bedrooms and baths.

Richard threw his arm up as though to embrace the room and asked, "Do you like it?"

My mother chuckled and I nodded; was that a question that had to be asked?

"This kitchen is not for cooking *akple* or pounding *fufu*," my mother said as she ran her hand on the shining island surface.

"You can cook *akple* on the stove, it's easy. And we have a special kitchen downstairs for pounding *fufu* in a mortar. Or you can use the *fufu*-pounding machine that's in the cabinet beneath the sink," Richard said from the other corner of the room where he was pressing some buttons on a white panel on the wall. A blast of cool air shot out from a vent above him.

"Even palm soup; in fact, anything with oil, you can't cook on this stove," she continued, as though Richard had not spoken. "Can you imagine palm soup bubbling over and spilling onto this glass stove?" she asked as she turned to me.

"It's like any normal stove, Afinɔ, you only have to wipe it clean," Richard said, trying to assure her. He reached for my suitcase and began pulling it down the short corridor. "Come and see the bedrooms," he said to us.

There were three bedrooms, two with en suite bathrooms, and one guest bathroom. We placed my bags in the biggest bedroom, which I thought was decorated rather simply. I would later learn that a bedroom does not need to have a dresser and a wardrobe and shoe racks and all the other things I had grown up seeing. Two brown doors interrupted the whiteness of the wall. A walk-in closet—big enough to hold a bed—was behind one and behind the other was the bathroom, which was white and had both a Jacuzzi and a glass-enclosed shower.

"Where are *Fo* Eli's things?" I asked after I'd inspected the closet in the second guestroom and hadn't found a single item of clothing. It was clear that no one lived in the flat.

"He doesn't keep his things here, you know he has many houses in Accra," my brother-in-law said very quickly, as though he had prepared for this question.

"Which house does he keep his things in?"

"Several, they are all over the place."

"But not this one?"

"I'm sure he'll start keeping things here," Richard said, walking back into the hallway.

"But . . ." I began before my mother pinched my arm to shut me up. I pulled my arm out of her reach.

"That is okay. There's nothing wrong with having more than one place to lay your head. In fact, it is a sign of God's blessings," she said loudly enough for Richard to hear. She then turned to me and frowned. I instantly knew not to pursue this line of questioning, at least not while she was there.

THE FLAT HAD been readied for our arrival. The fridge was stocked with everything imaginable, including *koobi*. The beds had been made, towels hung on racks, potted plants on the balcony watered.

"Who did all of this?" I asked Richard as he waited for the lift to take him down.

"We have people for these things; you'll see them," he told me. I nodded. Who were these people? Was this their full-time job? Watering flowers and buying salted fish for people they had never met? Would they be doing this every week or would we have to go to the market ourselves? And where was the market and how could we get there?

As if he could read my mind, Richard said, "I'll send a car to take you shopping at the end of the week." He then handed me a crisp wad of notes. "Take this for anything you need to buy," he said. I slowly extended my hand for the money. Gifts from the Ganyos usually passed from my mother to me.

"Thank you," I said. I had brought all of my savings, tucked into my handbag, but had been thinking about what I would do once it was gone. Was this wad of cash a monthly allowance? If

I knew how often it would come I would know how to budget. I did not ask him this, but I did ask again about my husband, now that my mother was out of earshot.

"He's coming back next week," Richard said.

"Coming here?"

"Partly . . . we'll see," he answered, his words halting. "You only need to focus on enjoying yourself," he said as he stepped into the lift with a big smile.

I stood in front of the silver doors long after they had closed. My fears pushed my excitement aside as they had done on my wedding day. I really wished that the Ganyos would tell me what exactly was happening instead of holding everything to their chests and only throwing scraps of information my way. I knew my mother would disagree, but I thought that they should have told me, before I even left Ho, that I wouldn't be living under the same roof as my husband. I had been under the impression that he would be in Accra when we arrived there. They should have told me that this wasn't the case; they should have told me when he would be returning from his Hong Kong trip. In fact, he should have called me to tell me these things himself; after all, I was his wife and he knew my phone number. Instead they had put me in this tower and given me pocket money like a schoolgirl. What was I supposed to do? Just sit in this building and wait?

MY MOTHER BECAME angry with me when I said this to her after we had cooked and eaten rice and beef stew with the ingredients we had found in the kitchen. She said that I was being ungrateful by asking so many questions and didn't understand why I needed to know everything the future held. "Isn't it enough to know that Elikem Ganyo is your husband?" she asked.

I became angry and retreated into my room to speak with Mawusi on the phone.

"I can't imagine marrying Yao and not living in the same house with him! You should ask Richard what's happening the next time he comes," she said.

"That's what I'm saying: he doesn't want to tell me anything proper, he's just talking in circles."

"You need to be firm when you're speaking to him, that way he'll know you're serious. They need to know you're not some small girl that they can play with."

"You make it sound so easy. What if Aunty hears that I'm asking all these questions and becomes angry? Then what?"

"Hmmm."

"I'm not trying to make trouble, I only want to know what's going on. How can I be a good wife with no husband by my side?"

MY MOTHER AND I settled into a routine. We woke up by six every morning at the latest and cleaned every inch of the flat. We had turned away the cleaners who showed up the morning after we moved in.

"We do it for everybody, Madam," one of them explained, but I still refused. We had never had servants, even when my father was alive. I simply wasn't comfortable with them in the flat. Besides, we could do it ourselves. We had nothing else to do.

"You know, it could all be a test," my mother said as she

mopped the kitchen floor and I wiped the windows with a blue solution I had taken from the cleaners.

"How?"

"Maybe they want to see the kind of wife you are; whether you are the type of woman who will sit down and relax while other people clean for you."

"Hmmm," I said; I hadn't thought of that. "But Aunty already knows me. Besides, if she wanted to test me she should have done it before I married her son, not after."

"You are young, you don't know," she said while shaking her head. The headshaking and her downturned lips told me that I would be receiving a lecture in the evening. The things I needed to know in order to succeed in this marriage were endless! I couldn't help but think that the other woman had it much easier than me.

A FEW DAYS before the wedding when Richard was visiting Ho, my mother and I had gotten him to tell us about this other woman. He said that Eli met her on his first trip to her country. He had recently graduated from the university with a degree in philosophy (a course assigned to him by the university, not one he selected) when Fred, his older brother who was then the national secretary for the governing party, sent him to Liberia to oversee his interests in a cement factory that he had opened with a group of investors.

"You will be my eyes and ears over there," Fred had told his younger brother when he saw him off at the airport. Eli would be staying in a flat that Fred had rented for him in Monrovia, and he would be driving a company car. He was ecstatic; it wasn't every day that a young man straight out of university got such an opportunity. But it had taken him a while to adjust to his new life: the way the English differed from ours; people's consumption of leaves that he hadn't known were edible; crumbling buildings riddled with bullet holes and green with moss due to years of war and torrential rains; the masses of unemployed youth with hardened eyes that told of unspeakable pasts and impossible futures. He empathized with the people and the harsh lives that many were forced to live. On the other hand, he had quickly grown to dislike the work his brother had sent him to do; his main task was looking over everyone's shoulder and reporting everything back to Ghana, a responsibility that didn't endear him to his colleagues. He wanted to work in a place where people didn't scowl and hunch over their desks when he appeared in their doorway. Besides, he knew that he was capable of much more.

After he arrived in Liberia, Eli carefully studied his surroundings for opportunities and had listened intently to what the new friends he had made had to say. He gathered that there was money to be made in Liberia. The war, which had crushed the country, had also created the need to reassemble it and to make sure that it functioned better than before. Roads had to be built, schools reconstructed, electricity turned back on, baby diapers and wheelchairs imported, oil drilled, and gold mined. And these things had to be done by people with money to fund their ventures and fill the bank accounts of the government officials who issued licenses and permits and selected who was awarded government contracts. Eli saw a place for himself in the chaos. He knew people who had money and he was confident in his ability to run a business. He and his siblings had helped their mother build up her small, one-mud-oven bakery into a flour distribution and retail chain. He knew that he could replicate that success in Liberia. He shared his ideas with Fred. Though initially reluctant because he worried that his interests in the cement factory would be left unattended, Fred had come around when his brother convinced him that they could earn ten times what they were making in the cement factory if they diversified.

A month later Fred sent Richard, who at that time wasn't sure what he wanted to do with his life, to Liberia with a bank account number and a directive to help Eli set up this other branch of the family business. The bank account held start-up money that they would use to purchase material and access. It was during this time, when the two brothers were knocking on the doors of government officials after regular office hours and inspecting the land for a real-estate project, that Eli had met the Liberian woman. Richard, who was there when the two first met, said that he hadn't given her a thought. She was nothing like the women Eli had dated in the past. She had been working as a secretary for a Lebanese hardware wholesaler who had sent her to their construction site to deliver an invoice. When Richard saw the woman in Eli's car and then two weeks later in their shared flat at 2:00 a.m., he questioned his brother.

"She's my girlfriend," Eli told him.

"Girlfriend?"

"Yes."

"Ehn?"

He hadn't understood what was happening. The woman was tall, almost as tall as Eli, and hard. There was no soft spot on her body; her bicep muscles were visible when she moved her arms, and her calf muscles sat round and high, like a sprinter's. There was a gulf between her compact, lemon-sized breasts, and her buttocks was as flat as a sheet of plywood. Plus she had no hips to speak of. Her skin was as dark as roasted coffee beans, and her face, the only soft part of her, was plain. She kept her hair in long braids and liked wearing skirts and dresses that showed off her manly features.

"To tell you the truth, I don't know what my brother sees in that woman," Richard had confided to my mother that day.

"His girlfriend in the university looked just like you, Afi. Beautiful face, flesh at the right places, and fair skin," he said to me while my mother shook her head at the travesty of it all, the idea of a man like Eli being hooked by such a woman. I, on the other hand, folded my hands in my lap in a useless attempt to cover my lower body. I was uncomfortable with the knowledge that Richard, and possibly the rest of Eli's family, had assessed my physical proportions.

"On top of it all, she smokes. Now every time you go near my brother, he smells like an ashtray," Richard said.

"The woman smokes?" my mother asked, her eyes wide with disbelief.

"And drinks hard liquor. She can outdrink any drunk in this town," Richard added.

"*Woh!*" my mother exclaimed and swiftly rose off the bench on which she was seated, unable to contain her shock.

"No wonder," she said, slowly shaking her head.

"No wonder O Afinɔ, no wonder. Why won't she keep producing sickly children?" he said sullenly.

But it wasn't the woman's appearance or her relationship with tobacco and alcohol that had led to Eli's family's distrust. It was the way she treated them. Even in the beginning when she was a secretary, she had shown no regard for the family. When Richard saw her in his and Eli's flat at 2:00 a.m. she had simply sashayed past him without so much as a "Hello" or "Sorry for surprising you in your kitchen at this hour." She never greeted him but would respond through her teeth when spoken to, and walked freely around the place as if she owned it, even when Eli was not there. By the time that Richard realized how serious the relationship was and alerted his family, Eli had rented a house and moved in with the woman. And by the time Fred came to Liberia to reason with him on behalf of their mother, the woman was pregnant; conveniently within six weeks of meeting a rich man.

I WAS BORED by the third day in Accra. I missed sewing on our verandah. I imagined how many orders I would have completed if I were there. I missed my customers who sat and chatted with me as I made the last stiches on their clothes, and the friends and neighbors who stopped by on their way from some place or the other to say hello and to talk about an upcoming funeral, a church event, or whatever it was that was of interest that day. Here, there was nobody, with the exception of my mother, who I feared was becoming addicted to the TV and who was only interested in talking about how I should behave with my husband and his family, and the guards at the gate. There was no one else for me to talk with. I imagined the scene at Togã Pious's, my older cousins sitting on the benches outside the compound walls and talking or fighting about something while the younger ones ignored their mothers' calls and prolonged their time outside as much as they could. I missed the noise, the endless chatter, the familiarity, the simplicity of it all, where every activity was a social one, where we girls strolled to the civic center almost every evening to buy *koko* from the women who cooked the porridge in cauldrons right in front of us and sold sugar, milk, and groundnut on the side. Even the walk to the dumpsite to empty the trash when we were teenagers had been a social one. At my new home, there was a garbage chute on each floor and the housekeepers threw the trash bags down it for you. I had insisted on doing it myself once I figured out where the garbage disappeared to.

I didn't bother to tell my mother that I missed Ho. I knew she would tell me to stop complaining and be grateful, so I soldiered on. Daily phone calls to Mawusi, who had gone back to school and was preparing to leave for a semester abroad in Côte d'Ivoire to study French, put some life in my days. I was happy when Richard sent a car and a driver to take us to the market and then the supermarket on Friday. My mother and I had been in awe at the selection of items on sale, and the prices too! In fact, the prices had left her upset and making plans for buying food from Ho and sending it to me when she returned. I was even happier when the driver, Mensah, did not leave after dropping us off.

"*Fo* Richard says that I'm now your driver. I will be here every day," he said after he had delivered the last grocery bags up to the flat.

I nodded but did not speak, afraid to show my elation. Instead I looked at the late-model silver Toyota Camry with new eyes. "Afi, this car is yours," I told myself. Technically the car wasn't mine; Richard had assigned it to me, of course, but that made no difference. It would take me wherever I wanted to go, wait for me as long as I wanted, and bring me back home. Now I just had to figure out where I wanted to go.

"I'm going to town," I told my mother the next morning.

"Where? For what?" she asked.

"I want to go and see the Accra mall."

"What are you going to see there? And what if your husband comes when you're away? This is not the time to be running around Accra."

"Ah Ma! If *Fo* Eli hasn't come since I've been here, why would it be this morning that he will come? I can't just sit around waiting for him."

"Why not? You have everything you need here. Look at this place. And what if Aunty calls and asks for you, what will I tell her?"

"Tell her I've gone to the mall. It's not like I'm going to a night club or to a party. I'm just going to the mall; it's less than thirty minutes away from here."

"Okay then, I will come with you."

I sighed loudly, eliciting a sharp look from her, but waited while she changed out of her TV-watching clothes, after which Mensah took us to the mall.

I'D HEARD SO much about the Accra mall from Mawusi but hadn't been there before. My mother had insisted that we do the wedding shopping at Makola, the huge open-air market in Accra where people, stalls, vehicles, and rubbish were in a constant battle for supremacy, while the scorching sun smiled with approval. But the mall was different. It seemed like everything shone and even though one couldn't walk from one end to another without bumping someone, the air-conditioning made it all bearable. Although I couldn't bring myself to shop, not with the prices that were quoted, I marveled at the display windows of the boutiques selling clothes and fabric.

"Do you want to buy it?" my mother asked when I wouldn't stop staring at a mannequin draped in a fabric with a peacock-feather pattern. Two-and-a-half yards of that fabric would make a beautiful party dress.

"No," I told her, without looking away from the mannequin. I had to be careful with how I spent my money; I didn't know when my in-laws would be giving me more pocket money and I couldn't afford to run out. Accra wasn't like Ho, where I could go next door to borrow money or ingredients for the evening meal from neighbors or from someone in Tɔgã Pious's house. Besides, I had yet to try on all of the clothes in the four large suitcases that the Ganyos presented at my wedding. Of course, this didn't mean that I couldn't fantasize about owning the shops I visited and everything in them.

THE NEXT FEW mornings, after breakfast, I went out to explore the neighborhood. My building was on a quiet street that was home to houses that sat behind high, electrified, barbwire-lined walls and a couple of two-story office buildings. The five- or six-feet wide pieces of land that separated the houses from the road were planted with grass and flowers and the branches of acacias grew over the walls and into the street, creating a shade for pedestrians. As people drove to work in the morning I had to be careful to walk on the very edge of the narrow road, which did not have a sidewalk, so that I was either in the road or in the open gutter. But that didn't bother me because I enjoyed the beauty of it all. It was not like anywhere in Ho, not even the Residency where the regional minister lived and where we would visit as children to peer over the fence at the peacocks strutting in the garden.

Our block transformed at a T-junction that connected it to a major street. Here, stores selling everything from wheelbarrows to milk lined the road along with so-called boutiques, banks, and a few smaller houses, less imposing than the ones on our street. Although cars were forced to drive at moderate speeds because of the presence of car-scraping speed bumps, it was still busier than where I was coming from. Farther down this road was a small market where women sold vegetables, fish, and grains in stalls at prices that would make people in Ho cry or laugh, depending on whether they were the ones buying or if they were hearing that I had used my money to shop there.

"It's because this area is for rich people," one of the security guards at my building told me. He was pimply faced and looked younger than me. He wore his uniform with pride but frequently spoke about when he would permanently take it off and move on to better things. On my way out and when I returned from my exploratory walks, I often stopped at the booth inside the fence that served as a guard post to chat with whomever was on duty. They had initially been guarded around me, knowing who I was, but within a couple of days they were answering questions that I hadn't even asked them. There were six of them assigned to the building, four men and two women, and they rotated during the day. I liked that the women were always on the day shift so that I got to chat with them more than the men. I learned that they mostly came from villages around Vakpo and worked for a security firm owned by Fred's brother-in-law. On my third day with the two women, Savior and Lucy, Savior asked me which bleaching cream I used.

"I want to buy it," she told me, gazing at my face as though I was a picture in a magazine.

"I don't use anything; my color is natural."

She responded with a frown that made clear her disbelief.

"Or is it a pill?" she pressed.

"No," I said, unruffled by her questions. People had been asking me the same thing for as long as I could remember. She asked me again the next day. When I gave her the same answer, she shifted to other topics. She told me that Fred owned the building. The furnished flats were rented mainly to expatriates for thousands of dollars a month. I had already noticed the foreigners leaving in their four-wheel-drives in the morning, some of them in the backseat and their drivers at the wheel. In fact, just that morning one of them had nodded at me and had left me wondering what it was that she had been trying to communicate.

Savior and Lucy were full of stories about the happenings in King's Court, the name of the building, which was written in gold letters on a black plaque affixed to the fence, but which I had not noticed when we first drove in. The two young women, who changed their hairstyles so often that I was tempted to ask them if they reused the artificial hair pieces, especially loved to gossip about the residents. They pointed out to me the civil servants who could miraculously afford to rent these flats on their meager government salaries, and the old white men who showed up with girls who were young enough to be their grand-daughters and those who showed up with the boys. They also showed me the foreign women who had a succession of dread-locked men visiting them and staying overnight. But most scandalous were the married Ghanaian men who rented the flats for their girlfriends and divided their time between two homes. The guards told me that there had been a huge fight some months before my mother and I arrived. A wife whose husband was a senior manager at one of the banks found out that he was keep-ing a woman at King's Court. She had driven over with two friends, deceived her way into the compound, and then stormed the girlfriend's flat.

"They would have finished her if we hadn't heard her scream-ing and rushed upstairs," Savior said, before doubling over with laughter.

"You are laughing? You know that they almost sacked us; we are only here because of God's grace," Lucy said, clearly rattled.

Savior dismissed her with a wave of her hand and contin-ued with the story. "It was in number fourteen, the flat next to yours. It's a good thing that her balcony door was open or no one would have heard her screaming. She moved out that same day," she told me. "In fact, she crawled out that same day because by the time we got there they had given it to her well."

I shuddered at the image of the mistress barely able to walk out of King's Court. "So the flat is empty now?" I asked her.

"No, *Fo* Richard's girlfriend moved in soon after."

"Richard? Richard Ganyo?"

"*Ehn.*"

Richard hadn't told me that his girlfriend was my neighbor. I itched to hear more but knew that it would be foolish to ask these two for information. Who knows what they would report back to the girlfriend, or even Richard?

"Her name is Evelyn," Savior volunteered as I walked away, deep in thought.

"I WANT TO enroll in fashion school," I told my mother that evening during a commercial break in the TV show we had been watching.

"Now?" Ma asked with a scowl. I was somewhat surprised because she had always been passionate about my education. Although she hadn't said this to me, I knew she had been deeply disappointed by my failure to make it to the university and had blamed herself. She had told me more than once that I would have fared better if she had bought more books for me and if she had hired a tutor to help me with the subjects I struggled with. When I failed a second time to gain admission into one of the public universities, she had proposed getting a loan from Aunty to pay for my enrollment in one of the private universities that were springing up like mushrooms and charging way more than they were worth. But I had refused, my confidence having sunk with each disappointing result. Also, I had grown to love sewing and begun to see it as a career. What I now wanted was to attend a proper fashion school. Sister Lizzie taught all of us well, but she taught us the basics. How to cut and sew a straight dress, or a dress with gathers or pleats, with a round, square, or V neckline; how to sew a simple skirt and top or a plain *kaba* and slit. But we hadn't learned how to sew trousers because in Ho few women ordered trousers and those who did went to the tailors. She hadn't taught us how to sew the kind of *kabas* that the tailors from Togo and Côte d'Ivoire made, the strapless kind and the kind with wires threaded through the fabric so that it formed every shape imaginable on the human body, or the ones where they cut patterns out of the fabric to create floral arrangements on the bodice or on the skirt. Those were the kinds of clothes that I wanted to learn to sew. The kind worn by the career women in *City of Gold*, the popular soap opera, where feathers and beads were sewn into dresses and leather and cotton were combined into the same evening gown. My mother had always approved of this desire to further my training. This is why her scowl was surprising to me.

"As soon as possible," I answered.

She sighed heavily and turned away from the screen to face me on the sofa.

"You just got married; it is better that you spend time at home, getting to know your husband and taking care of him."

What husband? I wanted to ask, but didn't because I knew it would annoy her even more. Instead I glared at her.

"Don't look at me like that. I am simply telling you what is best for you. There is no need to rush, the school will still be there next year. You are a new wife only once." She turned back to the screen, the commercial break over.

I went into my room. In a few weeks my mother had changed from a friend into a dictator and her transformation was unexpected and troubling. And even though she kept saying that she was doing what was best for me, I had begun to feel like I was not her first priority, that her desire to please the Ganyos came first. It was a good thing that she would be leaving soon, going back to Ho. Despite what she had said, I was determined to begin my training as soon as the vocational schools began admitting a new crop of students. I couldn't imagine spending all my days in this flat, waiting for Eli, my dear husband, to one day come and see me.

WHEN MY MOTHER went to bed, I listened out for Evelyn. I looked through the peephole when I heard the lift stop on my floor and saw a woman get off. She moved so quickly that I only caught a glimpse of her. She had on a black skirt suit and heels that looked like they could easily injure a person. In one hand she held what looked like a computer case and in the other she carried a handbag, the large kind that had become fashionable. The side of her head that I saw was covered with softly flowing waves that reached past her shoulders. As I heard her key turn in the lock I considered stepping outside and speaking to her, but then thought better of it. What exactly was I going to say to such a woman? Besides, if Richard did not tell us about her then maybe we weren't supposed to know about her. I wasn't going to look for trouble.

IF THERE'S ONE thing I knew about my brother-in-law, it was that he didn't hold back when he chose to tell a story. I still remember how his face had contorted in anger as he described the misery the Liberian woman had caused his mother.

"She has done something to your brother," Aunty had lamented when she spoke to Richard and Fred. This was when they finally gathered the courage to tell her that Eli had moved into a house with the woman, abandoning Richard in their flat.

This was after she announced she was pregnant and less than two months after she first met Eli. "This is not natural," Aunty had added wearily.

Fred had grunted in agreement, he had been thinking the same thing. Because why else would Eli, a man who previously had introduced his only serious girlfriend to his older brother and sought his approval, suddenly move in with and impregnate a woman who didn't want his relatives around? Eli had always been the sweet brother. The middle brother who walked alongside his mother in the market after school, balancing a wooden board stacked with bread on his head, and never complaining. The one who, as a boy, cried whenever his mother fell sick, and who came home from the university to be with her when she slipped in her tiled driveway and sprained her ankle. The one who consulted his older brother before making any major decisions and kept a stern eye on his younger brother, who was prone to recklessness. No one could ever have imagined him with this woman. There had to be something behind it. She must have done something to him, something to turn him away from his family and get him to follow her blindly. Fred only had to discreetly ask a few people before he began to hear about the potions that young women, desperate for a way out, put into men's food to scramble their brains and get them to forget their wives and children and buy houses and cars for women whose last names they didn't even know. The same medicine men who had given the rebels invincibility potions to rub on their bodies during the war were now brewing love potions.

But Richard was skeptical. Not because he didn't believe in the power of the supernatural but because his brief encounters with the woman had convinced him that there was something intrinsic to her that had netted his brother. The way she carried herself, sinewy shoulders held high and face shuttered close as though she thought the whole world stunk. Her rude confidence could not have come from any love potion; it came from within, from some barren and rough place inside. And the only person who knew her well enough to explain her actions was only interested in defending her, or perhaps in saving her.

Eli assured his family that once they got to know her, they would love the woman as much as he did. But her hostility increased with the size of her belly. She sucked her teeth and rolled her eyes when Richard came to visit and stayed away the first day that Aunty visited, coming home late at night, long after the old woman was asleep. And she had no excuse because she had quit her secretarial job the week after meeting Eli. When Aunty asked to meet her family, the woman had brought two cousins who were not more than twenty years old. Aunty had left after that, unable to countenance such disrespect. Eli, of course, had continued to make excuses for the woman.

"She just needs to get comfortable with you," he had assured his mother on the drive to the airport. The woman had pled morning sickness and stayed home, to Aunty's relief.

"Are you okay?" she had asked him worriedly because of a sudden fear that this would be the last time she saw him, that this woman would somehow make him disappear from their lives. She had spent most of the previous night on her knees, praying for God to break this hold that the woman had over her son, this hold that made him almost unrecognizable to her.

"I'm fine, Ma," he had said, and unleashed the smile that she loved so much. "She's a good woman. You'll see."

"Okay," she had said without attempting to reason with him. It had become clear to her that this battle would be fought in the spiritual realm; she silently entrusted her son to God as they parted at the entrance to the airport. "It is well," she had continuously reminded herself on the almost two-hour flight from Robertsfield to Kotoka. But no matter how much she prayed, it wasn't well. And that is when she thought of me.

FOUR

When Richard came by on Saturday I told him about my plans to attend fashion school.

"That's a great idea," he said. "Ask your husband when he comes."

"When is he coming?"

"Tuesday."

"This Tuesday?"

"Yes."

"He's coming here?

"Ah, Afi. I said he's coming, he's coming," Richard said with a smile, as though speaking to a troublesome but lovable child.

That bit of news pushed thoughts of design school to the farthest corner of my mind. I finally knew which day I would see my husband! But how in the world was I supposed to welcome him? Would he knock on the door or did he have his own set of keys? Would I have to go to meet him at the airport? What would I wear? What should I prepare for him to eat?

"Who will pick him up from the airport?"

"Don't worry about that, it's all taken care of."

"What does he like to eat?"

"Eli eats everything, he won't complain about anything you give him."

"But does he have a favorite food?"

"I know that he likes yam a lot, yam and any kind of stew."

"Okay. What time will he get here?"

"As for that I can't say, he always has a lot of running around to do so you just expect him on Tuesday. Or do you have somewhere to go on Tuesday?"

"No, I will be here."

"She's not going anywhere; she will be right here," my mother piped in. She had been in the bathroom and I hadn't even heard her enter the sitting room. These soft carpets could get a person in trouble.

WE SPENT THE next few days preparing for Eli's arrival. I scrubbed and mopped and swept and wiped, even though there was really no need to do these things because we kept the flat looking like a display in one of the posh furniture stores that were advertised on TV. I went to the market, the one near our house where the prices were high because the sellers believed that rich people had money to throw away, and bought two tubers of *puna* from two different sellers. Two tubers just in case one of them turned out to be bitter and two sellers because hopefully they wouldn't have gotten their yams from the same farmer. I was torn between garden egg and *kontomire* stews. I thought garden egg was basic but then I had never tasted garden egg stew that wasn't delicious. *Kontomire* on the other hand could go wrong easily; a slight bit of overcooking and you would have a pot of tasteless greens on your hands.

"Then cook both of them," my mother said impatiently when she tired of seeing me pace between the stalls of the *kontomire* and garden egg sellers. So that is what I did.

IF ONLY IT was that easy to quell the turmoil within me. I was nervous beyond words. On Monday night when I spoke to Mawusi, I could barely hold myself together.

"Have you done your hair?" she asked

"It still looks fine," I said.

"Are you sure? Have you washed it? You know these weaves are worse than braids, they start to smell after a while."

"I didn't wash it," I said, on the verge of tears. What if this was one of those weaves that turned frizzy as soon as they came into contact with water and had to be tamed with all kinds of hair products that I didn't have? But how could I welcome this man with a head of smelly hair?

"You can still find a salon and wash it first thing tomorrow morning."

"But I don't know what time he will come tomorrow. What if he comes in the morning?"

"Then use rubbing alcohol to clean your scalp."

"What if he's one of those men who don't like women with artificial hair?"

"Well, that is what you have now . . . don't worry about that. All you can do is find a way of cleaning it."

Her words didn't make me feel better. After I hung up, I imagined the Liberian woman hugging Eli, her head on his chest, her sweetly scented, natural hair tickling his chin.

I FIRST HEARD about the woman in my final year of secondary school. When Aunty and Eli's uncle went to Liberia to outdoor the baby girl after the woman gave birth, she refused to let them touch the child; her baby would not be subjected to any outmoded foreign customs. No libation would be poured to any gods or ancestors, and the child would not be named by the visitors from Ghana! She had thrown a fit when Eli tried to reason with her, so Aunty, not wanting to upset a new mother, had boarded the next flight back to Accra, Eli's old uncle by her side. Sickly from the day she entered the world, the poor child died two months later. Fred and Richard represented the family at the funeral. It was only after this that Eli succeeded in convincing the woman to visit his family in Ghana. He had hoped that she would learn to like, or at least respect, them if she spent more time with them. I was away at boarding school and only heard the stories from my mother after I returned. While she hadn't seen the woman, my mother had heard other workers at the depot whisper about the strange woman that Eli had brought back with him.

SHE HAD REFUSED to stay in Aunty's six-bedroom house and had instead insisted on staying in a hotel. When she visited Aunty's during the day, she would sit pouting in a corner, her face covered by sunglasses the size of a car windscreen, until Eli abandoned all who had come to visit him and came to her side. She refused to taste any of the food prepared in Aunty's house and instead brought food from the hotel each morning. She wouldn't even answer when people came up to her and playfully tried to speak Eʋe to her. A friendly *"Ŋdi"* or *"Èle abgea"* would only elicit a dead stare even though Eli had been teaching her Eʋe since they met. She refused to wear any of the three suits of *kaba* that Eli had asked Sister Lizzie to sew for her despite his exhortations. "Only country women tie cloths . . . where I come from," she had told Aunty when the old woman inquired why she was wearing a pair of tight jean trousers at the durbar for the yam festival. Even the American tourists at the durbar knew not to come dressed in jeans.

The final straw was when the woman ejected Yaya, who had recently returned from South Africa, from their hotel suite because she wanted to take an afternoon nap. Yaya had been excited to see her brother again and to meet his partner, but the woman hadn't shared her excitement. Although Eli had begged his sister to stay, she had left the hotel in tears and reported the incident to Aunty and Fred. They had called Eli to a meeting the following morning, the old uncle in attendance; the family could not go on like this.

"I'm leaving her," he had said before either of them could ask him to reassess his relationship with the woman. "I've had enough. I'm leaving her," he had repeated dejectedly, like a person who had prepared well for a test but had failed to get even one question correct. His mother had hugged him, happy that he would finally be escaping the dark cloud that had hung over his life for the past two years. But the woman had no plans of pulling her claws out of Eli. She had announced she was pregnant again as soon as they returned to Liberia and he had, therefore, been unable to bring himself to pack his bags. She had given birth to another sickly baby, another girl, Ivy, and had refused Aunty's offer to come and help care for the child, even though she was obviously not good at it. Exasperated, Eli had insisted that they move back home. He wanted to be near his family and closer to their investments in Ghana, which were now generating more revenue than their Liberian holdings. She moved to Ghana reluctantly, her cigarettes and booze clutched in one hand and her baby in the other. Since then, her relationship with Eli had been a series of starts and stops. She had moved out of their shared home more times than anyone cared to count and dragged her poor, sickly child behind her each time she did. In fact, she had resorted to using the little girl against Eli, so every exchange they had ended with her threatening to take Ivy away. I really didn't understand why Eli couldn't simply take the baby and send the mother back to where she came from, to working as a secretary and delivering documents to construction sites. After all, she wasn't the one who cared for the baby. It was the two *housegirls* who did most of the work. The latest stunt she had pulled was taking Ivy to Spain for vacation while Eli was in Beijing on business. He only found out when his call to one of her cellphones was answered by one of the *housegirls,* who told him that she had not seen her madam for three days. He had become worried upon hearing this because he knew the woman wasn't able to care for Ivy by herself. When he called and told this to his mother, she had become enraged and immediately decided that the woman had to be permanently cut out of Eli's life. As long as she was there, he would not know a moment of peace or happiness. But she knew her son; he was blessed and at the same time cursed with a good heart, so no matter how miserable she made him, nothing the woman did would cause him to turn his back on the mother of his child. It was up to Aunty to put an end to this.

So she had invited my mother into her small office at the flour depot after work and told her as much as necessary for her to understand the situation (Aunty was not the kind of woman to cry on anyone's shoulder). Then she had added the most relevant piece, the reason for which she had called Ma: she wanted Eli and me to get married.

"Afi is respectful and hardworking. And she is a beautiful girl," she had said as my mother listened with mouth agape. When she finally gathered her composure, my mother had said a breathy, "Yes." And that was how I came to be married to Elikem Ganyo. Now I was waiting for him to show up and be my husband.

WHEN TUESDAY MORNING came my hair (yes, it was mine; I paid for it) was washed, dried, brushed, and held back in a neat ponytail. My mother peeled one of the yams for the fire and then sliced the *kontomire* because both foods gave me an itchy rash on my hands when I touched them. As the *kontomire* and garden eggs simmered in separate pots on the stove, I set one place at the table. Then I took three serving bowls and spoons out of the cupboard and placed them on the island. I would dish out the food when he came so that it didn't get cold while we waited for him.

"Go and have your bath," my mother urged me as I stood surveying the kitchen, convinced that I had forgotten to do something. She was poking a finger into the pot of boiling yam to test if it was ready; if overcooked it would break apart and form a gooey mess.

"Okay. How is the yam?"

"It is fine; it is sweet," she said. She was now chewing a small piece that she had taken out of the pot.

I FINISHED SHOWERING in no time. Not having to boil water in a pot, pour it into a bucket, and take it to the bathroom shortened the process; here I only had to twist a knob and hot water would flow out of the tap. I wore the same dress that I had on when we first moved to Accra. I used a bit of face powder and squirted perfume into the air in front of me and ran through the droplets with eyes closed; now my whole body smelled like flowers. My mother interrupted my preparations to tell me that everything was set in the kitchen and that she was going to have her bath. She looked me up and down and smiled when I turned to face her. I was ready.

ELI CAME AT 1:36 P.M. I knew the exact time because I was sitting and staring at the analog clock on my phone when the doorbell rang. The sound startled me and I dropped the phone; I hadn't heard the lift stop and open on my floor. My mother rushed out of her room and mouthed "Go" while pointing to the door. I hesitated; for some silly reason I wanted to fish my phone from under the chair before I answered the door.

"Ah, open the door," she said with sound this time.

I stood up and smoothed my dress over my hips. My armpits were moist; it was a good thing that the fabric was light and patterned so that my sweat stains would not be visible. My feet felt heavy so that I needed extra effort to lift them. I imagined that I looked like a marching soldier. The frown on my mother's face told me that she was displeased. The bell rang a second time. She flashed her eyes as if they had the power to physically push me toward the door. My hand was so damp with sweat that it slipped off the round doorknob when I tried to turn it. I wiped my hands on my dress and tried again. This time I was successful.

ELI BROKE INTO a smile that reached his eyes when he saw me. He was leaning against the doorframe like someone who had been waiting for a long time to be let in.

"Please, good afternoon," I managed to say in a near whisper. Should I shake his hand, should I hug him, a kiss on the cheek? Last night I had imagined hugging him but now no greeting seemed right for this almost-stranger who was also my husband. It didn't help that he was jauntily leaning against the doorframe and openly staring at me, his smile intact.

"Afternoon, Afi," he said, his eyes never leaving my face. I lowered my eyes to look at my hands, and then my feet. Anything to avoid the intensity of his gaze.

"Please come in, *Fo* Eli," I heard my mother say from somewhere behind me. Only then did he look past me into the flat. I breathed a soft sigh of relief and stepped aside to let him in.

HE WAS SEATED in one of the armchairs, his feet splayed, his arms resting on the armrests, and his lips slightly curved in a smile. In his hand were two large cellphones. He had a beard; I didn't remember him having a beard before. It was so neat that it looked as if it had been trimmed by someone using a measuring tool for accuracy. I assumed that the same person had trimmed his hairline. He had on a white shirt folded up to his elbows and tucked into black trousers. The brown leather belt at his waist matched his shoes.

"Let us bring you some water," my mother said. I was thankful for her words because I would have otherwise just sat and stared at him like a fool. I followed her into the kitchen as though we both needed to carry a glass of water. I decided at that moment that I hated the open floor plan of the flat because I really wanted to say something about the situation to her but Eli could see and hear me from the sitting room. So instead I took a jug of water out of the fridge and she a glass out of the cupboard, all without speaking to each other. I set the two items on a small silver tray and carefully walked back to the sitting room with my mother behind me. I placed the tray on the side table closest to Eli and poured the water into his glass. He lifted it to his lips and I went back to sit on the edge of the couch with my arms folded in my lap.

"*Woezor,*" my mother said when Eli set the glass down.

"*Yoo.*"

"How was the journey?" she asked him in Eʋe.

"It went well."

"Your siblings?" she continued.

"They are well."

"*Woezor,*" my mother said.

"*Yoo.*"

"You are the ones looking after people," she said, nodding her head.

"You as well."

"You are the ones who have worked so, so, so, hard," she said, still nodding, as though agreeing with herself.

"You as well."

"Are you well?" he asked. He looked at my mother, then at me, as he said this.

"We are well," she replied. I remained quiet like a child in the presence of two adults having a conversation. "Well, I brought your wife and decided to stay with her as she waited for you," my mother continued.

"Thank you," he said.

"Are you well?" he asked again, this time looking directly at me. I nodded and managed a weak smile. He nodded as though satisfied.

"Your wife cooked something small for you," my mother said.

"Oh, thank you," he said, his eyes on me.

"Please, you are welcome," I said.

A moment later I felt a sharp pinch on my back. It was my mother. She swiveled her eyes in the direction of the kitchen when I turned to look at her. I shot to my feet.

"Please, I'm going for the food," I mumbled and hurried to the kitchen. He chatted with my mother as I heated the stews, but twice when I looked over at them he was staring at me. I lowered my head and only looked at him again when I went to announce that the food was ready. I noticed how tall he was when he stood up. I had been too flustered when he first walked in to note this. He was taller than six feet, which when compared to my five-feet two-inches was a lot. He seemed bigger than when I last saw him, his chest and shoulders broader, but unlike Richard he did not have a paunch. He moved easily, like a much smaller man, but when he sat at the table, he was imposing. Maybe it was because he was sitting at the head of the table.

"Aren't you going to eat?" he asked me when I remained standing.

"Please, I've already eaten," I lied.

"But I can't eat alone so come and sit with me," he said, pointing to the chair nearest him.

"Yes, sit with your husband; I'm going to my room," my mother called from the sitting room. When I turned to look at her she was standing out of Eli's view and was blinking rapidly. I knew that she was warning me not to do anything that would displease him, or her, or Aunty, or everyone in Ho who had chosen me as the solution to the problem. The sweat from my armpits began to drip down my sides.

I sat on the edge of the dining chair and began to take slices of yam out of the Pyrex bowl and place them onto his plate as I had seen my mother do for my father when he would come back from work.

"That's okay," he said after I had placed the fourth slice on his plate.

"Please, do you want garden egg or *kontomire*?" I asked in a small voice, suddenly worried that he would not like either.

"I will start with the *kontomire*," he said.

I quickly began to scoop the greens onto his plate, careful to drain the excess palm oil out of the spoon before serving him. I hoped that my fast movements would prevent him from noticing my shaking hand. He began to eat as soon as I finished. He smiled after swallowing the first mouthful.

"Very good," he said and dug in again.

I beamed, pleased with myself. I wished my mother had been there to hear him, and Aunty as well.

"So how are you liking it here?" he said to me in English.

"Please, it's fine."

"It's quiet, ehn, not like Ho?"

I nodded and then smiled, but my smile faded as I began to believe that he would take offense at what I had said. I didn't want him to think that I was complaining about Accra.

"But I like it very much," I said quickly.

He looked up, his eyebrows arched. I think he was surprised by the force with which I spoke because I had been whispering and mumbling since he came in.

"What have you been doing?"

"Please, walking around the area, going to the market, housework."

He was quiet for a while and then asked me, "Isn't there anything else that you want to do?"

"Anything else?" I asked cautiously.

"Yes, to keep busy."

I paused as I remembered my mother's rapidly blinking eyes and her suggestion that I wait a year before starting my training. But I really wanted to start, and Richard hadn't discouraged me when I told this to him. In fact he had said that it was a "great idea." Why would his brother react any differently?

"Please, I want to go to fashion school . . . sewing school."

"That's good. Which one?"

"Emm . . . please, I'm still thinking about that."

"Okay. I will ask Yaya to help you look."

"Thank you," I said, relieved. It was only after this that I realized that we, as husband and wife, had just had a conversation. My relief disappeared when he insisted on helping me take away the dishes and leaned on the counter beside me as I washed them. His presence was disconcerting and made the hairs on my arms stand up.

"Why don't you use the dishwasher?" he asked.

"Please, it's faster this way," I said. I didn't tell him that I hadn't tried to use the machine before—mainly because my mother thought we would break it—and was embarrassed to try to figure it out in front of him.

We went back to the sitting room after this but he didn't sit down. Instead he picked his phones off the center table and told me that he was leaving.

"Now?"

"Yes, I have a meeting. Please call your mother so I can tell her bye."

I wanted to ask him if he would be coming back later but I didn't dare. I rather went to get my mother and stood behind her as they spoke.

"Afi, thank you for lunch," he said.

"Please, you are welcome," I responded. I didn't follow him out into the hallway to wait for the lift despite the jerky movements that my mother's eyeballs were making. I needed to sit and think. I needed to make sense of the afternoon. Was this it? Was this my marriage? The short visit, the awkward conversation? This wasn't what I had imagined; it certainly wasn't what I wanted. It is true that I was afraid of messing everything up but I also wanted to be given the chance to try to make it work. How else would I repay Aunty and create the life I dreamt of?

FIVE

I did not see Eli again for two months, though he called every day, even when he wasn't in the country. The day after his first visit, he called me around noon as I stood at the guard post listening to Savior and Lucy describe an attempted armed robbery that occurred during the night at one of the big houses on our street. The robbers had thrown poisoned chunks of meat over the fence to the owners' Boerboels but had underestimated the dogs' resilience and the security guards' level of commitment to their job. It was while Savior described, with exaggerated facial expressions and hand gestures, how one of the security guards had aimed and fired his unregistered hunting rifle at the robbers, that my phone rang and an unknown phone number appeared on the screen.

"Afi?"

"Yes?" I answered.

"It's me, Eli."

"Oh! Please, good afternoon, *Fo* Eli."

"Good afternoon, how are you?"

"Please, I'm fine."

"Good. I've spoken with Yaya. She gets back from Tamale today and will come to take you to see the fashion schools tomorrow. She knows some of the owners."

"Thank you very much."

There was then a short silence during which I briefly thought that he had hung up. I wanted to ask him where he was or what time I would see him at King's Court that day but couldn't gather the courage. I had cooked for him again—this time *omo tuo* and groundnut soup—and needed to know when he would be coming to eat. But how could I ask a man like Elikem Ganyo to answer to me? And even if I could, the last thing I wanted was for him to feel like I was nagging. I imagined him complaining to his mother: "I've only seen her once and she's already demanding to know my every move." But at the same time, the food couldn't be left on the stovetop indefinitely in the hopes that he would eventually show up and eat it.

"Please, I have prepared *omo tuo* for you."

"*Omo tuo*? Thank you. But I'm sorry I can't make it today. I'm very busy at work; things are hectic. You know I just returned so there's a lot for me to do here. I'm really sorry I can't come."

"Okay," I said, my voice flat. I was disappointed. Disappointed and worried about what my mother and Aunty would say.

I think he sensed how I was feeling because he quickly added,

"But I will call you when I'm coming. So don't bother to cook for me until I call to say I'm coming."

"Okay," I said, even though that promise didn't make me feel better. In fact it made me feel worse because he was indirectly telling me that we would not be living together; that I wouldn't be seeing him every day.

"But expect a call from Yaya soon."

"Okay. Please, is this your number?"

"Yes, it's one of my numbers. You can call it if you need to get a hold of me."

"Okay. Thank you."

"And no need to call me *Fo* Eli, just call me Eli."

"Okay. Thank you."

As expected, my mother blamed me when I told her that Eli would not be coming that day.

"What did you do yesterday when I left you with him?" she asked, while stabbing at a button on the remote to mute the volume on the TV.

"Nothing, I didn't do anything," I said, my voice tight. It seemed like the tone of our conversations was getting more strained by the day. If things continued like this, we would soon be screaming at each other.

"Then why isn't he coming? How can a newlywed man say that he won't come and be with his wife?"

I shrugged and went into the kitchen where I began to loudly scrape the still-warm food out of the pots and into plastic containers. I could feel her eyes on me as I did this but refused to look up at her.

"But won't we eat?" she asked when I opened the fridge, a plastic bowl in hand.

I slammed the fridge shut, tossed the bowl on the island, and walked out of the kitchen and to my room, all without looking at her. I came out after a long nap to hear her telling someone on the phone that Eli wasn't coming that day. I only had to listen for a few more seconds to know that it was Aunty.

"What should we do?" my mother asked, her voice shrill with worry.

I didn't hear the rest of the conversation because I went back into my room and locked the door.

YAYA CAME TO pick me up the next morning. She had called the previous evening to say that we would be visiting four fashion and design schools. I hadn't told my mother because I didn't want to hear more of her thoughts on my decision to start training immediately. In fact, I knew she would say that it was this decision that had caused Eli not to come yesterday; never mind that he had prodded me to tell him my plan and seemed pleased with it. I also didn't want her accompanying us, something I knew she would offer to do so that she could keep an eye on me and police my every word and action. So I had breakfast and showered as usual and then put on a pair of jeans, a three-quarter-sleeve shirt, and black, flat shoes. I only came out of my room when I heard the doorbell.

"But you didn't tell me Yaya was coming," my mother said accusingly. Yaya was standing beside her in slim-fitting trousers made out of a Woodin fabric, the type with gold motifs superimposed on it. On top she wore a fitted black T-shirt and a multi-colored, multi-strand beaded necklace, and her red wedges matched her tote bag.

"*Woezor*," I said to her but did not respond to my mother's accusation.

"How are you?" Yaya asked, stretching out her arms for a hug.

"We are going out," I said to my mother before she could invite our guest to sit.

"Oh! To where? But why didn't you tell me? I'm not ready," she said, looking down at the cloth around her waist and her rumpled blue-and-white Women's Guild T-shirt.

"I thought you would want to watch TV instead," I said, evading her questions.

She furrowed her brows so that folds were added to the lines on her forehead. "No problem, I can bathe quickly," she offered, already walking toward her room.

"Ma, it will take too long. And then you will have to get dressed and eat; it will take too long. Why don't you relax? We will return soon," I said and then looked to Yaya for support. The impassive look on her face told me that she didn't care either way. Before my mother could utter another word, I opened the front door.

"Oh?" my mother said. The sharp look she gave me told me that she knew exactly what I was trying to do.

"We are going and will return," I called over my shoulder. Yaya said the same and began following me. I didn't wait for my mother's response.

YAYA'S CAR WAS a silver Camry, the same model as mine. How many of these did the family own? I was surprised to see no driver in it; she drove herself. I hadn't even known that she could drive. In Ho she always sat beside her mother or in Richard's car. But now she was overtaking cars on single lane roads and stubbornly refusing to give way to the *trotro* drivers who tried to force their scratched and dented bumpers into our lane after picking up passengers on the shoulder of the road. I was in awe and a little bit afraid. She laughed when she noticed my hand gripping the door handle.

"Don't worry, you'll get used to Accra driving."

I managed a close-mouthed chuckle.

"So, how is it going?" she asked.

"Everything is fine."

"Do you like it here?"

"Yes, it's nice."

"How did it go with *Fo* Eli?"

"Oh, it was fine. He liked the food I cooked."

"That's good," she said and fell silent.

I was thankful for this because I knew that she had not simply been making conversation, she had been assessing my performance and my mother had already done enough of that.

THE FIRST SCHOOL was in Dzorwulu, less than thirty minutes away from King's Court.

"This is one of the best," Yaya told me as we climbed out of the car on a side street. I was surprised to hear her say that because the place was not impressive. It didn't look anything like the images that I saw on the style channels that I would watch when my mother released her hold on the TV's remote. In fact, it was somebody's house that had been converted into a place of business. We entered through a small gate and onto a flowerpot-lined walkway, shaded by mango trees that led to a large shed where a hive of people was measuring, cutting, pinning, sewing, ironing, and hanging fabric. Several headless dummies lined one wall and a variety of electric sewing machines, button makers, and pressing irons sat atop tables that were lined up under the shed. Yaya said, "Good morning," and those standing closest to us responded. The familiar whir of the sewing machines became louder as we weaved through the tables to enter the house. We bypassed a kitchen and came to a small room that had been converted into an office. In it was a large woman whose face broke into a smile when she saw Yaya.

"*Atuu,*" she said and stretched out her arms.

Yaya bent over and hugged her.

"I can see that you are doing well," Yaya said to the woman.

"By God's grace," the woman said, pointing to chairs that were piled high with swatches of every color and pattern imaginable as well as with fashion magazines. Yaya introduced me after we had transferred the fabric and magazines from the chairs onto a table and sat down.

"Sarah, this is my sister-in-law, Afi. She's the one I told you about."

"Ehn hehn, ehn hehn," Sarah said, nodding her head, which appeared to be attached to her shoulders instead of her neck.

She was a jovial woman who had been two years ahead of Yaya in secondary school—which meant that she was much younger than she appeared—and had been trained at a fashion school in London. I sat up straighter at this bit of information; this woman had been educated abroad, in London. I didn't even know that Ghanaians went abroad to study fashion. I knew that people traveled to study medicine and such, but not fashion design. Sarah was impressive! Although hers was a relatively new establishment, she had already begun to make a name for herself, Yaya told me. To confirm this, Sarah handed me glossy magazines that featured a host of famous people wearing her designs: Ghanaian and Nigerian actresses and musicians, CEOs and important women in government, a South African TV personality, our First Lady! She showed me a picture of the outfit she had sewn for the vice president's daughter's traditional wedding ceremony. I don't think I had ever seen a piece of clothing fit a person as perfectly as that blue-and-white *kaba* fit the second daughter. You couldn't see a fold, caused by poor cutting and excess fabric, anywhere on the bodice. By the time I finished looking at the pictures, I was in awe of Sarah.

"Sarah doesn't just accept students," Yaya said. She obviously thought highly of her.

"At all, only four of those people out there are under training. The rest I have hired to do small, small things around the shop and might select one person from among them after my next student graduates. I'm very selective because I like to devote time to training my students who, you should know, are all graduates who learned to sew before or after the university. My good friend here," she said, tapping Yaya's thigh, "says you're very good so I'm happy to make an exception and take you on."

"Thank you," I said. Was I supposed to make a decision now?

"We are going to see a few other places and will get back to you after that," Yaya told her before I could decide on what to say.

Sarah nodded in understanding, her jowls jiggling. But I still didn't see her neck.

BACK IN THE car, I didn't share my disappointment in the setup with Yaya. They were obviously friends and I didn't want to risk offending either of them. But I had imagined a glass building with high-ceilinged rooms painted white in which designers decked in all-black bent over work tables with sewing chalk and scissors in hand. The next place we visited fit that description almost perfectly. It was in Ridge and was run by an older male designer whose name I had known even before I started sewing. But his works, which were displayed on mannequins in glass cases along a narrow corridor, were not as remarkable as Sarah's and his demeanor was even less appealing. He kept us waiting for an hour and a half and then when he finally called us into his office, it was for four minutes. He stood behind a large work table in a Chairman Mao–inspired suit, sketching, and even as he spoke to us he remained hunched over the table, eyes trained on the sheet of paper before him. When he did lift up his head, he spoke only to Yaya. After telling her that he was "Ghana's king of fashion," he directed her to his assistant for any other information that she might need and went back to his sketching.

Yaya sucked her teeth as we walked out of his office. "That one is such a diva," she said. I raised my eyebrows in question because I had only heard female singers referred to as divas. I didn't know that a man could be one too. Anyway, we both agreed that his wasn't the place for me. The next two schools we visited fell somewhere between Sarah's and the diva's. By the time we went for lunch, we had both agreed that Sarah's would be best for me.

"And it's close to the flat," Yaya said over a plate of pasta. She had insisted that I order the pasta because it was the best dish on the menu and I had agreed even though I would have preferred *jollof* or fried rice. Now as she spoke, I struggled to get the pasta, which I had only known as macaroni before that day, to stay on my fork long enough for me to put the fork in my mouth. She pretended like she wasn't seeing the doughy strings sliding off my fork and landing with a plop in the plate. If I were at home I would have eaten this with my fingers. Around us, all of the other patrons appeared to have control of their food.

"When will I start with Sarah?" I asked Yaya.

"Anytime. You can even start tomorrow if you want."

"That's good. Thank you so much.

I picked up the fork again and tried to imitate Yaya by twisting it in the plate until there was a roll of pasta on it. This time I was able to get most of the food into my mouth.

"Are you also in the fashion business?" I asked her. I wouldn't have been so bold in Ho, but now as we both faced each other in the restaurant, I felt comfortable enough to ask her that question.

"No," she said laughing. "I manage my mother's distribution centers in Accra and Tema and I also help my brothers." She didn't seem bothered by my question so I continued.

"Do you live around us?"

"I'm quite close by, in East Legon, near *Fo* Eli's . . ." She paused abruptly and looked down at her plate as though something of interest, besides the pasta, had suddenly appeared on it. "I'm about fifteen minutes away from your flat," she finally said, her eyes trained on a spot beyond my head. We both fell silent after that.

So, Eli lived only fifteen minutes away from me.

MY MOTHER WAS waiting for me when I arrived home. I imagined that she had been sitting in the same spot since that morning, glaring at the door, ready to pounce. She didn't even say "*Woede*" when I walked in. Instead she narrowed her eyes and said, "Be careful, Afi, be careful."

"What have I done this time?" I dared to ask her. I sat in

one of the dining room chairs instead of beside her in the sitting room; the farther away the better.

"I am your mother and I know what is best for you. You are not smarter than me."

"*Yoo*, I've heard." I was taking off my shoes as she spoke.

"Don't think that you now know everything because a big man has married you and you have come to live in this palace in Accra."

"*Yoo*, I've heard."

"I am warning you."

"*Yoo*, I've heard." I stood up and began walking to my bedroom, desperate to escape her lecture. But I was not lucky this time around because she followed me and for the next hour, railed about how my stubbornness would only create problems for me, for all of us.

It was a phone call from Eli, who wanted to know how my day with Yaya went, that brought an end to her talking. That night as I lay in bed, I thought of the peace of mind I would have when she left and also about how it would feel to live by myself. I also thought of how good it would feel to have someone by my side at that moment. I imagined Richard with his secret girlfriend next door. How I envied them.

WHILE I DID not have what Richard and his girlfriend had, I didn't have to wait long for my mother to leave. Aunty came to Accra on Saturday and my mother went back to Ho with her. As I had expected, she delivered another lecture on the morning of her departure; a lecture that I did not listen to, despite my constant nodding. At least Aunty seemed happy with me. She did not blame me for Eli's failure to return to the flat. She told us that once again, the problem was the Liberian woman. She had finally decided to return to Ghana with their daughter Ivy and had been fighting with Eli since she heard about our marriage. Not only had she vowed not to move out of Eli's house, out of our house, but she was doing everything she could to prevent him from coming to see me.

"She has started following Eli around town in her car and has paid people to spy on him. She also threatened to run away with Ivy if he comes to see you. She has even threatened to harm herself!" Aunty told us. We were standing around the dining table, which I had set for lunch. The irony of it all, a girlfriend, in fact, an ex-girlfriend stopping a husband from seeing his wife!

"But what kind of problem is this?" my mother asked, seemingly more worried than Aunty.

Aunty only shook her head; we all knew the kind of problem it was.

I wanted to ask her why Eli didn't simply take Ivy and send the woman to live in America or one of those other countries she enjoyed visiting. After all, it was his child and she was an unfit mother. From what I had heard, Ivy would be better off separated from her. And what could she possibly do to Eli if he took the girl away? No judge would side with her if she decided to take the matter to court. And even if one tried to, Eli would only have to slip him a wad of cash for a favorable ruling. There was no reason for this situation to drag on. And all that talk of harming herself was just bluff; that woman enjoyed spending Eli's money too much to take her own life. But I knew better than to say any of this to Aunty, a woman who still saw me as a child. So instead, I promised her that I would continue to do my best. A promise that was for me as much as it was for her.

"You are already doing a lot, my dear. And don't lose heart, this is all temporary. The end is coming for that woman," Aunty assured me. Her words lessened the anxiety that I had been feeling. I had all along been thinking that the woman was still abroad, but now she was back and at it again. Well, at least now my mother would stop berating me for driving Eli away.

I BEGAN AT Sarah's the next week, almost one month after I moved to Accra, and immediately immersed myself in my training, which was to last for one year. Her workshop and the showroom at the front of the house, which I had not seen on my first visit, made up Sarah L Creations. She told me that her parents had given her the house after they retired and moved back to their hometown. She was constructing a multistory building nearby, to which she planned to transfer her workshop, and promised to show it to me when she had the time. From my first day, Sarah treated me differently from the other students. Even though I called her Sister Sarah, she regularly invited me to join her for lunch in her office and chatted freely with me. The other students—three men and a woman—only got instructions and directions out of her. Still, they were all smiles and welcomed me into their midst. As the days went by, we became friendlier and I would even give a couple of them lifts home in the evenings. Their reception was a relief because I was insecure about working with people who had university degrees and likely knew much more than what Sister Lizzie had taught me. I didn't want to embarrass Yaya, who had personally vouched for me, and I definitely didn't want to disappoint Eli who seemed invested in my training.

My driver, Mensah, who lived a thirty-minute *trotro* ride away, was waiting for me downstairs every morning at seven.

When I sat in the car, he would say a quick prayer under his breath, switch on the radio, and then we would set off. Even though the workshop was about seven kilometers away from King's Court, it always took us more than thirty minutes to arrive. Rush hour traffic in Accra was like nothing I had ever seen. Cars so close together that bumpers touched, people looking for shortcuts so that they drove on sidewalks and in illegal lanes such that a one-lane road suddenly had two lines of cars and no one, not even the police officers stationed at these choke points, could figure out which lane was the approved one. The *trotro* drivers, who were the worst offenders, wreaked havoc. In a bid to easily pick up passengers, they drove on the shoulders of the road and displaced pedestrians in the process, not caring that getting out of the way meant falling into an open gutter. When they attempted to force their way back into the regular lane, there were ear-splitting honks, scratches, dents, broken side mirrors, and smashed tail lights. And, of course, obscenities from all sides. It didn't help that Mensah also sometimes drove like a *trotro* driver and never allowed them to cut in front of him. On many days, I held my breath, gripped the door handle, and prayed that I arrived at work with the Camry intact.

Sarah expected us to be at the workshop at eight. I usually got there at least twenty minutes before, giving me enough time to buy *Hausa koko* and sugar bread from a woman a few houses down. Unlike Sister Lizzie, Sarah did not expect her trainees to sweep, mop, fetch water, and run errands before the start of work. The other workers did those things; all I had to do was come up with designs, cut, and sew. Sarah didn't treat us like apprentices, she treated us like employees. We didn't wear a uniform and even though her kitchen was a few feet away from where we worked, she never asked us to cook for her. Her professionalism was such that when work began at 8:00 a.m., and we always began at 8:00 a.m., it was as though we were in a glass-paneled multi-story building with high-ceilinged offices.

I OCCASIONALLY BROUGHT lunch from home but I usually bought lunch from a food stall nearby that was owned by the *koko* seller's sister. By the end of March, Eli had twice sent over his driver with an envelope of cash, which I had begun to think of as my monthly allowance. I kept most of this money wrapped in a plastic bag in one of my suitcases but had enough left over to see to my daily needs, send money to my mother and once to Mawusi, and to shop in the boutiques near my flat if I wanted. On most days, I bought lunch for Mensah too. In the beginning, I would send him home and tell him to come back for me at five but Richard later told me to have him wait for me until I finished work.

"But what will he be doing for nine hours?" I asked Richard, alarmed.

"He's a professional driver, he knows what to do." he said. "What if you need to go somewhere in the middle of the day and he's not there?"

But where did I have to go? My life consisted of going to school and coming home. Thanks to the traffic, it was always almost dark when we drove through the gates of King's Court. The only variation in this routine was on the weekends. On Saturdays Mensah drove me to the market, the Madina market, not the one near me with the inflated prices. There I did my shopping for the week with a *kayayo* by my side, balancing my purchases in a basin on her head for a small fee. I was always happy to leave the market with its throng of people, all of whom seemed to be going everywhere and nowhere at the same time. I bumped into someone every time I twitched. Sellers incessantly called out "Madam" to passing shoppers so that I soon learned not to turn my head, no matter how persistent the call. Many of them had set their tables in the pathway meant for shoppers and motorists so that when vehicles drove into the market, everyone, buyers and sellers alike, had to scamper out of the way, goods in hand. No one moved fast enough for the drivers who drove with one hand on the horn and the other on the wheel. Their persistent honks combined with the cries of the market women and the shouts of the shoppers as they were crushed against pickup trucks loaded with goods and livestock.

All of this was made worse when it rained. Black mud, combined with filth, flew from under the spinning tires of cars and tried to swallow up sandals or slippers. All of this happened in a pungent cloud of raw meat, fish, and rotting fruits and vegetables. The chaos was unlike anything I had seen in Ho. Our big market, even on market days, had far fewer people and was so much cleaner. I always immediately hopped into the shower and then took a nap when I returned home. With my mother gone, there was no one to tell me that women didn't sleep in the afternoon or that fish should be descaled and gutted before being placed in the freezer. The remainder of my Saturdays was spent watching films and reading books and magazines I borrowed from Sarah. On Sunday mornings, I went to the Catholic church in Adenta, taking a taxi because Sunday was Mensah's day off. I then cooked enough food for the week when I returned home. I would have liked to cook for Eli too but he had clearly told me not to do so, unless he called to say he was coming.

I spoke with Mawusi every day. She had promised to come visit in June during the long vacation, before she began her semester abroad. I also spoke with Eli every day. He made sure to call me during lunchtime or after work. In the first few days, our conversations never lasted beyond one minute and consisted mainly of him asking me how I was and me telling him that I was fine. But they grew longer as the days passed. I soon found myself discussing minute details of my life with him—what I had for lunch, something funny Sarah said at work, something I'd seen on TV. He too began to open up, mostly telling me about his projects, his business partners and employees, and his many travels. Those conversations were the highlight of my day and I always waited eagerly for his number to appear on my screen. The only topic that was never on the table when we spoke was the other woman. He quickly made it clear that he had no desire to talk about that other part of his life. Not with me. He would briefly say something about Ivy, especially when she wasn't feeling well and when he was worried about her health, but he never mentioned her mother.

When I asked when I would next see him, he was noncommittal: "Soon, I will come soon." As much as I enjoyed and looked forward to his calls, and felt like I was getting to know him, I was unhappy about his absence; phone calls, no matter how long, how friendly, and occasionally bordering on the romantic they were, couldn't make up for the fact that I hadn't seen him since he first visited. Worse still, the phone calls made me long to be with him in person; if I enjoyed speaking to him on the phone so much, imagine how much I would enjoy his company. I found some consolation in Aunty's promise that the situation was temporary: The woman was behaving erratically,

Eli feared for his child, he wanted to decisively end one relationship before beginning another, she told my mother. These messages, when relayed to me, made it a bit easier for me not to dwell too much on the fact that I was a married woman, who since her wedding day more than two months ago, had only seen her husband, who lived fifteen minutes away, once.

"They are working on it. Aunty, *Fo* Richard, *Fo* Fred, everybody, they are all working on it so don't worry," my mother assured me after three weeks of only phone calls from Eli.

"This Liberian woman must be truly powerful if all these people are needed to get rid of her," I said, half jokingly.

"I have told you that this thing is spiritual. Do you think that it is natural for a man to defy his whole family, even the elders, for the sake of a woman, especially that kind of woman? You have to be patient and as you wait, call on the Lord to open your husband's eyes and cause him to come to himself."

"Okay," I said, even though I didn't need her to tell me to pray. I had been praying about almost nothing but this since the day she told me that I would be marrying Eli. But the prayers were no longer giving me as much hope. I began to panic by the sixth week after our one meeting; I had been married for almost eight weeks and there was still no husband by my side! How in the world was I going to turn things around when I wasn't even being given the chance? And how much longer were the Ganyos going to accept me as a wife who couldn't perform my duties? Would they eventually tire of my failure and ask me to pack my things and go back to Ho? Would I be able to show my face in Ho after all of this?

DURING THIS TIME, Yaya invited me to go out with her often. I think she felt sorry for me. One Friday after work we went to the cinema. I normally wouldn't have enjoyed the film because it did not have a happy ending, but the experience of seeing it on a large screen, while I ate warm, buttered popcorn, made the ending bearable. Afterward, we spilled out of the theatre with the crowd of mainly young couples and headed to the parking lot. But instead of taking me home, Yaya drove to a house in West Airport where one of her friends was hosting a party. I would have said no if she had first asked me if I wanted to go. I had only begun to be a bit comfortable in her presence; I didn't need the stress of spending time with her posh friends.

The parties I attended in Ho usually had limited soft drinks and beers, which guests who arrived early enough had to grab straight from the crate or from ice chests; they also had limited food—usually fried or *jollof* rice with a single piece of chicken or beef—served in Styrofoam containers to the eldest, the first to arrive, and the most persistent, while music boomed from loudspeakers that could be heard blocks away. But our parties had a lot of dancing. Dancing until clothes were wet with sweat, until palm wine was served to the revelers to energize them because the few bottles of beer that they had snatched from the crates and ice chests might as well have been water. Dancing until fatigue set in, or inebriation took over, the kind that caused people to stagger to the music and wake up from deep sleep the next morning, still on the dance floor. Unlike those parties, this rich-people party did not have any of this kind of dancing. Instead, guests stood around in small groups chatting and swaying to the music. I stayed close by Yaya's side and smiled each time she introduced me to someone new, including the hostess, who was a tall woman with thick locks that grazed the small of her back and bangles that tinkled with every movement of her slender hands.

I marveled at how almost every person at the party, male and female, resembled a piece of artwork; colors mated with patterns and cuts and produced styles that I couldn't put names to. Necks, wrists, and fingers were decorated with gold ornaments that were interspaced with strands of beads, some of which glittered under the glow of the room's recessed lights.

I sighed audibly when I looked down at my faded boot-cut jeans and striped three-quarter sleeve button-down shirt. I had five of those secretary-appropriate tops, and before that evening had always considered them dressy. I had believed myself to be very lucky when I found them, almost brand new, in a pile of clothes that a second-hand clothing dealer had for sale. I didn't feel so lucky now and wished I could just become invisible.

"Why don't you go and get something to eat; I'm going to the bathroom," Yaya whispered to me.

"I will wait for you," I said, involuntarily pressing my back into the wall behind me.

"Don't wait for me, get some food and mingle," she urged, pointing to a long table on which were spread dishes that didn't resemble anything I was used to seeing or eating.

"Okay," I said so quietly that she probably didn't even hear me.

At the table, I picked up a plate and looked around for the stern-faced individual who would stop me from taking too much by latching onto the serving spoon and dishing the food onto my plate. But there was no such person; it was *serve yourself*. The item closest to me looked like raw octopus! I almost ran past it; I had no intention of eating that slimly looking thing. The next item was some kind of soup, but nothing like what I was used to, so I bypassed it as well. I paused when I came to white doughy balls. I picked one of them up with a tong and began to bring it up to my plate but then changed my mind midway and set it back down. No need to embarrass myself.

"Those dumplings are really good," a man standing next to me said in an accent that was not Ghanaian. He was heaping some of the octopus onto his plate.

"Oh, okay," I said and put one dumpling onto my plate.

"Only one?" he asked. He was now standing directly opposite me, on the other side of the table.

"No," I said quickly and put another dumpling on my plate. Maybe dumplings were like fried yam or plantain; no one eats only one at a sitting.

I placed the tong back into the dish and looked up at him expectantly. I wondered where he was from. Thanks to the Nigerian movies that were broadcast on every Ghanaian TV station, and now on my twenty-four-hour African movie channel, I knew he was not Nigerian. He looked to be a few years older than me but had a bald head, which needed to be wiped to get rid of the shine.

"The rice is also good, try it with the shrimp sauce," he said with a smile.

I felt my facial muscles relax when I heard "rice," and skipped several unfamiliar dishes until a dish that had the color of fried rice but had no vegetables in it was in front of me. I scooped several spoonful onto my plate and followed that with the shrimp sauce. Across from me, the bald man stood watching, still smiling as though we shared a happy secret.

"What's your name?" he asked me as I picked up a fork and a knife, which were wrapped in a white cloth napkin.

"Afi," I said, finally smiling with him. I was happy to have him by my side because I didn't know what to do now that I had the plate of food in my hand. I couldn't see Yaya and without her, I would have to stand in a corner and eat because I could not imagine inserting myself into any of the groups of people who were standing or sitting together and eating.

"My name is Abraham."

"Nice to meet you," I said.

"Join us outside," he said and began walking through a pair of sliding doors, as though confident that I would follow.

I scanned the room for a second time but still did not see Yaya, so I followed Abraham onto the patio.

"Everyone, this is Afi," he said as he sat down at a table with five other people.

A couple of them nodded at me, and a woman with a ring in her nose said, "Hey." If my mother had been there she would have whispered to me, "Why, is she a goat?" I said, "Good evening," and sat in a chair beside Abraham.

"I'm Uchenna," the woman with the nose ring said, even though I had not so much as glanced her way. "I manage Ghana Online," she continued, determined to answer questions I had not asked. "Have you heard of us?" she asked, forcing me to look directly at her nose ring, which seemed like such an uncomfortable adornment.

"No, I haven't," I told her.

"We are the largest online retailer in Ghana; you can get anything, and I mean anything, from our online store," she said, and then handed me a flyer from a small stack on the table. I thanked her and placed the glossy paper in my bag without looking at it.

"I hope you will visit us," she said with a glint in her eye.

I nodded, even though it had been more than a year since I last went on the internet. That time it had been to open a Facebook account because Mawusi insisted that I had to have one, and there was nothing drawing me back there. Besides, I wasn't even sure how one went about purchasing an item off the internet.

"Uche never stops working, always trying to sell something, always hustling," Abraham said to me with a familiar laugh. His gaze lingered on my face and then traveled down my body, as though he was appraising an item that was up for sale. I knew that look; I'd been receiving it from men since my breasts started growing when I was about eleven.

"I beg O, Abe, I'm only introducing myself, which is the polite thing to do," she replied, also with a smile. "In fact, let me introduce her to everyone else," she said. "This is Tina and this is Hajiratu; they are doctors at the military hospital," she said, pointing to two women who didn't look a year older than me. They both nodded and returned to their conversation. "And this is K.K. and Akuba. K.K. works with the World Bank and Akuba you might know from the evening news on ZTV," Uchenna said of the other two people at the table, who smiled. "And Abe, you already know. So tell me, what do you do?" she asked, her chin resting on her interlocked fingers, her eyes expectant.

"Nothing," I whispered to my own surprise and quickly shoved a forkful of rice into my mouth; maybe she would leave me alone if I started eating. Where had this lie even come from? As I chewed, I realized that I was embarrassed to tell these people, these managers, and doctors, and World Bankers, and whatever Abraham was, that I was a seamstress's apprentice and had only begun fashion school. I had always been comfortable with what I did; in fact, I had been proud that I was training with Sarah, a woman who had studied fashion design in London and sewed for the First Lady. But these people's accomplishments made mine seem insignificant, even laughable, and I suddenly felt small. If I told them what I did, they would immediately know, if my clothes hadn't already made it clear, that I was not one of them, that I didn't belong.

"Are you a student? she persisted.

"No."

"Ok, then," she said, then turned to Abraham who had been following our exchange with interest and asked, "When do you leave for Peru?"

"Who's going to Peru?" the World Banker piped in.

"I am, I leave on Wednesday; we're in talks with a company over there," Abraham answered, his gaze moving away from me for the first time since we sat down.

"No way! I'll be there on Saturday," the World Banker said.

"If either of you is traveling on British Airways, let me know; I have miles that are about to expire and I need to give them out," one of the doctors offered.

"You can only transfer miles to relatives, and I don't even think they expire," Uchenna, the manager, said and rolled her eyes.

I put more rice into my mouth as the conversation shifted to airline travel, and miles, and priority boarding and then to how expensive the London Underground was in comparison to the New York subway. By this time, both Uchenna and Abraham seemed to have forgotten that I was there, and I was happy for that. I feared that anything I said would reveal my ignorance of the matters they were discussing. After a while, I looked down at my plate and saw that it was empty; I had been shoveling food into my mouth like a robot.

"Ready for dessert?" Abraham asked me during a lull in their conversation.

"I'm okay," I told him, my arms folded across my torso. I didn't want to have to go back to the table and try to figure out what I could put on my plate. I had eaten and enjoyed the dumplings but that was enough adventure for the evening.

"You sure? Come on, they have ice cream," he persisted.

"Okay," I said, the offer of ice cream proving to be very persuasive. I stood up and spotted Yaya as soon as I walked through the glass doors; she was chatting with a white man whose hair flowed in shiny waves down his back and could vanquish my weave in a silkiness competition.

"I was about to come looking for you," she said when she saw me.

"I was outside," I told her. If she had been someone else, maybe Mawusi, I would have asked her why she hadn't come earlier. How long did it take her to use the toilet?

I noticed that she was staring at Abraham. I took two steps away from him.

"Hi," he said. "I met Afi at the buffet table and we are on our way back there for dessert," he continued and stretched out his hand for a shake.

Yaya shook his hand and gave him a close-mouthed smile. I exhaled quietly.

"Okay, well I was about to leave but why don't you get dessert first?" she said to me.

"Oh, that's okay, I'm ready," I told her and then turned to Abraham and did my best to apologize to him with my eyes.

He got the message and wished us goodnight.

"Did you enjoy yourself?" Yaya asked in the car.

"Yes," I said, though I had enjoyed the clothes, not so much the company. I felt out of place with these people.

"You'll get used to it," she said.

I smiled.

"Was Abraham good company?"

"Oh, you know him?"

"I've seen him around at these things. Accra is smaller than it looks."

"He was nice; he introduced me to some people outside."

"Well that's good, it helps to know these people."

I nodded, even though I was fine knowing only the people I had left behind in Ho.

IT WAS PAST midnight when she dropped me off at King's Court. I paused briefly to chat with the young man at the front desk before walking toward the lift. As I waited for the door to open, a woman came to stand beside me.

"Good evening," I said, taking in her tight dress that showed off every curve of her body.

"Good evening," she lifted her eyes from her phone before we stepped into the lift. She stood nearest the doors and pressed the button to the fifth floor, her fingernails blood red.

"You are going to my floor," I said, taken aback; apart from Richard and my mother, I'd never had anyone get off on my floor with me.

She stared at me for a couple of seconds and said, "Afi?"

"Yes," I answered, and then before I could stop myself, said, "Evelyn?"

She nodded and flashed a smile as the doors opened onto our floor.

"I've been meaning to come over since you moved in, but I always get home so late and don't want to disturb you," she said. I had not expected her to be friendly. The glimpses of her through the peephole had led me to paint a picture of a sophisticated woman. If there was one thing I knew, it was that sophistication was often accompanied by haughtiness and hubris.

"Richard told me about you; I'm his girlfriend," she said, misinterpreting my silence.

"Nice to meet you," I said, surprised at how freely she revealed her connection with Richard when he had not bothered to tell me she existed.

"Why don't you come over tomorrow?" she asked me as she searched for her keys in her woven clutch.

"I will be going to the market," I told her.

The even arch of her eyebrows shot up and she asked me, "All day?"

"No," I said and frowned. Why would she think that I would spend all day in the market?

"I'm only joking," she said after letting out an airy chuckle. "I'll be home until about nine so come by any time before then."

I nodded and we said goodnight. My brows remained furrowed as I entered my flat; I didn't know what to make of this Evelyn.

SIX

After the market the next day, I asked Mensah to drive me to a hair salon that one of my fellow trainees had recommended. It was one of those posh ones where the air conditioner blew nonstop, the equipment still carried the factory shine, and the latest issues of fashion magazines were neatly stacked on glass tabletops. There I paid (more than I ever had) to have my weave removed and my new growth retouched. I had changed my weave the week after Eli came to visit. Today, when the hairdresser was done, I admired my reflection in the mirror, pleased with how much my hair had grown since the wedding. The soft black waves, the tips full and even after being trimmed, fell slightly below my shoulders and were almost as thick as the weave I had worn. The hairdresser barely used any pomade, unlike the one in Ho who oiled my hair until it was limp, and instead had used a spray that left my hair bouncy. She even asked to take a picture of me for the salon's album when I was about to leave.

I knew my mother would have been happy to see how good I looked. I called her as soon as Mensah drove me home, and I described to her how my natural hair was so thick and long that it looked unnatural. She asked me to send her a picture and made me promise not to allow the hairdresser to trim my hair the next time I went for a touch-up. She also had much to say about the family. One of my cousins, Uncle Excellent's oldest son, was getting married to a girl I had attended primary school with, and my father's people, led by Tɔgã Pious, were preparing for the wedding. According to my mother, there had been a disagreement about the number of items on the list; the family was asking for too much (they even wanted a flat-screen TV) and Tɔgã Pious was having none of that, but the matter had been resolved, with the intervention of Father Wisdom. How my uncle loved to receive but not give! He hadn't protested when the Ganyos were handing out fat envelopes at my wedding and brought extras of everything. After laughing at my uncle's antics, my mother and I moved on to discussing the Ganyos. My mother reported that there was no news from them, although Aunty inquired about me daily.

"She asks for you every morning, even after church on Sundays," she said with satisfaction, as though that alone was enough, as though it was all that I deserved as a wife.

She's my mother-in-law. Why doesn't she just call me? I wanted to ask, but didn't to avoid angering my mother. This was one of the more pleasant conversations that we had had lately and I didn't want to ruin it. Some evenings after I had eaten and bathed and ceased busying myself, I missed her. Before hanging up I promised to call her the next day.

I called Mawusi after that and we brought each other up to date on our lives. She was eager to be done with school and to settle down with Yao, although the two were practically married already. Their halls on campus were less than five minutes apart and they ate supper together every day. Lately, she had been talking less about her relationship with Yao. I knew that it was because she didn't want to make me feel worse about my situation.

"Has he come?" she asked.

"Eli?"

"Yes."

"Hmmm. He still hasn't come. Only phone calls, everyday phone calls. That's all I get."

"Ah, has he traveled?"

"Traveled? He's right here in Accra with me, breathing the same air, but almost two whole months and nothing. I really don't know how long I can continue like this."

"Maybe you should go to his house."

"Ehn?"

"Yes, didn't Yaya say that he lives close by? Just go there."

"Go there and then what? When he asks who told me to come there, what will I say? And when he goes complaining to his mother, what will I do? Please, I don't want any trouble."

"Then all you can do is wait for him to come to you."

I mentioned to her that I would be going to Evelyn's later and she advised me to be careful about what I revealed to the woman.

"You don't know the kind of person she is; I have heard that the family doesn't like her."

"When did you hear this? Who told you?"

"Yao is friends with one of her cousins; they were classmates. Why do you think she wasn't at your wedding? Wasn't Fred's wife there?"

"Well, thank God I'm not going over to her flat to marry her," I said laughing. Mawusi laughed too. I appreciated my cousin's advice but I didn't need it; I hadn't discussed my life with anyone since I came to Accra, not even Sarah or the other trainees at the school. If there was one thing I agreed with my mother on, it was that one could never be sure about a person's intentions, no matter how kind that person seemed.

Later when I knocked on Evelyn's door she opened it with a big smile and waved me in. Dressed in shorts so short that the lower part of her bottom hung out, and a tank top so tight that her nipples poked through the thin fabric, she resembled a teenager. I wondered how old she was.

Her flat had the same layout as mine and was similarly furnished. On her center table was a bottle of wine and an assortment of nail polish. The scent of nail polish remover was heavy in the air.

"I just finished changing the color on my toes," she said to me as she sat on the sofa and raised one foot onto the table so that I could see the shiny purple color expertly applied to her toenails.

"It's very nice," I said to her.

"Thanks. What can I get you to drink?" she asked and reached for the bottle of wine. "Wine?"

"No, thank you," I said before she could pour me a glass.

"Juice? Water?" she said when she put down the bottle, a smile tugging at the corners of her mouth.

"Yes, water, please."

"How can you come to visit me and only drink water?" she said as she made her way to the kitchen. "I have some pastries; would you like to try them?" she asked from across the room. I shook my head, refusing her offer. "Oh, you have to at least try the cakes, they are delicious," she insisted before opening a white box on the marble-topped island, taking out several cupcakes, and placing them on a saucer.

"Thank you," I said when she set the plate in front of me along with the water.

"So how are you?" she asked, her eyes gleaming.

"I'm fine," I answered, making it clear that I had no intention of telling her anything.

"How's the school?" she asked. She wasn't lying when she said that Richard had told her about me.

"It's fine."

"Great, great. Sarah is a very good designer; she's made a few outfits for me. But her prices are something else."

"Yes, she's very good," I said. I didn't know enough about Sarah's pricing to comment on that and even if I did, I didn't think it appropriate to join a stranger in criticizing my madam.

"And Accra, how are you liking Accra?" she asked before picking the remote off the table, switching on the TV, and navigating to a sports channel where a football game was in progress.

"Accra is fine, I like it," I told her.

"Great," she said, smiling. "You know, once upon a time, I was like you, new to Accra. But I wasn't lucky enough to have all of this," she said with a wave of her hand.

"Really?" I said, surprised. I couldn't imagine her as anything but this well-off person in front of me.

"Yes. My mother sent me to live with an uncle who promised to send me to school, but instead he and his wife decided to make me their maidservant, cooking for their children, cleaning up after them. Everything you see in the Nigerian films, they did to me."

"Ehn? How did you manage?"

"I ran away. I stayed with friends for a while, slept in people's kitchens, and once in a kiosk in Kaneshie market. But I met a man who took me in—his wife lived in Kumasi at the time—and put me in school. Of course, I had to pay him in kind, but you know that nothing is free in this city."

I was listening intently, my eyes wide.

"Anyway, I know what it's like to be new and alone."

I bristled. Did she think I was alone?

When I didn't say anything, she turned her attention to the screen where two Premier League teams were playing. I picked up one of the cupcakes and studied the rainbow of colors in the icing. I wondered what flavor it was under all that sugary paste.

"Are you a football fan?" she turned away from the screen to ask me.

A piece of cake in my mouth, I shook my head.

"What would you like to watch?"

I swallowed the mouthful of sugar and told her I didn't mind if she watched the football game.

"So how are you holding up with everything that is happening?" she asked me.

"Everything?"

"Yes, with you, Eli, and Muna," she answered.

"Muna?"

"Yes, Elikem's . . . the . . . the woman."

So, the Liberian woman's name was Muna. I let this sink in, repeated the name in my head a few times, and decided that I hated the sound of it. What kind of name was Muna? It sounded like a lump, an object that was thrown onto the floor and left there, a person that sat in a corner with spit dribbling out the corner of her mouth.

"Richard told you?" I asked.

"Yes, and I'm really sorry that you are in this position," she said. Her eyes looked sad. I figured she was probably pretending. "So what are you going to do?" she asked me after taking a sip of her wine. I bristled at the question. Did this woman think that she could just poke her nose into my life? It was Richard's fault; Richard who did not bother to tell me about his girlfriend next door but had no trouble laying out my life before this same girlfriend.

"Nothing," I said and bit into another cupcake.

"Nothing? Hmmm!"

Against my better judgment, I asked her how she knew the Liberian woman.

"Well, we've met at a few functions and I've been to the house a couple of times, most recently when the little girl was sick and had to be rushed to Korle Bu."

"I see," I said, when what I really wanted to say was, tell me more.

"She's . . . nice," Evelyn said carefully.

"Nice?"

"Well, yes, she's nice," she said, this time more firmly as though she had no other choice. "The few times I met her she was very friendly and she has invited me to their house again.

But I'm just too busy to be visiting people and the woman always has one foot in the airport anyway."

"I see," I said again, willing her to continue.

"We first met at some business award ceremony, I can't remember which one—there are so many of them these days and they are mostly worthless because people pay to win. Anyway, we sat at the same table, Richard and I, and she and Eli. I was actually seated beside her and we chatted a little. One strap on my dress gave out during the ceremony," she said, smiling and cupping her breasts which were too large for her palms, "and she lent me her scarf to cover up and insisted that I keep it at the end of the evening. And it wasn't a cheap scarf, I'm talking silk, probably bought from a boutique in Italy or somewhere like that. We met again at a mutual friend's birthday party a few weeks later. She brought Liberian food, lots of greens; it was all very tasty. I even brought some home. And last time when I went to the house with Richard to visit while Ivy was sick, she seemed happy to see me."

I snorted before I could stop myself. I wondered if she was one of the spies that Aunty had mentioned. Maybe the woman had asked her here to keep an eye on me, and Richard didn't even know it.

"You're behaving like Richard. But I'm only telling you what I've experienced," she said in response to my stony face.

"Then your experience has been different from everyone else's," I said.

"Mmmm," was all she said before she turned back to the football game on TV. But I kept staring at her. Something about the confidence with which she spoke caused me to suspect that she had even more information that I did not have. Now I was stuck between not wanting to make my life a topic of discussion and wanting to hear what she really knew, even if I didn't believe all of it. But Evelyn didn't go back to discussing the woman. After a few more minutes of football, she switched to a music channel and we both watched silently as half naked women wriggled their well-oiled bodies against fully-clothed men.

"I know that guy," she said when a musician appeared on the screen, dressed in a fur-lined hoodie and baggy jeans dancing on a street in Accra, grabbing his crotch to the beat of the music.

"Really?" I asked, my curiosity getting the better of me; this woman really knew how to hook me. A few minutes later I was shaking my head in disbelief as she described how the rapper had hounded her for her number at a nightclub and then hurled insults at her when she refused to give it to him. For the rest of the afternoon she regaled me with stories of her life in Accra. She worked for an advertising agency and got the chance to meet a lot of famous people because of her job. In fact, that was how she met Richard: her company handled the advertising for King's Court. I began to find her candor refreshing; her life seemed to be an open book. She told me about the men she was with before Richard and the things about him that she loved and hated. Did I know that Richard liked to spend Saturdays in bed, cuddling? Did I know that Richard had a room in his house that was dedicated to his shoes? She told me about the plots of land she owned in Accra, including one on which she had started a cement block factory. She told me these things with complete nonchalance. I ended up eating dinner with her and taking the rest of the cupcakes back to my flat.

That night I thought about our conversation but couldn't decide how I felt about her. She had seemed so straightforward and open about her own life that I had left her flat feeling like I had known her for a long time. My mother would surely dislike her if they ever met. A person who talks so freely about her own life will talk just as freely about yours, I imagined her saying. Regardless, there was something about Evelyn that intrigued me, so that before I fell asleep, I admitted to myself that I was looking forward to seeing her again and hearing more about her life, and about what she knew about mine.

ELI CAME TO my school the next day. He hadn't said anything about coming to see me when we last spoke. I was on my way to the food stall where I planned to eat *red red* with one of the other girls when I saw across the street a tall figure leaning against a white Land Cruiser and waving. I had to draw closer to realize it was him. I still didn't know him well enough to remember his form and movements. But when I did recognize him, I began to walk faster and forgot the person at my side, who eventually went on without me.

"Good afternoon," I said, surprise causing my voice to come out louder than I had intended.

"Good afternoon, Afi. How are you?" he said, smiling down at me.

"I'm fine, thank you," I said, smoothing the tail of my secretary top, wishing I had known that he was coming.

"I came to take you to lunch. I'm sorry, I should have called first but I just finished a meeting in the TLZ building and thought this would be a good time."

I nodded, happy that he had come but unsatisfied with his explanation. I climbed into his car, which was all tinted windows and leather seats. When seated, we both looked at each other. He stared openly before starting the car while I stole glances when I thought his eyes were on the road. He was so handsome! The white shirt contrasted perfectly with his beautiful brown skin, and his voice was deeper, warmer in person than over the phone. When he smiled at me, my stomach fluttered and I looked away, unable to hold his gaze. I started talking to ease the tension. I told him that I had successfully cut and sewn my first pair of trousers that morning, and he told me that he had been meeting with investors, of which he was one, who were building a mall near the airport. I was impressed but not surprised—I knew the kind of man that he was. When finished, the mall would be better than any we had in the country; there would be underground parking, a helipad on the roof, a five-star hotel. Every major business in Ghana would have space there so that shoppers could get everything done in one place, and those who could afford to would sleep over and continue shopping the next day.

"You could open a boutique there to sell your clothes," he looked away from the road to say to me. I grinned and glanced away. A few minutes later I was still grinning as we stopped at a traffic light and our car was immediately descended upon by hawkers. Wait till my mother heard this! Wait until she heard that I might have a store in a new luxury mall. Even more, wait till she heard I was about to have lunch with Eli; maybe I could go to the bathroom and call her when we arrived at the restaurant.

Eli took me to Red Oasis. The staff seemed to know him and without asking, directed us to a table at the poolside. I asked him if he was a regular.

"Yeah, I come here for a lot of my lunch meetings; it's not too far from my office," he told me.

"Oh. Please, where is your office?" We had never discussed the location of his office in our phone conversations.

"It's on the bank road, after the first traffic light. It's bigger than the offices in Monrovia, Nairobi, New York, and London combined."

"Are you traveling again soon?"

"Yes, but short trips, nothing like the last time," he said, his finger lazily rubbing the sweating glass of sparkling water. "Do you want to come?" he asked.

"Me?" I replied, my glass of Coke halfway between my mouth and the table. I had never thought of traveling abroad, with or without him.

He chuckled at my reaction. "I think that's a good idea, maybe on my next trip to Europe. Do you have a passport?"

I shook my head. I had never had a reason to get a passport.

"Okay, I will arrange for someone to get one for you. I will have Joanna buy the forms and bring them to you."

"Joanna, your assistant?"

"Yes."

"Okay, thank you," I said to this offer of a European trip and help from Joanna.

Our food came after that and we began to eat. I had ordered rice and beef sauce and he had *akple* and okro soup with goat meat. My food tasted fine, but his soup looked thin without the *adem*ɛ and other leaves that would thicken it and make it tastier. It was such a shame that he had to come out to a restaurant to eat *akple*, all because that Liberian woman didn't know how to cook our food.

"Is it tasty?" I asked him, suddenly pained, like a mother who had caught someone maltreating her child, because the mad woman gave him no option but to eat this inferior restaurant food. I wouldn't have been surprised if it was cooked with boxed corn and cassava flour instead of proper corn and cassava dough.

"It's fine," he said as he dipped a ball of the white paste into the soup.

"You should let me prepare *akple* and okro soup for you," I said, daring to look directly at him.

He was silent and unmoving for a couple of moments and then he reached across the table for my hand, the one still holding the fork. The contact startled me and I dropped the fork onto the red tablecloth.

"I know things haven't been the way they should. I know and I'm really sorry. I'm having some difficulties but I'm fixing everything. Soon . . . things will change. I want to be with you, to see you, to come home to you. It's just that . . . well you know I've been with someone else and we have Ivy and we live together and she is . . . and Ivy is sickly, very sickly, Ivy is very sickly and I have to think about her before I do anything. But I want you to know that things are going to change for the better. I know that calling you isn't enough; I know that you are my wife and this isn't how it should be. I want you to be happy and have everything you want. I will make sure that you are happy and have everything you want. I promise you." His gaze and voice were soft when he said this, as though he and I were alone instead of sitting poolside at a hotel during the busy lunch hour. His hand remained on mine, lightly brushing, as he stared at me. I realized that he was waiting for an answer.

"Okay," was all I could whisper. My heart was beating faster than it ever had, and I knew that if I tried to say anything more, only nonsense would spill out of my mouth. I couldn't believe what he had said and how he had said it. I wanted to put my arms around him and tell him that it was okay, that I could wait for a few more months, that I knew about the difficulties he was having with the woman, that I respected how much he loved his daughter and cared for her well-being, that most men would have thrown the woman out a long time ago without a second thought, that I would wait for him, as long as he wanted me to. But instead, I interlaced my fingers with his and gazed at him and I did this without any shyness or fear. I looked at him like a woman looks at her man, like a wife looks at her husband, because for the first time, I felt like his woman, like his wife.

We finished our meal in silence and he drove me back to work. Parking a few houses away from Sarah's, he reached into the glove compartment and pulled out two wads of crisp bills that still carried the bank's seal.

"Your driver brought me money last week," I said when he put the money on my lap.

"It doesn't matter, use it to go shopping, go out to eat, whatever you want," he said.

I reluctantly stuffed the money into my bag and thanked him.

"When will I see you again?" I asked him, my eyes meeting his.

He hesitated before answering, "This weekend."

I nodded, satisfied. The weekend was only four days away.

I said "thank you" again and reached for the door handle; I had overstayed my lunch break and Sarah would not be happy. But before I could open the door, he reached out and pressed a hand on my knee. I turned to him, my eyes questioning. But without saying a word, he pulled me closer and brushed his lips against mine. My body reacted with a hunger that I did not know I had been feeling. I pressed against him, at least as much as I could with the gear box between us, and my tongue slipped out of my mouth to meet his. I didn't care that people could see us through the windscreen or that Sarah would be angry that I was late. All I cared about at that moment was the feel and taste of him. When we finally parted, we were both breathing heavily and I had to take a couple of minutes to compose myself while he held my hand.

"I'll see you on Saturday," he said softly.

I DON'T EVEN know how I made it through the rest of that day, but after supper I called my mother and told her that Eli had taken me out for lunch. I told her about our conversation in the car and at the lunch table. I, of course, left out what had happened between us at the end. It was too intimate a moment. Maybe I would tell Mawusi, but for now it was my beautiful secret.

"God is so good," she said, her voice shaking. "I've been so worried, Afi, so worried," she said to me. She was crying now.

"It's okay, Ma, there's nothing to worry about. He's coming here this weekend," I told her, knowing the news would make her happy. I so wanted her to be happy. She had suffered greatly since my father's death. I understood that my marriage to Eli was already changing her life and giving back to her some of the dignity and respect she had lost with the death of my father. I understood that this marriage was also her way of paying back Aunty. I understood that because of all these things, I had to make this marriage work. If only she would recognize the depth of my understanding and my deepest intention not to disappoint her. As she wept softly on the phone, I decided then that I would be more patient with her. After all, I was all she had. Before we hung up, she made me promise to call her the next day. I knew this meant that she was going to deliver a progress report to Aunty and would come back with the woman's response.

As I was about to dial Mawusi's number, Tɔgã Pious called. He had taken to calling me several times a week, always to ask how I was doing, how my husband was doing, when I would be coming to visit. Today, after exchanging greetings, he asked why he had not yet heard from my in-laws.

"Heard from them?" I asked him, not fully grasping his meaning.

"Since the wedding, they haven't come to visit, and when I go to Aunty's house, it is as if I'm not your father. As if I'm not their in-law," he said angrily, as though I was the one who had offended him. "Since the wedding, they have not come to ask me how I am doing, how I am managing. Why are they treating me, your father, like this?"

I then understood. The Ganyos hadn't given my uncle any money or gifts since the wedding, and neither had I. My mother had informed me over the weekend that Eli had sent a driver to deliver provisions, including three sacks of rice and three gallons of oil, to her. He had also sent her several yards of cloth and some money. She had shared some of these gifts with her closest friends, including *Daavi* Christy, and now it appeared that Tɔgã Pious had heard of this bounty and wanted to know why he hadn't also been a recipient. I honestly felt no pity for the man; had he already finished spending the money that he got from my wedding? Were it not for his position as our family head and his age, I would have given him a piece of my mind.

"And I hear that other people are being given things. Are our in-laws trying to say that they don't know that a child belongs to her father and not her mother?" he said, all bluster and indignation.

I didn't try to answer this question. He did not have the audacity to say such things to Aunty or her children, but, of course, he felt comfortable calling me.

"Afi, you know I'm an old man, but you are not asking how I'm managing to eat every day. You are not asking how I'm paying for my hypertension medication. It is not easy on me, it is not easy at all."

"Tɔgã, I'm sure my in-laws have not forgotten you."

"Then why have I not heard from them?"

"You know they are busy people."

"Hmmph! Busy people. Make sure to remind them that I, your father, am here. Remind them that I have children to feed and illnesses that need treatment."

"*Yoo.*"

"And you yourself have to remember that I'm here. You can send anything to me through *Fo* Kekeli at Tema Station. He can be trusted to bring anything."

"*Yoo.*"

"I am expecting to hear from you soon."

"*Yoo.*"

"Okay, stay well, bye-bye."

As if I didn't have enough on my mind, now this. I didn't know why my in-laws were ignoring my uncle and I didn't care.

I too would ignore him if I could but for the talk and accusations that would follow my mother and me. I knew that people would say that I was now rich but was refusing to perform my duties. That I had abandoned my father's people, especially Tɔgã Pious. I shouldn't have cared what anyone thought, especially because they had stood by as my mother and I suffered. But our extended family and community still had a pull on me. Everyone knows that a person is nothing without family, even a family headed by a selfish man. I decided that the next day I would send Mensah to Tema Station with some money for my uncle.

Mawusi and I spoke before I fell asleep and I told her about the kiss. What did it mean? Was he leaving the woman? Would I be moving in with him? I confessed to her that I had considered the possibility that Eli didn't want me, that he did not find me attractive, but that kiss had changed my mind. We both marveled at the restraint he had shown since we got married. How many men would resist even touching a woman who was their wife, simply because they wanted to first resolve problems with another woman? I had not known before this that a man could show such restraint. I wondered what had made him finally kiss me.

I got a partial answer the next day when I spoke with my mother. She told me that the Liberian woman was leaving that weekend. She was getting on a plane and going somewhere again. There had been a big fight in which the woman had threatened to kill herself. Madness! Yaya had been at the house when it happened. But was she leaving for good? Or was this just one of her tantrums?

"No one seems to know, but don't worry about that. You

have the man now; do everything to ensure that he stays with you forever."

I nodded in understanding. I finally had my husband and I would do everything to make sure that no other woman ever took him away.

"That is the life of a wife, especially a wife of a man like Eli," Aunty said when she surprised me with a call the next day. "If not that woman, there will be another one sniffing around, trying to steal what is yours, and you cannot sit down and let that happen. You have to learn to fight for your husband, never let your guard down. You are lucky that my son is not like other men. But even good men can fall, and women have become desperate in this country, especially those Accra women. There is no time for sleep in marriage."

"Yes, Aunty," I said.

"I know you will not disappoint us; in fact, I am not worried," she said cheerily.

"Yes, Aunty," I said.

I SKIPPED SCHOOL on Friday with Sarah's permission and spent the day cleaning and cooking in preparation for Eli's arrival. I sent Mensah to the market, because I was too busy to go myself and when he came back I sent him to the supermarket so that my fridge was fuller than it had ever been before. I began preparing three meals for the weekend: *akple* and okro soup, *fufu* and light soup, and yam and red fish stew. I prepared the soups and stew on Friday; the accompanying starches would have to wait until at most an hour before the meal was to be eaten. I knew that my mother would not approve of me cooking the day before and refrigerating the food, but Eli hadn't given me a time, and I didn't want him arriving at the flat hungry and have to wait while I peeled vegetables and steamed meat. After cooking, I went to the salon to have my hair washed and styled and then said "yes" when the nail technician asked me if I wanted my nails done. I got a manicure and a pedicure and had him fix acrylic nails onto mine. When I slipped into the bath that evening I was tired but felt happy with all that I had accomplished.

ELI ARRIVED AROUND 6:00 p.m. on Saturday. I had been dozing on the sofa, a book in my lap. He was wearing khaki shorts and a polo shirt. We hugged at the door and then he made himself comfortable on the sofa, his phones and keys on the center table. I brought him water and asked if he was ready to eat. He decided on yam because it was too late to eat anything heavy, and he watched CNN while I peeled the yam, immersing my hand in salt water after I was done to stem the itching and the red rash that was forming.

"You should have let me peel it," he said when he saw the rash on my hand as I dished the stew onto his plate. He held my hand, turned it over, and asked if I had a balm to rub on it. I told him that the rashes would disappear in a little bit. He complimented me on the food, and the fact that he went for seconds and thirds confirmed that he enjoyed it. After we had eaten, he insisted on helping me clear the table, but I would not let him help with washing the dishes.

"Please go and watch TV," I told him as he hovered in the kitchen with a dish towel in hand, ready to dry what I washed.

He agreed to sit down only after I had served him a dessert of fruit salad. I hurriedly cleaned the kitchen while he ate and then joined him in front of the TV. From some unknown country, a reporter in a helmet and flak jacket was describing, with a great deal of yelling and a finger pressing into one ear, an armed offensive while explosions lit up the landscape behind her. Eli sighed and switched to a movie channel.

"Why are you so far away from me?" he asked in a mocking tone, his eyes lazily studying me, his large frame relaxed on the cushions.

"Sorry," I murmured, and rose from the armchair to sit beside him on the sofa.

I sat so close that our arms touched and I could smell him. I can't describe his smell—it wasn't like any cologne or soap I had ever smelled but it was warm and clean and made me want to rest my head on his shoulder.

"I told Joanna about the forms; you should hear from her next week," he said.

"Joanna?" I asked.

"My assistant, your passport," he said.

"Okay, yes, thank you," I said, embarrassed. I drew away from him slightly and hoped that he did not notice the effect that his presence had on me.

"I'm going to go take a shower," he said, standing up abruptly.

I stood up with him, surprised. But without waiting for me to speak, he picked his phones off the table and disappeared down the corridor. I heard my bedroom door open and close as I remained standing in the same spot, thoughts bouncing in my head. He was going to shower! In my bathroom! That meant that he was going to sleep over. Yes, yes, yes! Why else would he be showering in my flat? But then he hadn't brought a change of clothes so he might be leaving after the shower. Or had he left a change of clothes in the car? But that wouldn't make sense; why wouldn't he have brought them into the flat? Should I follow him into the bedroom, into the bathroom? Well, it's not like he needed me to fetch or heat water for him; everything he needed was in the bathroom. Would he know to look in the hamper behind the bathroom door for clean towels? Would he use my towels that were hanging on the rod? I wouldn't mind if he used them. Should I go and wait for him in the bedroom? Yes, I should go and wait for him in the bedroom. Oh, but I had sweat while I stood over the pot of yam. Ah, but I could dash into the guest bathroom and freshen up.

I went into what briefly had been my mother's bathroom, ran a face towel under the tap and wiped down my body under my dress. I rubbed the towel in my armpits and then between my legs. My hand froze as I did the latter. Why hadn't I thought to shave down there? It had been almost a month since I shaved. How could I go before Eli looking like this? I dropped the towel into the sink and began frantically searching for a shaving stick or a pair of scissors. I opened the medicine cabinet that was hidden behind the mirror but it was empty. The hamper behind the door was also empty. I went into the bedroom and checked the drawers and wardrobe; they were all empty. My mother hadn't left anything behind!

When I walked into the bedroom, Eli was sitting at the foot of my bed, a towel around his waist. He smiled and patted the space beside him when he saw me and I gingerly did as he asked.

"Are you okay?" he asked.

"Yes."

"Are you okay with me staying?" he asked, clarifying his question, his hands on his thighs.

"Yes," I said again. But what was I going to say? He was my husband and was sitting on my bed, almost naked. He hadn't dried himself properly and drops of water clung to the hair on his chest, and now the rose fragrance of my Lux soap mixed with his scent so that he smelled like both of us combined.

He interrupted my observations with a kiss that began on my lips and trailed over my dress, down to my belly. I jumped off the bed when he began to move lower, knocking his head with my knee in the process.

"Sorry, sorry," I said, mortified.

"What's wrong?" he asked, rising to his feet before me, one hand rubbing his forehead. He looked concerned.

"Nothing," I said, then added, "Please, I want to switch the light off."

"Okay," he said reluctantly and watched me as I scooted to the bedside to switch off the lamp. I lingered there after the room went dark, contemplating my next move.

I soon sensed him behind me and then felt his hand tugging at my zipper. I stood still as he peeled my dress off, his hand touching, caressing. When I was naked before him, even though the air conditioner was running at full blast, I felt hot, as though I had a fever, and this time when he kissed me, his lips made contact with my skin, my nipples, my belly, and that place between my legs where I lose all sense of myself, where everything but my body ceases to exist. I forgot about the hair, about not having showered before. It was only after as I lay on his damp chest, after he had slid into me and caused me to moan so loudly that I feared the security people at the gate had heard me, after he had chanted my name while moving inside me, his eyes half closed, his breath ragged, it was only after all of this that I wondered if he had expected me to be a virgin. I hoped not.

SEVEN

I woke up to the savory aroma of frying sausages. The air conditioner was on, the room was cold, and I was naked beneath the comforter. Eli was not beside me. I jumped up so quickly that I began to feel dizzy as soon as my feet hit the floor. When the dizziness passed, I put on my dress from the previous night, which had been lying on the floor, and went outside. I found him in the kitchen, whisking eggs in a small plastic bowl as though it was something he did every morning.

"Good morning," he said when he saw me, a huge smile on his face. He wore nothing but his boxers.

"Good morning."

"Breakfast is almost ready."

I walked over to where he was and took the spatula that was in the frying pan. "Please, let me do it," I said through tight lips.

Why hadn't I brushed my teeth before coming outside? He had obviously taken a bath.

"That's okay, I've got it," he said, holding his hand out for the spatula. How could I have let this happen? The kitchen clock read eleven. I had slept until 11:00 a.m.! The poor man had to make his own breakfast. And this was the first time that he had stayed over. The very first time! Thank God my mother was not there to see this. I imagined her, a frown on her face and a finger wagging in front of my nose, asking me: "What kind of woman sleeps while her husband cooks?" I resolved that she would never hear of this embarrassment. Though, to be fair, he had woken me up late in the night and again around six that morning, the second time with his tongue in places that even my fingers had not gone before. That time I buried my face in the pillow and stifled my moans, fearing what he would think of me.

Now he softly pulled the spatula out of my unyielding hand and nudged me with an elbow. "Go sit down, the food will soon be ready."

"Let me do it," I insisted. He shook his head firmly, a smile still softening his face.

Conceding defeat, I began walking back to the bedroom. I needed to brush my teeth and take a quick shower.

"Don't stay in there too long or your food will get cold," I heard him say as I closed the bedroom door.

He didn't seem annoyed that I overslept. I just had to make sure it didn't happen again. My conversation with Aunty came to mind; there were so many women who would wait on this man hand and foot, and I didn't want to give him a reason to go looking for one of them. And I definitely didn't want to give him reason to think that I was some sort of corrupted girl, some sex maniac. I scrubbed myself harder with my *akutsa*, as though in penance; the moaning, the writhing, the thrusting, the grabbing, the biting. Why had I done all of that? Where had those things even come from? I had only been with two men before, and honestly, I had never felt the urge to be that way with either of them. But last night I had bitten Eli on his shoulder. Bitten him! He hadn't seemed upset. In fact, he had pulled my hand away from my mouth when I tried to stifle my cries. But who knew what he was thinking behind that smile?

Breakfast was uncomfortable for me. He was still mostly naked and after we both started eating he asked if I was okay. I knew what he was asking and was embarrassed by the question; I didn't look up from my omelet, which was surprisingly good, as good as what I would make.

"How are you?" he asked again.

As I hesitated, I realized that this was an opportunity to redeem myself. "I'm fine but my here is hurting," I said, stroking the air above my stomach and crotch.

His brow knitted in concern at my answer and before I realized what was happening, he was on his knees beside me. "I'm so sorry. I should have brought you breakfast in bed. I'm so sorry. Yes, last night was too much. Have you taken a painkiller?" His hand hovered above my abdomen as though transmitting healing energy.

I nodded, even though I hadn't taken anything.

"Let's move to the living room so that you can relax in the armchair," he said. He rose to his feet, picked both our plates off the table, and led the way. Of course, I wasn't really in pain;

I was only feeling a slight bit of discomfort because it had been over nine months since I was with my former idiot boyfriend. Honestly, last night had been so good that the discomfort didn't matter. I was already looking forward to tonight.

WHILE ELI WATCHED the news, I went into my bedroom and called my mother. She answered on the first ring.

"Ehn hehn, Afi?" she answered.

I told her that Eli had stayed the night, that he was watching TV in the other room as we spoke.

"Praise God," she said. I could sense her smile.

"He stayed in your room?"

"Yes, Ma."

"With you in your room?" she probed.

"Yes, we were together," I said impatiently. My mother and I had never talked about sex before; she had always pretended that it was something that I would never do. Now she couldn't bring herself to ask me if Eli and I had sex.

"Together?"

"Yes, together. We did it," I blurted out, desperate for these questions to end.

"Good, very good," she said. "I will tell Aunty."

"Ah, Ma, why?"

"What do you mean by why? Aunty has to know."

I fell backward onto the bed with the phone in my hand. Now the whole Ganyo family was going to discuss what I did in my bedroom and would applaud me for it. I wouldn't be surprised if Richard showed up, clapped me on the shoulder, and congratulated me for finally sleeping with his brother.

Eli left after breakfast and to my delight returned in the evening, with a traveling bag that held clothes and toiletries. I met him at the door and offered to carry the bag to the bedroom but he refused. He would do it himself. He also brought food. Rice and pork, chicken and chips, *akple* and tilapia, in aluminum take-out containers.

"For dinner," he said as he set the two plastic bags of food on the kitchen counter.

"Thank you, but there's food here," I said, disappointed. This tendency of his not to allow me to be a woman, to be a wife, was troubling. Clearing the table after meals, washing dishes, cooking breakfast—next he would be washing my clothes and sweeping. That is not how things were supposed to be.

"You need to rest," he said and placed a hand on my belly. I shivered at his touch. "How are you feeling?" he asked, misinterpreting the slight movement of my body.

"Better," I said.

"Good, I also bought you a hot water bottle," he said and turned to fish the bottle out of his traveling bag.

Hot water bottle! This is what lying had gotten me. Now I would have to lie in bed like an invalid while needlessly burning my stomach. As I had feared, we only cuddled that night. He wouldn't do anything more, no matter how much I pressed my backside into him. I could have tried harder, done more, but then it would have been obvious that I wanted sex. I fell asleep with a frown on my face.

OVER THE NEXT few weeks, Eli and I settled into a routine. I woke up early and made breakfast while he showered. We ate breakfast together and then he left for work while Mensah drove me to school. I usually got home before him and prepared supper, which we often ate in front of the TV. We chatted a little after that, usually about his work or my school or about something we had seen on the news or read in the newspaper. He then turned his attention to work, reading, approving project plans, emailing partners and employees. Some evenings he disappeared into one of the bedrooms to answer calls. After that we bathed, sometimes together, and then retired to bed. We went out on the weekends. In the first month, he took me to a Highlife music show at the National Theatre and then to a jazz night at a club in Osu.

"Some of my friends will be there," he told me on Thursday, the day before we went to the jazz club.

"Which friends?" I asked. He had told me a bit about some of the people he knew.

"Mainly people I've met through work. Fred and Cecelia will also be there."

"What should I wear?" I asked Mawusi later that day. I wanted to make a good impression on his friends and his brother and sister-in-law.

"Wear something nice, something stylish."

"Like what?"

"Wear a dress and high heels. Don't wear African print and don't wear jeans. Some of these rich people's clubs won't let you in if you're wearing jeans."

"I don't have any nice dresses that aren't made with African print."

"How about the silver one, the short one you wore to the

New Year's party at the hotel in Ho last year? Don't you have it with you? Everybody liked that dress, don't you remember?"

The dress in question was strapless, sat mid-thigh, and was so tight that I couldn't eat a proper meal while wearing it. Everybody had indeed liked it, some a bit too much. It had caused a fight between a couple; the woman hadn't been happy with her man's wandering eye.

"That dress is too short and tight."

"It's sexy. Wear it with your black strappy sandals, the ones with the pencil heel. It will drive him crazy."

"He's already crazy for me," I said proudly.

"Well, you want it to remain that way."

I tried on the dress while Eli was in the bathroom and it fit just as snugly as when I had last worn it. All I needed to do was polish the sandals, wash and style my hair, and I would be ready to go.

HE WAS UNABLE to stop staring at me when I walked into the sitting room. He was dressed in a blue blazer, black shirt, and black jeans with black suede loafers.

I asked him if he liked my outfit. I was still a bit shy to be speaking to him like this.

"You look beautiful," he said, before hugging and kissing me. I had to reapply my lipstick.

We left in a silver Mercedes that matched my dress, a car I hadn't seen before. The club was in Osu, on a lane with several other nightspots. Even though it was almost midnight, the street was congested as though it was midday. Revelers were everywhere and had turned the entire street into a pedestrian walkway, blocking all vehicular traffic. We had to park several blocks away in a bank parking lot, and Eli gave the security guard money to keep an eye on the car. I leaned on Eli for support because I could only walk comfortably in my shoes for a few minutes before my ankles began to ache and I began to wobble. The club was already packed when we got there and there was a long line of people waiting outside. But the bouncer, who knew Eli, let us in, ahead of those in line. We then made our way across the dimly lit room to the table where our party was seated. Everyone at the table stood and began speaking at the same time when they saw Eli, even Fred. "Eli! Good to see you, man! You made it! Welcome, big boss! Looking sharp as always, man! Eli, Eli!" They each reached out to shake his hand and then mine.

"This is my wife, Afi," Eli said when he introduced me to the four people I was meeting for the first time.

"Nice to meet you. It's such a pleasure to meet you."

There were three couples around the table, including Fred and Cecelia. The first couple seemed to be in their early thirties. The man, like Eli, had on a blazer, and the woman wore a white silk blouse with a silver necklace. Her hair was held back in a bun. Next to them was a Lebanese couple, the man in a linen shirt and the woman in a black dress without any visible jewelry. Fred also wore a blazer and Cecelia had on an African print dress that looked like something Sarah would sew. No one was wearing a sparkling silver dress that fit like a bandage and rode up every time they twitched in their seat. I drew nearer to the table to hide my bare thighs and then turned to Eli to see if he had noticed the difference between me and the other women. He was busy talking to the couple in their thirties.

Cecelia hugged me. "We finally get to see you," she said. She was seated closest to me.

"How are you doing, Afi?" Fred asked. He was seated next to Cecelia. I didn't think I could ever feel completely at ease in his presence.

"I'm fine, thank you."

"Eli said you're training to be a fashion designer," Cecelia said.

"Yes, I am," I said, speaking carefully, not wanting to say the wrong thing.

"How do you like it?" she asked.

"I like it very much. I'm working with Sarah, at Dzorwulu."

"Yes, I know Sarah; my seamstress copied this design from her," Cecelia said and then laughed. "Please don't tell her," she added, still laughing.

"Oh, no, I won't . . ." I began before Eli gently tapped my arm. I turned to him.

"What would you like to drink?"

"Can I have a Coke?"

"A Coke? You cannot come out with me and only have a Coke," he said, teasing.

"Try the cosmo, it's what I'm having," Cecelia said.

"Or do you not drink alcohol?" he asked, in a low enough voice that Fred and Cecelia did not hear him.

"I do, but nothing too strong."

"Ok, then try the cosmopolitan, and if you don't like it you can try something else."

As soon as he placed the drink order the band started playing and the conversation died down around our table. I knew nothing about jazz but even I could tell the band was good. My drink came before they finished the first number and I had drunk the entire thing before they finished the third. Why didn't we drink cosmopolitans in Ho? This drink was good!

"You like it," Eli said when he noticed my empty glass. I nodded and then giggled. He smiled and lightly kissed me, right there in front of his important friends and his brother and sister-in-law. I leaned my head on his shoulder and he put his arm around me before ordering another drink for me and for himself. He had a gin and tonic while I had a red harmattan.

"It's better than a cosmopolitan," he said when he saw my look of disappointment when the drink arrived. And he was right. The red harmattan was fruitier and tasted like it had no alcohol in it, but I was tipsy before my glass was even empty. I leaned my head onto Eli's shoulder, slipped my hands into his, and allowed myself to be carried away by the rhythms of the saxophone and the bass; it felt like the band was playing just for the two of us. Later, I chatted with Cecelia some more, and with the other two couples. Cecelia showed me pictures of their daughters on her phone and regaled me with tales of their travels. They had just returned from a safari in Botswana and found the desert beautiful. I had never thought of the desert as beautiful, but they actually made me want to visit.

The band started up again and Eli ordered another red harmattan for me. We left soon after I had finished this drink; Eli had to fly to Tamale early the next morning. The brothers were building a shea butter processing factory there and he was going with Richard to inspect the project.

The ride home was so smooth that I dozed off and only woke up when we reached King's Court.

"Can you walk?" he asked.

I nodded and took off my shoes, which I then passed to him, along with my purse. He held my hand as we entered the building, and the lift, and then the flat, only letting me go when I was on the sofa.

"Did you have a good time?" he asked. He poured a glass of water for each of us.

"Yes, but you should have told me not to wear this dress." My words were a bit slurred.

"What is wrong with it?" He was standing in front of me, smiling and looking at the dress.

"What is wrong with it?"

"Yes, what is wrong with it?" he said, kneeling on the couch so that I was between his legs.

"Didn't you see what the other women were wearing?" I said, giggling. His breath against my neck was ticklish.

"Who cares about what they were wearing? I only care about what you have on," he said, now nibbling on my neck.

"It's too tight, too revealing."

"It's perfect, you're perfect," he said while tugging on my dress until the elastic was no longer above my chest.

WE WENT TO Baobab, a popular club, the following Friday, this time only joined by Fred and Cecelia. There was a DJ spinning; the dance floor, which was really the sidewalk outside, was packed with foreigners, most of whom had no respect for the beat. This time I was appropriately dressed. I'd gone shopping with Shamima, one of the girls from my school, and had picked up several outfits that I could wear for evening outings and to special events. I had no intention of repeating the silver dress debacle, regardless of what Eli said. This evening I had on skinny jeans and a cropped blouse that showed about an inch of my stomach.

"I love this," Eli had said when he saw me. He wasn't the only one. He had drawn his chair closer to mine when he noticed a group of young men at another table gawking.

We were seated around oil drums that served as tables. Because the club had spilled into the street, cars drove slowly on the other half of the road that hadn't been taken over. This time I knew what to order and felt less nervous talking to Cecelia. We went to another place after that. Here too the bouncer knew Eli and let us in after saluting him. We had barely taken our seat in a cordoned-off booth when Fred and Cecelia disappeared onto the club's smoky dance floor. Eli turned to me, indicating he wanted to dance. When I hesitated, he held my hand and I had to follow him. He didn't dance like the younger men I'd dated. He didn't seem to know the latest moves, there was no *azonto*. Instead, he mostly held me close, even when the music was fast, and when he pulled away, it was to show off some Highlife moves. We couldn't help smiling as we danced and we were still smiling when we arrived home. We were so happy together.

WE VISITED FRED and Cecelia's for lunch the next day. They were friendly and made me feel at home, but the talk around the table was all about politics. Cecelia was thinking about running for office now that their daughters were getting older. She wanted to be a member of parliament for our district in Ho and was thinking about kick-starting her campaign in time for the next national elections.

"Have you ever thought about politics?" Fred asked me.

"Never. It's not for me."

He laughed. "That's what Cecelia used to say and now here we are."

"We'll give her a few more years," Eli said, smiling at me.

The conversation went on for so long that we ended up staying for dinner. They made me promise to visit again soon, with or without Eli.

MAWUSI CAME TO visit the next week and I had so much fun with her. Sarah agreed that I could work half-days and so I took my cousin to all of the places that Yaya and Eli had taken me before. We went to the cinema, ate at Red Oasis, and shopped at the Accra mall.

"I can't wait to be done with school and to have a proper job, so that I can afford to do all of this," she said. We were at a newly opened lounge that required a reservation to get in and charged as if people didn't have to work for money. Some of the entrees on the menu cost more than my mother made in a month.

"Have you started applying?"

"There are no jobs to apply for in this country. Nothing! You have to know someone and even then, you're not guaranteed a good one. My friend who started working last year with an ad agency on High Street spends almost half of her salary on transportation. Can you believe it? Half of her salary goes to taking *trotro* and taxis. The pay is not good at all. I need something better than that. And Yao too. And we need to start saving for the wedding."

"Find the job first before you start worrying about the wedding. I hope you're not planning anything big."

"Me? Big? Please. I have better things to do with my money. I want the wedding to be small but nice, classy. I will have to spend some money, but not too much. I'm not going to be like those people who are going into debt to pay for their wedding."

"Well, like I said, find the job first."

"I know, you don't have to tell me."

We went somewhere new every day and Eli joined us most evenings and on Friday took us to a rooftop hookah bar. He taught us how to inhale the vapor and then let it out in a minty cloud. Only a coughing fit caused me to take a break from the pipe but then I started up again as soon as it died down. Mawusi giggled through the entire evening; her alcohol tolerance was even lower than mine. When she first arrived, she had been nervous around Eli, but by the third day, she was clinking glasses with him and joining in our after-dinner conversations, offering Eli public relations advice that he appeared to be taking seriously. On her last evening with us, she asked if he could help her get a job and he promised to ask around on her behalf.

"You're so lucky," she said when he went into the bedroom to make some calls.

"I know." I was grinning.

"This is like a fairytale."

"Fairytale? Really?" My cousin was too much of a romantic.

"Well, almost. Has he said anything about moving?"

"No, but I'm sure it will happen soon."

I gave Mawusi some money and rode with Mensah to drop her off at Tema Station. We waited for her bus to get full before driving away. I immediately began to miss her. She was going to spend a few weeks in Ho before leaving for her semester in Côte d'Ivoire.

THE NEXT WEEKEND, Eli and I stayed at a hotel that overlooked a golf course and the weekend after that we went to a members-only riverfront resort in Kpong. I met more of his friends, among them, Chris and Ade, his business partners visiting from Nigeria. It was obvious that he had spoken to them about me before because there was no look of surprise on their face as they shook my hand and asked how I was. They were very friendly, especially Ade, who joked that I was too beautiful for Eli and asked why Eli hadn't told them he was married to Miss Ghana. After questions about how I was and how I was enjoying the resort, they sent me off to join the wives who were relaxing by the river, their bodies coated in mosquito repellent spray, their eyes curious. Chris's wife was Emefa, and Ade's was Vimbai. Both women had that monied look that I was becoming used to: silky hair, perfectly arched brows, skin without a single blemish, French manicures, an assortment of gold jewelry and authentic beads—not that fake stuff from China—large leather totes with designer logos embossed onto them, sunglasses with gold letterings on the sides, and dresses that would most likely reveal designer logos when turned inside out. They both spoke with a polished accent that is easily mistaken for a proper English accent by those who, like me, had never been to England. Like their husbands, they were friendly, but they did not hide their curiosity. They wanted to know everything about my life with Eli and I told them as little as I could without seeming unfriendly.

"How are you enjoying married life?" Vimbai asked. We were relaxing on three chaise lounges, with me in the middle one.

"It's fine, I'm enjoying it."

"That's good. Do you get to see a lot of Elikem? He's so very busy, isn't he? With his finger in so many pies," Emefa said.

"He's not too busy; I see him."

"Well, that's good. So there's nothing else stealing his attention?" Vimbai asked.

"No, not really."

"Really, so you have him all to yourself?"

"Yes," I said, and quickly stood up. These women would not be happy until they squeezed some information about the Liberian woman out of me. I had to get away from them.

"What's the matter?" Vimbai asked. She sat up in the chaise, lifted the sunglasses off her nose and squinted up at me.

"Nothing. I need to make a call, my phone is in the room," I said, lying.

"Okay. We'll be here for about another hour and then go for a dip in the pool, so join us when you're done," Emefa said.

I nodded and then dashed in the direction of our chalet. But when they were out of sight, I made a right turn to the restaurant. I had noticed ice cream on the menu when Eli and I had lunch and I wanted to try it. I bought two scoops of chocolate ice cream and climbed to a deck on top of the restaurant, which overlooked the Volta River. It had comfortable chairs and low tables and green and yellow hedges were planted to form a cubicle around each set of chairs. There was no way Emefa or Vimbai would spot me if they decided to come to the restaurant. I settled into one of the chairs and pulled out the spy novel in my calico bag that I had sewn with some leftover fabric the week before.

About thirty minutes later, long after I had finished the ice cream, I heard Eli's voice. For a moment, I thought he was talking to me, but then realized he was in the cubicle next to mine with Ade and Chris. I was so engrossed in the novel that I hadn't noticed when they came. They were having an animated exchange about bonds issued by the Bank of Ghana so I decided to wait until they were done to announce myself. Ade was still recounting a conversation with the bank governor when Chris interrupted with news about the sale of one of the local airlines, which had just popped up on his phone.

"I flew it two weeks ago to Tamale," Eli said.

"Really. How was the service?" Chris asked him.

"Alright. But the equipment was old. I don't know who they're going to get to buy such old equipment," Eli said.

"Did you go with the wife?" Chris asked.

"Which of them?" Ade asked, and then burst into laughter. Eli and Chris did not join in the laughter.

"So how are you handling this thing with Afi and Muna?" Chris asked him.

I closed the book and put it on the table, alongside my bag.

Eli sighed heavily. "It's not easy, my brother."

"Your mother is still giving you a hard time?" Chris asked.

"Will she ever stop?" Eli said. "But now it's about more than what my mother wants. You know?"

"So now you want to be with her, with Afi?" Ade asked him.

"Why else would I bring her here?" Eli said, his voice laced with irritation.

"And Muna?" Ade continued, undeterred.

Eli sighed again but said nothing.

"You have to choose one of them just for your own peace of mind. I saw what my father went through trying to maintain two homes and keep two women happy. I wouldn't wish that on anyone," Chris said.

"That's your father. He and Eli are not the same person; you can't compare them. My brother, you don't have to choose; man wasn't made to be with one woman. You're a lion, you should have an entire pride!" Ade said.

"My friend, just stop with that," Chris snapped at him.

"I will sort it out," Eli said, as if to bring an end to the back and forth and then he redirected the conversation back to the sale of the airline.

I remained frozen in my seat. There was no way I could reveal myself after this. I didn't even open my novel again, afraid that flipping a page would alert them to my presence. When a waiter came twice to ask if I wanted anything, I frowned and shook my head, eliciting a look of annoyance from him. I breathed a huge sigh of relief when they left about an hour later.

BACK IN OUR chalet that evening, I wondered how to broach the subject with Eli. Should I confront him on what I'd overhead? What if he accused me of eavesdropping?

"I had a good time with Emefa and Vimbai," I said. We were in bed.

"Good, they're nice. But they were looking for you in the afternoon to join them in the pool."

"Really? I decided to do some reading."

"Okay. Good book?"

"Yes. You know, they were asking so many questions, about us . . . about our situation."

"They are harmless," he said, nibbling on my earlobe, a hand caressing my belly.

"Are they her friends?" I asked him.

He froze.

"That doesn't matter."

"But it does . . ."

"Am I not here with you?" he asked before getting up to stand beside the bed. This was the first time that I had heard him raise his voice, the first time I had seen him narrow his eyes and harden his face.

"Eli . . ." I began but he stalked off to the sitting area, which was separated from the bedroom by a porcelain tub. I followed him there, naked. He was standing and pouring brandy from the minibar into a glass.

"I'm sorry," I whispered.

He glanced at me and then looked away without saying anything. His face was so tight that I imagined it would feel like a wooden mask if I touched it.

"Eli, I'm sorry," I said, my voice pleading, not wanting to lose everything I had gained in the past few weeks. What would I tell my mother? What would I tell his mother? But most importantly, how could I go back to being separated from him? I stood on my toes and kissed his stiff neck, his jawline, and then his lips. I could taste the bitterness of the drink. He didn't kiss me back but he didn't push me away either. I caressed his face with one hand while the other snuck beneath his boxers. He inhaled sharply and then his lips softened against mine. I pulled away from him and sank to my knees. When I looked into his eyes again, he was no longer angry.

EIGHT

If I had had any doubts before, Eli's behavior that night made it clear that any mention of the Liberian woman was out of bounds. I was to pretend that she did not exist. Every once in a while he let something slip about Ivy: what the girl liked to eat, how she stayed up crying through the night, how she clung to him in bed. But those slips were followed by heavy silences tinged with regret; the countenance of a man who had disappointed himself. The uncertainty circled like a mosquito that is buzzing in a dark room, always threatening to land so that its victim can never know peace. I told Mawusi about what happened and she too was bothered that Eli was still pretending while he was with me that the woman did not exist while acknowledging to his friends that she was still in the picture. I was also troubled that I was yet to enter his house, that at the end of each week he took the traveling bag away, filled with dirty clothes, and returned in the evening with a fresh set of clothing.

"What's happening?" I asked my mother, hoping that she would have heard something from the Ganyos.

She didn't have an answer. "Just focus on taking good care of him. That is what will get you into his house. Do your best to make him happy and everything will be fine."

I sighed; I was already doing everything I could. I was cooking every one of his favorite dishes, even when it meant that I had to leave school before closing time. I timed my cooking perfectly so that the food was warm and the table set as he walked into the flat. I washed, starched, and ironed his clothes whenever he would allow me to, and after he had taken his evening bath and was poring over the documents he usually brought home from work or was typing away on his laptop, I tried to make myself useful. I hovered nearby, ready to respond to his every wish.

"I'm fine," he would usually say without lifting his eyes from his work, "don't worry yourself, get some rest."

But how could I rest? Resting would cost me my marriage, my husband. There could be no rest. I did my best to stay up with him, watching TV or reading novels while he worked, then rising to go to bed with him as soon as he put away his documents and laptop. The bedroom part was still a bit of a challenge. I didn't want to be loud and enthusiastic but he seemed to like it, to enjoy my pleasure, to find nothing wrong with it. So I reluctantly allowed myself to show how I felt, all the while hoping that it would not come back to haunt me.

But when it came to the woman, I could not show how I felt. I asked Richard one day as we stood in the hallway waiting for the lift, what was going on between his brother and the woman. He had come by to drop off some building plans and I had followed him outside under the pretext of seeing him off.

"Nothing, that woman is not even in Ghana," he told me. He was wearing another shirt so tight that I wondered how the sleeves had not yet cut off his blood circulation.

"But when will I move into his house, when will I leave here?"

"Ah, but isn't this also his house?" he asked with a forced laugh.

"You know what I mean."

"Afi, these things take time. What's the hurry? Besides, are you not happy here?"

What kind of a question was that? I was a married woman who was not being allowed into her marital home.

"But Richard," I began, but the lift doors opened and he hurried away.

"There's nothing to worry about," he said.

I sighed heavily as the doors closed and tears began to well up in my eyes. I turned away from the lift to enter my flat and noticed Evelyn's open door. She was standing right inside it, this time wearing a mini-dress that could pass for a negligee.

"Have you been spying on me this whole time?" I snapped at her.

"Spying? Please O, my door was open before you even came outside."

"And you didn't see the need to close it?"

She laughed. "Afi, I'm not fighting with you so please don't take your frustration out on me."

I sucked my teeth and turned away from her, not wanting to anger myself even more.

"Muna is gone on vacation, that's why he's here. She's coming back soon," Evelyn said. I turned; the smile had disappeared from her face. Now she just looked like a woman who was forced to deliver sad news.

"Vacation?" I said, my voice a whisper.

"Yes, and she's coming back soon," Evelyn said. "They don't want to tell you. They don't want to admit that they haven't been able to get him to leave her. This thing that he's doing here, I don't know if he's also on vacation or what, but don't be fooled into thinking that he's left Muna. You just tell him that you want to move into his house and hear what he will tell you."

I inhaled deeply and held my breath to stop myself from bursting into tears. I knew immediately that everything she was saying was true, he had confirmed it in the conversation I overheard at Kpong. I felt so humiliated standing in front of Evelyn, so insignificant, the small town girl who had been brought to the big city but had failed in playing the game like the city girls, like Evelyn who had Richard but didn't seem to care if she only had a part of him or even if she lost him.

"It's okay," she said, stepping outside. I bowed my head to hide my tears and she put a hand on my shoulder. I flinched and she took the hand away.

"Why don't you come inside?" she said.

I shook my head. "Eli is inside," I said. Why was I even bothering to explain anything to her?

"So? My friend, come inside," she urged.

I gave up and followed her, this woman who I mistrusted but felt like I needed.

In her flat, we sat on the couch. She muted the volume on the football game she had been watching.

"You'll be fine," she said.

"How?" I asked. I could not think of how I could do more to make him see that I was all he needed, that the Liberian woman was not worthy of him.

Her gaze wandered to a spot behind me as she tried to come up with an answer.

"Well, I think you have to talk to him. You know, just be direct, straightforward."

"He got angry when I tried."

"Then try again; you have the right to know. Besides, marriage is not always full of laughter, sometimes it is anger and tears. Don't back down."

I looked at her through my tears. It was so easy for her to say this, to say that I should knowingly provoke my husband. She had nothing to lose. Richard was just a boyfriend, one who she would have no problem replacing. But me, where was I going to find another man like Elikem Ganyo to marry?

"Afi, you can't be afraid of your husband. If you can't share your fears with him then who can you share them with? You are his wife! Ask him to tell you what is happening with him and the woman. Ask him."

I stood up after she said this. "He's waiting for me," I said even though I knew Eli would still be working and would not even realize that I was not in the flat.

Her lips moved as if to speak, but she said nothing, just shook her head sadly.

I left, a mixture of emotions roiling inside me: frustration, betrayal, anger, disappointment.

ELI EVENTUALLY NOTICED my quietness.

"What's wrong," he asked me one evening as we snacked on a bowl of cashew nuts.

"Nothing," I told him.

"Are you sure? You seem down," he said, reaching for me.

"It's nothing, I'm just tired from work."

"Then let me get you someone to help with the housework."

"No, that's not necessary. It's only because we are very busy at school this week. Sarah has a fashion show coming up and we are all working overtime. But I cooked for the week over the weekend so we are fine." It was true that Sarah had a show coming up in Dakar and we had been fitting the models for most of the week, but of course that wasn't the reason for my quietness. I could tell from his furrowed brows that Eli didn't entirely believe me so I faked a yawn and said goodnight before he could ask any more questions. His hand lingered on mine, reluctant to let me go. That was the first time that I went to bed without him.

ON THURSDAY OF that week, I returned from work to find Tɔgã Pious waiting for me in the lobby, a small Ghana Must Go bag at his feet.

"Tɔgã?" I said, my surprise preventing me from greeting him.

"Afi, are you well?" he asked, as though there was nothing unusual about him being here unannounced. Had something happened to my mother? I hadn't spoken to her since the day before.

"How is home?" I asked, expecting bad news.

"Home is well, everybody is well, they all send their greetings," he said cheerfully.

"My mother?"

"Afinɔ is fine. I saw her in front of the post office this morning. She's fine."

"Okay, thank God. *Woezor.*"

"*Yoo.*"

We remained staring at each other after this, he with a wide smile.

"So where is your house?" he asked.

"It's upstairs," I said and picked up his jute bag. It didn't weigh much, thank God. I hoped it meant that his would be a very short visit.

"Pious Koku Tekple, look at where you are," he said under his breath as the doors of the lift opened. Inside, he nodded and smiled at his reflection in the mirrored walls. While my mother's awe of King's Court had pleased me, his only irritated me. In my flat, he ran his hands over every surface, even the white walls, as though to confirm what he was seeing. He followed me into the kitchen and peered over my shoulder as I fetched a bottle of water out of the fridge for him. All of this was accompanied by a running commentary.

"This is not a fridge, it is a provisions' store! Everything is shiny, shiny. This chair is so soft that my whole body is entering inside. This TV is more than a cinema."

Bush man!

When we were seated in the sitting room, I welcomed him again.

"Thank you, my daughter."

"I hope all is well," I said, still wanting to know what had brought him here.

"Everyone is well, it is nothing bad. I only wanted to come and see where you are, to spend some time with you."

"How did find your way here?"

"But you told me over the phone where you live. Have you forgotten? Besides, am I not your father? How will I not know where you, my daughter, live?"

I frowned. I had no memory of telling my uncle where I lived. But that didn't matter, he was in my house and Eli would soon be coming home. Why did he have to visit now, when I was already so stressed out? I offered him food, and while he ate, I took his bag into the guestroom and made up the bed. I ran to the door as soon as I heard Eli's key turn in the lock and told him my uncle was visiting us, and I was happy to have him, but that I hadn't known he was coming. I wanted him to know that Togā Pious had surprised me, but at the same time, I didn't want my uncle to look bad in front of my husband. It was one thing for my mother and me to mock him; it was another for people outside the family to do it. But Eli didn't seem to mind. He chatted with an obsequious Togā Pious when the old man came out of the bathroom, shirtless, as though he was in his own house. But after dinner, Eli retired to the bedroom while Togā Pious clicked through all the TV channels.

"What do you want to watch?" I asked him, annoyed. I wanted to join Eli in the bedroom but didn't want to leave my uncle alone outside. I had to be a good host, and I feared that the nosey old man would search through every corner of the flat as soon as I turned my back. I could already imagine the stories he was going to tell when he returned home. I wouldn't be surprised if another uncle showed up next week.

"I want to watch everything," he said, laughing and placing his ashy feet on the center table. He wouldn't have dared to do this in Eli's presence. At that moment I wished that my husband would suddenly open the bedroom door and surprise the old man. Imagining his frantic reaction brought a smile to my face.

"Look at how happy you are, I should have come a long time ago," he said.

My smile faded. He didn't seem to mind.

"Well, since I'm here, I might as well tell you that I have some land near the new hospital and I want to build something small there," he said after clearing his throat.

"Something small?"

"Yes, somewhere I can lay my head. The family house has been taken over completely, there is nowhere I can call my own. A man my age needs a place he can relax peacefully."

"I see," I said, nodding. Although what I really wanted to say was: "Who is in the family house? Is it not your wives and children and renters who pay rent to you?"

"Ahn hahn, so I've come to hear what you have to say, what you plan to do. My daughter, I am in your hands."

The callousness of this man! The audacity! After denying my mother and me a place to live, he was now coming to ask me to build a house for him.

"Tɔgã, please, I don't have that kind of money."

"But I'm not asking you to give me everything today. You can give it to me small, small."

"I haven't even started working yet, I've gone back to sewing school."

"Ah! Afi, what are you talking about? Look at where you are. Look at who you are married to," he said, stretching his arms out wide.

"I will see what I can do," I said quickly, wanting to end the conversation.

"Ahn hahn, you are now sounding like my daughter."

I had no intention of building a house for him, but I did have to give him money to encourage him to leave my home. I couldn't stand having him around, eating everything, talking cheerily as though he and I were the best of friends, referring to me as "my daughter" when he had never treated me like a daughter. I felt so relieved when he left on Saturday that I took a four-hour afternoon nap, waking up in time to prepare supper, yam chips and kebabs. Eli washed the dishes, despite my objections, and we retired to the sitting room.

"I won't be able to sleep over here regularly . . . for a while," he said. I was sewing strips of batik onto a leather handbag that would be modeled in the Dakar show.

I tossed the bag onto the sofa beside me. "Why?"

"Well, you know . . . I've already explained my situation to you; I told you that I was having some challenges."

"But that was before, before you moved in. Before everything happened between us. And now all of a sudden you are telling me that you are leaving." The ferociousness of my response surprised me. I clasped my hands in an attempt to restrain myself, to put my emotions in check.

"I didn't say I was leaving."

"Then what are you saying?" I snapped and stood up. I had obviously failed in calming myself down.

"Afi, please understand, this is not easy for me either," he said, standing up too.

"Then why are you doing it? How can I understand when you haven't told me anything? Eli, I don't know what is happening. I don't know, I don't know what you want, I don't know what you want me to do." I was gesticulating wildly as I spoke to him and tears were running down my face. I hadn't known that I could burst into tears so quickly.

"I'm asking you to be patient," he said.

"Haven't I been patient enough?" I screamed, not caring if I upset him, or my mother, or his mother, or his entire family. "I am tired, Eli, I am tired," I sobbed, snot mixing with my tears and ruining the perfect image I had presented to him since he first walked into the flat.

He seemed surprised at my outburst, like he hadn't thought it possible for me to express anger.

"I'm sorry. I have to think about Ivy too," he said, trying to hug me.

I sidestepped his embrace.

"You know she's sickly," he said in a pleading tone.

"I don't know anything!"

"She has sickle cell anemia. She needs care."

"Why can't that woman take care of her?"

"Afi, I have to be with her, she's my daughter. I'm going to the States tomorrow to bring them back."

"Them?" I yelled.

"She needs her mother too."

"And how about me, how about what I need?" I asked him as I wiped my face with my nightgown.

"It's temporary; I just need to sort things out with her."

"What things? Tell me."

"I don't want to get into that today, it's not going to do us any good," he said, looking at me as if I was being unreasonable. What was unreasonable about me wanting to share a home with my husband? What was unreasonable about me not wanting to share him with another woman?

"You can't do this, Eli, you can't leave me." I was gripping the hem of his T-shirt now.

"Darling, don't be like this. It's only for a short while, until I figure things out." He tried to frame my face with his palms but I pulled away.

"What is a short while? How many days? How many weeks?"

"I don't know yet; I just need time."

"Eli, I love you, please don't leave me," my tears were blurring my vision so much that I couldn't see the look on his face.

"I love you too, darling, you know I do. That's why I want to sort things out with her."

"But do you have to live with her to sort things out? Why do you have to be in the same house with her?"

"It's complicated."

"It's not! It's very easy. You're the one making it complicated!" I snapped.

"You don't understand."

"Then make me understand, make me understand why you keep going back to her."

"Afi," he began, reaching out to me.

"Don't touch me," I yelled, spit flying out of my mouth.

"Afi," he said, his eyes pleading.

"If you're going, go. Stop calling my name and go to her. Go!"

He left that night and afterward I could not sleep. I sat in the sitting room throughout the night, and for most of the following morning. I ignored the phone when Sarah called, and again when I heard the special ringtone I had assigned to my mother. I began dialing Mawusi, but hung up before her phone could ring. Finally, that evening, I found myself knocking on Evelyn's door.

"Come in," she said quietly when she saw my face.

I surprised myself by telling her everything.

"I'm sorry," she said when I had finished speaking. "So what are you going to do?"

I shrugged. I did not have a plan. I realized then that I would have had a plan by now if I had spoken to my mother or Mawusi. Of course, my mother's suggestions would not have been hers but would have come from the Ganyos, packaged as words of concern and encouragement. I wanted none of that.

I fell asleep in Evelyn's guestroom after an evening of eating and drinking but very little talking. She had no more news on the woman and seemed to be out of advice. She, however, had ample wine, so for the first time I drank good wine, not the sugary nonalcoholic kind that I was used to. I woke up with a dry mouth and a sense of disorientation. Evelyn had already left for work but had left breakfast on the kitchen counter for me. I ate, showered, and went in to work. Sarah was less than pleased when she saw me.

"I was calling you all of yesterday. What happened? Did you forget you had the bags?" she said, a tape measure around her neck and a pin precariously tucked between her lips.

"Sorry. I wasn't feeling well," I said. The effects of the wine combined with the heartache made my excuse close to the truth.

"But you could have answered your phone, you could have sent your driver to deliver them," she said, the pin still between her lips so that she whistled some of her words.

"I'm sorry," I said and walked to my work station, embarrassed. I managed to place Eli in the farthest corner of my mind as I pushed myself to finish sewing the batik on to the bags. I felt bad about letting Sarah down; I had begun to see her as a friend. Luckily for me, her frown was replaced by a smile when I handed her the bags at lunchtime, and by the end of the day, we were huddled in her office, signing invitation cards for celebrities she hoped would attend the show.

Eli called six times while I was at work and three more times when I got home. I ignored all his calls but answered when my mother called; the last thing I needed was her coming to Accra to find out what was happening to me.

"He has left," I told her unceremoniously.

"What do you mean he has left?"

"He's gone back to the woman."

"Afi, you don't listen! What did you do?"

"I did everything you told me to do, everything that you and Aunty told me to do. I cooked, and cleaned, and smiled, and spread my legs as wide as I could, but he still left!"

"Why are you talking like that, what is wrong with you? Have you forgotten that I am your mother?"

"You asked a question and I answered it. Are you not the one who said that as long as I took care of him he would stay? I did that, and even more, and he still left."

"You are not yourself, I'm coming to Accra."

"There's no need for you to come to Accra, there's nothing you can do here. Besides, the man is flying to America this evening to go for his woman and child. This same woman that you people said would disappear."

"Stop shouting. Why are you shouting?"

"My husband has left me."

"Afi, I'm sure it's nothing, I will call Aunty right now to tell her what is happening."

"Call Aunty, but know that I'm not interested in receiving any more advice or encouragement. What kind of marriage is this? Afi, do this and he will choose you. Afi, do that and you will win. Is he a husband or a prize? Ah, Ma, I'm tired, I'm tired."

"Afi . . ."

"No," I said cutting her off. I hung up and shut my phone off. It was only then that I realized that I was crying. I had never felt so alone and small as I did at that moment. I wished I knew how to turn things around. It hit me then that I was hopelessly in love with him, that more than anything, I wanted to be by his side. Not because of his mother, or mine, but because of how I felt when he looked at me, when he said my name, when he held me close. At that moment, I wished more than anything that I hadn't fallen in love with him, that I didn't love him.

YAYA AND RICHARD came to see me at work the next day, and although they arrived separately, they came with the same message: this is nothing to worry about; he will be back. I listened quietly as they spoke about their niece, my stepdaughter, about how much Eli loved her, about how incapable the woman was of caring for her.

"He's doing all of this for the little girl, not the woman," Yaya said, trying to reassure me. We were seated in her car because there was no space in the workshop where we could talk privately. I was stoic as she spoke, not caring to pretend like I wanted to hear what she was saying. I had allowed them to pull me around by the nose long enough. I had had enough.

The only person who had been straightforward with me from the beginning was Evelyn. Though it went against everything I believed, I started spending more time with her. She recommended a foreman from Kpando to work on the house I was building in Ho, on my mother's land.

"He's going to steal a bit from you, they all do, but he will make sure the work is done and he will stop the other workers from stealing. The only other way is to sit on the construction site yourself, every day from morning to evening, and oversee the work. And even if you were to do that, they could still steal from you without getting the work done. Do you know how many times I've caught workers leaving my site with boxes of nails stuffed into their boxers? Nails! You need someone who's used to dealing with these people."

She was right. Within a week of bringing in the foreman, the house was at the roofing level and my costs went down; the bags of cement and everything else were lasting much longer

But advice on the house wasn't the only area where Evelyn helped me. One Friday she took me to a reception at her office. It was for their top clients so everybody who mattered was there, even many people from outside Ghana. I recognized some of the business people Eli had told me about, but I was more interested in the celebrities, their clothes, and their entourage. The first person I spoke with was the anchor from the evening news on TV2.

"Did you tell her about your boutique?" Evelyn asked me, a glass of wine in hand. She had noticed me talking with the woman.

"What boutique?"

"The one you will soon open."

"Ah, Evelyn."

"Don't ah me. This is the time to start advertising your work. Tell them you will soon be graduating from Sarah's and opening your own place. Tell them about some of the pieces you've designed, and also tell them Eli is your husband. Everybody knows him and they will remember you because of that. There's Lady X over there, let's go talk to her." I followed Evelyn, confident that she would do most of the talking and she did. But my cheeks were still sore from smiling when we returned home that evening. I really did not know how Evelyn did it.

THE FOLLOWING SATURDAY she asked me to accompany her to a funeral because Richard had refused to go with her. It was the funeral of some rich woman's father and everyone who was everyone was going to be there.

"I might find Richard's replacement there," Evelyn said jokingly as we entered her car. But then I knew three women who had met their husbands at funerals, so I knew there was a kernel of seriousness in what she was saying. It was one of the many reasons why the highways were clogged over the weekends with people going to and returning from funerals, dressed up in the latest fashions.

Before we went to the church, we stopped by Evelyn's block-making factory, which was in Adenta, to inspect the work being done.

"You own all of this?" I asked in awe as I surveyed what seemed like hundreds of rows of cement blocks lined up like soldiers on a parade ground, gray and grainy and drying in the sun. Young men, most of them shirtless and glistening with sweat, shoveled cement and sand into three yellow concrete mixers, while another group shoveled the mortar into blue block-making machines, leveling the mortar as they put it into the mold to get rid of the excess. Each of them stopped to greet Evelyn as she walked by in her black sheath dress, stepping gingerly so as not to get mortar on her high heels as she inspected the open space that served as the factory. The foreman stood with his arms behind his back, as though he were a student addressing his headmistress.

"Did Richard set it up for you?" I asked when we returned to the black Escalade that seemed to intimidate everyone on the road, even policemen, who never dared to stop her for made-up road infractions because they assumed she was a big man's wife, girlfriend, or daughter.

"Richard?" She laughed long and hard. "Please, I started my business before I met Richard," she said as we crawled in traffic down Legon Road toward the 37 Military Hospital; the funeral service was at the Holy Spirit Cathedral.

"How?"

"How did I start?"

"Yes, how were you able to start?"

"Small, small. I saved money from my first year of working at the agency and bought the land. I had planned to build a house. In fact, that is why I bought the first block machine, but other people building in the area kept asking to buy my blocks and I figured I could make good money selling to them. I didn't even have a mixer when I started; the boys used to do everything by hand, but I've since been able to upgrade. And let me tell you, the money is good. I've already built three houses out of the block factory, one in Accra, one in Tema, and one in Kpando. That's why I don't even bother with that so-called Aunty and her nonsense. Behaving like she's the only one to ever give birth to sons. What kind of mother insists on choosing girlfriends and wives for her sons? And Yaya! Yaya who acts like she's not also a woman, like she's not also going to one day marry someone's son." She sucked her teeth after she said this, and then became quiet. But her words hung over us, even as we attended the funeral reception that was so glitzy that minus the black clothes, it could have passed for a wedding reception. The drumming and dancing that followed the reception was still going on when we left. When we returned to King's Court that evening, I asked her about what she had said earlier.

"Look, they are your in-laws. I've never wanted to bad-mouth them to you. There's no need to make you feel worse than you already do. I shouldn't have said anything today."

"It's not bad-mouthing; it's the truth," I said, wanting her to tell me more. We were sitting around her dining table sipping perfectly seasoned goat light soup that we had brought back from the reception in plastic bowls. Evelyn knew the caterer, who had insisted on giving us food to bring home. She had changed into shorts and a T-shirt, but I was still in my *kaba* and slit, which, from what I had seen that afternoon, appeared to be the attire of older women at Accra funerals. Almost all of the younger women had shown up in sheath dresses, fascinators, and high heels that would make for dangerous walking in a regular cemetery—where there were no footpaths and it wasn't unusual to step on unmarked graves—but did not pose much difficulty in the new private cemetery where the burial took place today, with its paved pathways and demarcated burial plots. At least I now knew what to wear if I was invited to another Accra funeral. I brushed invisible dirt off my top as I waited for Evelyn to speak.

"Look, Afi, you should know the kind of woman Aunty is by now," she said with a sigh.

"It will surprise you to know that I've had very little inter-action with her, especially since the wedding. My mother is the one she talks to." I sounded like a teenager trying to deny a friendship in order to appear cool.

"Well, I will tell you this: Aunty is controlling. She behaves like she is God. She wants to tell everybody what to do, how to live, even strangers. But I don't blame her, I blame the people who keep bowing down to her; beginning with her sons who have never had the courage to open their mouths and say 'no' to her, not once in their whole lives. I cannot understand how men like Richard and Eli allow themselves to be treated like small boys. You should see how Richard jumps to answer the phone when she calls, and then drops everything to carry out her orders. I'm not joking. Even if he's on top of me, pumping away, he will stop and hop off like a kangaroo to speak with her and do her bidding. Can you believe it? And Eli, hmmm. As for Eli . . ."

"What about him?"

"Do you know that Aunty ordered Richard to dump me as soon as she found out we were together? Ask me why."

"Why?"

"She said my father once insulted her. My late father who has been dead for twenty-two years! A man who died while I was in primary school! She once came to Kpando to buy palm nuts and took offense that my father wouldn't accept the price she was offering. So because of something that happened when I was a child, an incident that I knew nothing about and had no hand in, she has ordered her son to leave me. Can you believe it? She told him I wasn't good for him because she was sure that I would have my father's ways. In other words, she was sure that

I would stand up to her." Evelyn rolled her eyes and returned to sipping her soup. A bead of sweat lined her upper lip; I didn't know if it was from the pepper in the soup or from the story she was telling me.

"I don't even know what to say . . . she has been very nice to us. To me and my mother . . ." I still couldn't bring myself to criticize Aunty in front of Evelyn.

"I'm not saying that she cannot be nice. I know for a fact that she pays school fees for more than fifty children in Ho. I've seen Richard stuffing the cash, fresh from the bank, into white envelopes to distribute to the families. But the fact is that the woman wants everybody to worship her. As long as you are doing her bidding, you won't have any trouble, but the day that you make a mistake and go against her is the day that you will see hell. My sister, you will see fire! And that is why I haven't placed my hopes in Richard; I'm not expecting anything from him. As long as his mother is alive, there will be no future for us. Did you know she wanted him to throw me out of this flat? He had to lie to her, telling her that I pay rent; that's the only reason she let the matter rest. And that's why we rarely go out together, because he doesn't want people to see us and tell his mother, even though I don't know why he bothers because there are people working in this building who tell her everything. I think it's one of the reasons he's happy to have you here; he can now use you as cover to come and visit me. And then there's Yaya, Small Aunty. She's her mother's ambassador in Accra and reports on everything that happens here. That family is too much for me." She sat back with a sigh.

Her description of Aunty was unlike any I had heard, but it rang true. I recognized the generous woman but also the controlling woman who gave with one hand and directed with the other. The only thing I had yet to see was the punishment that she meted out to those who offended her. My heart clenched when I thought of my mother working for Aunty, living under Aunty; I couldn't go against the woman. And as for Eli . . .

"What about Eli, he's like Richard, ehn? I asked.

Evelyn gave a frustrated laugh. "Are you not married to the man? Are you not seeing what's happening?" she said, getting up to take her soup bowl to the kitchen. "You don't need me to tell you about him, my dear."

I watched her as she walked away, hoping she would tell me something else than what I had begun to believe, than what I had begun to see as the truth. When she didn't say anything more, my gaze slid down to my soup. Brown chunks of goat meat, skin still on, floated in it, as did a layer of oil. I didn't think I would be able to chew and swallow a single piece of meat if I tried. My jaws felt locked and my throat constricted. I could see no way out of the mess I was in and couldn't think of anyone who could help me. But my spirits lifted and I became optimistic when I found out a week later that I was pregnant.

NINE

"I'm pregnant," I said to Eli, as though this was something I announced every day. I had practiced this several times in front of the bathroom mirror and then while seated and holding up a hand mirror. I decided to say it sitting because that position made me appear softer, nonconfrontational. And I really didn't want a confrontation. I wanted this to be a new beginning for us. A happy one.

Eli was seated in the armchair, his phones spread out on the table before him to form an electronic arc, and his legs spread around the table's sharp edges. It was early August; two days since he had returned from America, one week since I found out I was pregnant. I waited to tell him in person.

"You are pregnant?" he said in an awe-filled whisper.

"I'm pregnant," I said again, resting my hand on my stomach.

"You . . . you went to the hospital?" he said as he moved from the armchair to join me on the sofa.

"Yes," I said. We were now face to face, his lips turned up in a smile.

I burst into a happy laugh, encouraged by his smile. He drew me into his arms and I went willingly. I began to cry when he kissed me; I had missed his touch. He placed a hand on my belly, which was still as flat as it had been when he last saw me.

I giggled. "It's too early, you're not going to feel anything," I said. I slowly removed his hand and wrapped his arms around me again.

"I love you," I whispered, as though the words were fragile.

He loosened his hold on me, drew away, and looked into my eyes. "I love you too."

We made love and then he left. But I wasn't upset. I knew that our situation wasn't going to change instantly. It would take time, but I was certain this pregnancy was going to bring him to me for good.

Everyone felt the same way. My mother, Mawusi, Aunty, Yaya, even Richard, who had been avoiding me since his visit to Sarah's. They all believed that once Eli had another child, the woman would no longer be able to use Ivy to control him.

"Not only are you his wife, his proper wife, but you are also the mother of his child. Let's see what she will be able to do then!" Yaya said over lunch in my flat. Since my pregnancy, she had been coming over more often, usually with home-cooked meals and maternity clothing she bought on her travels. My mother also wanted to come for a visit, but I convinced her to

wait until I was further along. I missed her but didn't want to
have to deal with her nagging until it was absolutely necessary.

"Okay, Mrs. Ganyo," she had said when I told her to hold
off on visiting, the joy she was feeling at my pregnancy carried
through the phone.

"Has he been coming to the flat?"

"Almost every day."

"And is he staying?"

"Sometimes. But I'm not worried. He spent five nights here
last week."

"Ahn hahn, very soon it will be seven nights." We both burst
into giddy laughter.

I BECAME EVEN more confident when my doctor
revealed that the baby was a boy. I was twelve weeks along and
Eli had come with me to the clinic in Achimota, which was
unlike anything I had ever seen—nurses smiling with patients!
Who knew that nurses could be so kind?

"A boy?" Eli asked the doctor, his eyes widening in wonder as he carefully followed the movement of her hand on the
ultrasound screen. "It's a boy," he turned to me and said, as
though I hadn't heard the doctor. I was still on the table, my
shirt bunched beneath my breasts, and the gel glistening on my
small but growing belly.

I nodded and began to cry.

"Don't cry," he said as we tried to hug each other without
getting the gel on him. His words made me cry even more. I was
going to have Elikem Ganyo's son. His first son! My mother
began crying on the phone when I told her, and I think Aunty's
voice broke, but I'm not sure.

"Everything will change now, you'll see," she told me. And she was right.

Eli fussed over me even more when he got back from the clinic. He insisted on dishing out the take-out food we had ordered and brought it to me on a tray while I sat in front of the TV.

"We should get you a maid, someone to help you around the house," he said. He had been going on again about getting a maid since I told him I was pregnant.

"There's no need; besides my mother is coming soon," I said with a mouthful of *mpoto-mpoto*, made with mashed sweet potatoes and sprinkled with sugar. Pregnancy had given me a serious sweet tooth. I had put honey in a stew I made the day before.

"You can't expect your mother to do everything when she comes."

"Let's wait until I move into the other house to get a maid. This place is too small for five people."

He looked away from me when I said this, picked up one of his phones, and began running his finger across the screen.

"So when?" I said, pushing him, determined to take advantage of this opening. It had been three months since I told him I was pregnant and all I had gotten so far was sleepovers and one small suitcase. But I wasn't going to allow that to continue. Not when I was carrying his son, his first son, his only son.

"When, Eli?"

"Look, these things . . ."

"I don't want a long speech, just give me a date. Say 'Afi, this Friday, you'll move out of this flat and into our house.' Finish."

"Afi, don't be difficult."

"Difficult?"

"You know what I mean."

I lifted the tray off my lap and plopped it on the center table with so much force that the *mpoto-mpoto* splattered, orange globs landing on the polished glass. I was surprised the glass did not shatter. He dropped his phone in surprise. "I'm not giving birth to this baby while living in this flat. I swear to God, if you refuse me, I will go back to my mother." I stood up and brushed past him.

"Afi." I turned around. "I won't have this," he said, as though he was speaking to a disobedient child. His words enraged me even more. I stomped into the bedroom and slammed the door. He didn't stay over that night.

I WENT TO see Evelyn after he left, and told her I would leave for Ho the next day.

"Don't force these things, Afi, let him do it because he wants to."

"What do you mean? How can you say that after all I've been through?"

"Don't misunderstand what I'm saying, you know I'm the last person to side with your husband. But I don't know if leaving will get you what you want."

"And staying here, what will it get me, and what will it get my child?"

"Afi, look around you, look at the life you have. A beautiful flat, a car and driver parked in front of the building; you even said he's promised you a boutique in the new mall. On top of that he's kind and loving. So what if he sometimes goes to stay with another woman? Men have side-babes, that's just the way it is. But it doesn't matter because you are his wife. You are the one his family and friends recognize, and that's what's important. I don't think giving him an ultimatum is the way to go. You have to learn to enjoy the money and ignore the man's faults. Enjoy yourself, go shopping, ask him to move you into a big house of your own, one with your name on the title, ask for a bigger car, a four-wheel-drive, in fact, ask for two cars! Invest the money he gives you, start your own business, help your mother start a business. Let him go and spend the weekend with another woman if he wants. You just live your life and enjoy it.

"It's not that simple."

"Because you're in love with him? Please, put love aside and be practical. Love will not put food on the table; it won't hold you at night."

"You don't understand, you don't know how it feels, how much it hurts. I wish I could be one of those women who are able to live with another person in their marriage, those women who proudly say that they are the farm and the other woman is only a garden. I wish I could be like them but no matter how hard I try I can't bring myself to accept her. I love him and I just can't share him with another woman, I can't."

I IGNORED EVELYN'S warning and the next day packed two suitcases. Mensah drove me to Ho.

"Why are you here?" my mother asked; it was obvious from my expression that this wasn't a happy visit. We sat in the sitting room and she offered me water. I'd walked through the door just as she was leaving for choir practice. Now her hymnal lay on her lap, its maroon cover blending into the cloths tied around her waist.

"I had to come home."

"Home? This is not your home anymore."

"Ma?"

"Does Aunty know you're here?"

"I didn't tell anyone."

"You didn't tell your husband?"

"No."

"You left your husband's house with two big suitcases and didn't tell him?"

"I don't live in my husband's house."

"You've started with this thing again, ehn? You've started again!"

"How will you have felt if Da had married you and never brought you to his house?"

"What did Aunty tell you?"

"I don't want to talk about Aunty," I said, then slowly stood up. I was beginning to feel heavier and was now doing everything slower than before. My mother stood up with me. She looked both worried and angry at the same time.

"I'm tired, Ma, I'm tired. I don't care what anyone says. If he doesn't kick that woman out and move me in, I won't go back to Accra."

"Afi, what is he doing to you that is so terrible? Is he beating you?" she asked. I refused to answer her; I wasn't going to play her game. "Is he starving you? Are you hungry? Tell me!" Now her face was close to mine. That might have bothered me before but not anymore. I simply walked past her and into my former bedroom, which was just as I had left it. She followed me.

"Ma, I'm not going back. You can go and tell Aunty. If he wants me back, he should get rid of that woman." I lowered myself onto the bed, which creaked under me.

"Where are you going to stay? In this house? Have you forgotten that this is Aunty's house?"

"We will move to the new house."

"Is that why you have been sending me money to finish the house? Was this your plan all along?"

"No, this wasn't my plan. I didn't plan for my husband to impregnate me and stash me in a flat while he lives with another woman in our home."

My mother grimaced and for a moment, I believed that my words were causing her physical pain, but I wasn't going to back down.

"Stay here, I'm going to Aunty."

"Okay."

"Stay here, don't go anywhere, don't call anyone. Don't call Mawusi. In fact, who saw you when you arrived?"

"I don't know, a few people. I stopped to greet the charcoal seller."

"What did you tell her?"

"Nothing, I only said I was visiting."

She exhaled loudly. "Stay inside. I will tell Mensah to go and park at Aunty's house before this whole town starts asking questions," she said, her voice hushed. Even in her anger, she didn't make the mistake of speaking loudly enough for anyone outside to hear.

I STRETCHED OUT on the bed when she left and winced when I felt the wooden slats press against my back through the mattress. I almost tumbled out of the bed when I rolled over to my side in search of a more comfortable position. Had the bed always been this narrow and the mattress this thin? Around me the room seemed old, dusty. The table with my mother's suitcases and boxes on it was unvarnished and sloppily assembled so that several unsightly nails were visible. I could see spirals scratched into the concrete floor where the mason had smoothed the cement mixture with a trowel and when I squinted, I saw dust particles floating around me. Every flutter of the threadbare doorway curtain sent even more dust my way. I'd never noticed these things before. In fact, I had been proud of the fact that I had my own room; how many young people living with their parents in Ho have their own room? All of my cousins shared a room with someone. Even Mawusi, when she came home during the holidays, shared a room with her mother. Now it all seemed shabby; that's what living in that gilded flat had done to me.

"WHERE ARE YOU?" my mother called as she entered the front door.

"I'm where you left me."

"Is it me you're talking to like that? Be careful!"

"I'm just saying . . ."

"I said watch yourself. If you're a big woman, you're a big woman only for yourself, not for me."

I rolled my eyes but said nothing.

She was now standing by my bed looking down at me. A deep wrinkle divided her forehead into two, and her hair, which she had recently dyed such that I could see traces of the inky dye on her hairline, was held in a tight bun. I knew she was waiting for me to ask what had transpired at Aunty's, but I refused; I didn't send her over there. When she tired of my silence she said, "I'm going to heat something for us to eat."

I sat up.

"Where are you going?" she said, snapping at me.

"To help you in the kitchen."

"I don't need help."

I HEARD HER plunk a pot onto the tabletop gas stove and then begin stirring; it sounded as though she was scraping the bottom of the pot with the ladle. I sighed; we were going to have aluminum for dinner tonight. The scent of spice-infused palm oil soon wafted through the doorway and pulled me out of my room. My mother dished our food into two enamel plates and set them on the scarred wood of our dining table. We sat on two mismatched chairs that had once belonged to Aunty. I looked down into my plate and frowned at the anchovies in the sauce.

"Keta school boys?"

"What's wrong with them?"

"You know I don't like them," I said in a whiny voice.

"Then you should have stayed in your own house and eaten what you like," my mother replied before breaking off a piece of cassava with her fingers, immersing it in the sauce, and eating it. After this, she picked several Keta school boys out of the sauce and chewed them.

She knew I didn't like anchovies. The fishmongers never cleaned them well enough before drying, so that every bite was laced with sand.

"Did I know you were coming? I made my stew to eat by myself and then you showed up. Do you expect me to throw away my food because you have decided to leave your husband's house?" She drank a mouthful of water from a large plastic cup.

I ignored her theatrics and instead went to the kitchen to wash my hands. I heard a gurgle when I twisted the tap but no water came out. It took me a moment to remember that unlike my flat that had huge overhead tanks to store water, my mother was at the mercy of the Ghana government, which rationed everything, including electricity and water. There was a tall, multicolored plastic bucket filled with water beside the sink, and in it was a plastic bowl with a long handle. I used it to fetch water to wash my hands. My mother could have easily cooked something else, especially because I was pregnant, but she had instead chosen to punish me with sandy fish. I looked around to see if there was something else that I could eat. I found a bowl of groundnut soup in the small fridge and warmed it on the burner; it would be groundnut soup and boiled cassava for dinner tonight.

WHEN I RETURNED to the table with my dinner, my mother was halfway through hers. She glanced at my food and shook her head as though my choice was too disgusting for words.

"I saw Aunty," she finally said, her hand resting on a cube of cassava in her plate.

"I see."

She glared at me; the brevity of my response seemed to increase her anger.

"She is very unhappy with what you have done. Very unhappy! She says I should tell you to go back to your husband first thing tomorrow morning. Mensah will drive you back."

"Ma, I'm not going," I said calmly. This is exactly what I had been expecting. I was prepared.

"You will disobey Aunty?"

"I'm not disobeying anybody, I'm just saying that I won't go back to living in a flat while another woman occupies my marital home and sleeps in my marital bed, with my husband. I won't do it, Ma."

She pushed her plate away so hard that it slid to the other end of the table, fell off the edge, and clattered off the floor, sending specks of palm oil everywhere. The noise startled both of us.

"What do you mean? Nonsense. You will go."

I stood up. "I am not going today, I am not going tomorrow. If Eli wants me to come back, he should come for me and take me to our house!" I banged the flat of my hand on the table as I spoke; my enamel plate danced.

"Hehn, what are you saying?"

"I am saying . . ."

"I know what you said, foolish girl. Are you mad?"

"I'm mad for wanting to live with my husband?"

"You are mad because you're talking like a madwoman. You expect Elikem Ganyo to come here and beg you to come back home? You have forgotten who you are and where you come from. You have forgotten when you used to sit right here at this table with your old Singer sewing machine, praying that someone will bring you a dress to mend and pay you a few coins. You have forgotten when we used to stand on that verandah waiting for Aunty's driver to bring us a small sack of rice and a chicken so that we could also celebrate Christmas, so that we could also have something to eat, so that we would not have to go to other people's houses to ask for food. You have forgotten all of that and you have decided to spit in her face. To shame me in front of this woman who has done so much for us, to shame me in front of everybody. Where in this town will I show my face after this, Afi? Where? How will I go to work after this? How will I go to church, to Women's Guild meetings? Tell me, Afi, where will I go to hide after this?" She was crying now. This too I had expected.

"Ma . . ."

"'Ma,' what? What are you calling me for? So you know I'm your mother but you won't listen to what I tell you? You are listening to people who only want to lead you astray, to tell you lies and destroy your life."

"Which people?"

"That Evelyn, who has also forgotten where she comes from."

"Evelyn? How do you know about Evelyn? She didn't tell me to do this, in fact, she told me not to leave."

"That is a lie. Aunty says she is the one putting these ideas into your head. Do you not know she is jealous of you? A woman who is past thirty with no husband in sight, why will she not advise you to leave your husband? She wishes she had what you have but you are too foolish to see that."

"Nobody told me to do this, Ma. Why aren't you listening to me?"

"Nonsense! Why should I listen to you? Are you the mother? Did you breastfeed me?"

She untied the shorter of two cloths that were around her waist and dabbed her eyes with it. Palm oil still glistened on her right hand but she didn't seem to notice.

"Afi, I am your mother, I have no reason to give you bad

advice. Why would I eat my own? Why would I destroy the only thing I have in this world?"

"I know, Ma. I know you want what's best for me."

"Then why will you not do what I am telling you?"

"Because I love him. Living in that flat without him is killing me, Ma. Knowing that he's with another woman while I lie alone in bed, it is killing me. Sometimes I feel like . . . like I can't breathe, like I'm going to choke on my sadness and die alone in that bed. I cannot keep living like this." Now I was the one crying. I sat on the nearby sofa and propped my head up with both hands as the tears ran down my face. My mother sat beside me and wiped my face with the edge of her cloth.

"I know it's not easy. I know. But it won't be like this forever."

"How do you know, Ma? It has been almost one year and nothing has changed. If I don't do something now I will be stuck in that flat forever. I have to fight for what I want, for what's mine."

"Afi, even if he is with another woman, it is not the end of this world. Which man, especially one like your husband, does not have another woman? Even your uncle Pious, as old and useless as he is, has a girlfriend, on top of his many wives."

"This is different. It is supposed to be the girlfriend who stays in the flat and gets to see the man once a week, not the other way around, not the wife. Ma, I'm not going back to that life. I'm not. Tell Aunty I'm not going."

"Afi, which mouth will I use to deliver this message to Aunty?"

ELI CALLED SOON after. His mother had told him I was in Ho.

"Come back and let's talk about this . . . this thing."

"Mmm mmm, I'm tired of talking."

"So what are you saying?"

"I'm not coming back to that flat. Our son will not live in that flat. If I come back it is to live with you, in our house. And you will have to come for me."

He hung up the phone. There was no turning back now.

THAT EVENING MY mother placed a low stool in the bathroom and I sat on it to bathe. It was too strenuous to repeatedly bend over to scoop water out of the bucket with a small plastic pail and empty it on my body. She offered me her bed, which had a new mattress, and I accepted even though she refused to share it with me. Instead she went to my room. I was too tired to argue with her so I let her go, but still I struggled to fall asleep. I was constantly aware of the whir of the faltering fan, and my cotton nightgown was soon drenched with sweat. Every time I managed to start dozing off, I was jolted awake by footsteps and voices as people walked past the window. This is what I had missed when I first moved to Accra, but now I longed for the cool and quiet of my flat. How was I going to survive here?

MENSAH CAME BACK the next morning. It was about seven and we were standing on my mother's verandah. I had hurriedly tied a cloth over my nightgown when my mother called out to me, but had forgotten to put on my slippers; I was used to walking barefoot on the plush carpet at King's Court. The concrete was cold beneath my feet. A light fog still hung in the air and one of the neighbor's teenage daughters was hurriedly sweeping under the almond tree while dressed in her school uniform; she should have swept before her morning bath. She would be late for school if she took any longer. Her palm frond broom kicked up a cloud of dust that thickened the fog.

"Aunty said I should take you back to Accra," Mensah said. I noticed that he didn't start with 'please.' Obviously, enough had been said about me yesterday to embolden him.

"Tell Aunty I can't go."

"You can't go?" he said, shock causing his mouth to hang open after he asked the question. I don't think he had ever heard anyone say no to Aunty.

I shook my head.

"When can you go then?"

"I'm waiting for my husband to come for me."

"So I should tell Aunty you can't go? That you're waiting for your husband?"

"Yes."

He left but not before giving me a look so sharp that had it been a knife it would have pierced me.

MY MOTHER WAS seated at the dining table when I reentered the house, her face still crumpled. Her cloth was tied across her chest and her chewing stick was slack in her mouth, as though it would fall as soon as she began speaking. Fortunately for me she didn't say a word, but then she didn't have to, her face said everything. On any other day, she would have been dressed and walking out of the door by then, but today she did everything slowly. She fluffed the thin cushions of the chairs in the sitting room, swept and dusted, and then decided to mop, even though she normally only mopped on the weekends. It was only after this that she filled a bucket with water from a barrel in the kitchen and carried it into the bathroom for her morning bath. I was seated in the sitting room when she finally came out of her bedroom, dressed for work.

"I am going."

"Won't you eat? I made oats."

"I am not hungry. I will see you in the evening," she said, barely looking at me. But she didn't leave immediately. Instead she stood in the doorway, readjusting her cloth, her headscarf, her blouse, anything to delay facing Aunty. It made me even sadder to see her suffer this way. For a brief moment, I considered asking Mensah to come back, but I steeled myself. This was necessary.

BARELY AN HOUR passed before Mensah returned; Aunty wanted me to come to the depot. Even though I had been expecting this, I felt my entire body become slack. I was tempted to ask Mensah how Aunty had received my message but I didn't; he was already beginning to see himself as my equal. Besides, I knew that everything I said or did would be relayed to her. So instead, I got dressed and rode with him to the depot, my head held high and my lips set in a tight line. Aunty's depot was opposite the main entrance to the big market and was one long block of rooms, most of which served as storerooms for flour, rice, oil, and other food products that she bought wholesale and distributed. Some of the traders in the big market bought their goods from her and resold them in smaller quantities; one sack of rice from the depot was later resold as thirty cups of rice in the market. The area was already buzzing with activity. On the street, taxis and buses honked incessantly as they ferried traders and shoppers, and pedestrians darted through the moving traffic in a bid to get to their destinations. At the depot, a queue of women waited in front of the cashier's office to make their purchases. Boys and young men, most of them shirtless and sitting on carts and in wheelbarrows, waited close by to carry the goods to the market. I recognized several of the women but didn't stop to greet them and didn't turn around when I heard one of them call my name. Instead, I dashed into Aunty's office, which was the last room in the row and one in which no one dared enter unless they were summoned by Aunty herself. When I entered, she was seated behind her desk and my mother sat in one of two straight-back chairs in front of the desk. The office was plain: gray filing cabinets lined one wall and a fan turned overhead. Piles of cellophane-wrapped receipt books occupied one corner, and beside them was a wooden stand on which sat a small TV with rabbit ears antennae. A gray landline phone and a filing tray were the only items on Aunty's desk.

"Good morning, Aunty," I greeted her, my shaky hands hidden behind my back.

"Good morning, Afi. How are you?"

"Please, I'm fine."

"Good. Sit down," she said, pointing to the empty chair next to my mother. Beside me, my mother sat on the edge of her chair, her hands tightly clasped in her lap.

"I hear that you have left your husband's house and have refused to return," she said without any inflection in her voice, as though she was asking me about the weather.

I nodded, my words stuck in my throat.

"Why?"

I cleared my throat, and told her what I had told my mother yesterday but with fewer details and in a less defiant tone.

"And this is why you are refusing to go back home?"

"Yes, Aunty."

She sighed with her whole body and appeared to sink into her swivel chair. My heart began to beat faster.

When she spoke again, it was in the same calm tone. "It is not right for you to come here and behave like this. To behave as if my son is some type of beast that has bitten you. Elikem has not done anything to you; how many men will do for you all that my son has done for you? How many? I have spoken to him and he's willing to take you back, because of the child, so go home."

"Please, to Accra?"

"Of course."

"Please, will I be moving to his house when I go back?"

For the first time I saw a flash in her eye. I was pushing her too far. "I said go home."

"Please Aunty, I cannot go back to that flat," I said, my voice quavering and my heart thumping. I heard my mother draw a sharp breath but I refused to look her way.

"Are you telling me that you won't go?"

"Aunty, please . . ." my mother began, but the woman immediately raised a fleshy hand and my mother fell quiet.

"I asked you a question."

"Please, it's not that I don't want to go, it's just that . . . it is what I explained to you." I was almost whispering.

She swiveled her chair to face my mother. "Olivia, do you hear what your daughter is telling me?"

"Aunty, I have talked, I have said everything, but her ears are hard. I do not know what else to do." The tremor in her voice told me that tears were not far behind. She then turned to me.

"Afi, my daughter, my only child, I am begging you, I beg you in the name of God, go back to your husband."

I shook my head. My eyes were now fixed on a spot behind Aunty's head.

"So you will disrespect your mother?" Aunty said.

I remained quiet.

"Okay then, go," she said.

In a flash, my mother pushed back her chair and fell to her knees. "Aunty, she is a child, she does not know what she is doing. I will talk to her."

The woman abruptly stood up and my mother followed her lead.

"She's your daughter."

"YOU'RE DOING THE right thing," Mawusi said, when I told her what had happened in Aunty's office. She was away in Côte d'Ivoire for her semester abroad. All of this turmoil would be more bearable if she were with me. I was even tempted to call Evelyn but didn't, not after I had ignored her advice to stay in Accra.

I PRETENDED TO be asleep when my mother returned that evening. In fact, I had been pretending to be asleep most of the day. By the time I returned from the depot, word had spread that I was in town. A stream of friends and relatives came looking for me at my mother's house. I'd refused to answer the door until Godsway, Mawusi's brother, walked to the other side of the house and saw me through my mother's bedroom window. I was forced to open the door to let him in. Tɔgã Pious had sent him to bring me. I told him I would come over as soon as I had lunch but I didn't. Instead I drew the curtains and curled up in my mother's bed. My uncle was the last person I wanted to see and I didn't want to have to answer questions about my presence in Ho. Besides, I didn't think my mother could handle knowing that I was out and talking with people, not after everything that had happened that day.

AROUND EIGHT THE next morning a wave of nausea forced me awake and sent me running to the toilet, but not before I became entangled in my mother's doorway curtain and had to steady myself on the doorframe. I noticed my mother in the sitting room, reading her Bible, when I came out of the toilet. All she had on was a cloth knotted above her breasts. Her scarf had slid to the crown of her head and didn't look like it would stay on much longer.

"You're not going to work?"

"Mmm mmm," she replied, without looking up from the book on her lap.

"Why?" I sat across from her. I was beginning to feel lightheaded.

She went on reading her Bible without answering me, her forefinger following the small print on the page. It was after she had finished her reading and closed the Bible that she spoke to me.

"Aunty said I should stay home until I convince you to go back." She didn't seem angry when she said this, just weary.

"Has she sacked you?"

"No, she said I should come back after you go to Accra."

"So no work?"

"No work and no guild meetings." My mother lightly ran her hand on the cover of the Bible as she spoke.

"She has banned you from church!" I exclaimed.

"Lower your voice," she said. She walked over to the window and struggled with the rusty lever before succeeding in shutting the louvre blades.

"You can't go to church?" I was on my feet beside my mother.

"She didn't say I can't go to church, she said guild meetings."

"But how can she do this? It's bad enough that she has suspended you from work, but church?"

My mother sighed heavily and sat down again.

"I will call Eli; he has to talk to his mother."

"Call Eli? The same Eli that you have left? You are not thinking properly, ehn?"

"But she cannot do this to you."

"If you do not want her to do this to me, you should go home."

THERE WAS VERY little conversation between us over the next few days. She went to the market and cooked for us but always shooed me away when I tried to help. When our neighbors asked why she hadn't been to work in several days, she told them it was because I was visiting, and she said the same when some of the women's guild members came to check on her after their bi-weekly prayer meeting. Aunty had made it clear that under no condition was I to speak ill of her son. My mother was desperate to conceal my marital problems, but she quickly realized that keeping me cooped up at home wasn't helping. Word soon began to spread that I was hiding indoors because I was ill. A few days after my return, Tɔgã Pious, who had tired of waiting for me to come to his house, came to mine.

"Afi, what did you bring for me?"

In the sitting room, I listened quietly as he complained about my neglectful in-laws and listed the many reasons why I had to give him money. I was wearing one of my mother's voluminous boubous that made me look like a sack of flour. "Nobody has to know you are pregnant; there are too many evil eyes," she had said earlier that morning while handing me a small pile of shapeless garments that could hide my pregnancy. Now I sat hunched over in the chair so that the boubou looked like a wearable tent that revealed only my toes. But Tɔgā Pious was not concerned about my appearance, he wanted gifts and cash and I didn't want to give him either. I reasoned that he would eventually leave when he tired of talking; besides, I had nowhere else to be. However, I underestimated my uncle's persistence and my tolerance for his relentless begging. Barely an hour passed before I went into the bedroom, fished some notes out of my bag, and gave them to him. The look on his face when I gave him the money was one of a child who was sent to catch a fat chicken but was only given a chicken foot after the bird was cooked.

"You will have to do something before you leave because this is only for wetting my throat," he said as he counted the money for a second time, licking his thumb after counting each note. I glared at his back as he walked out; that money was almost as much as my mother earned in a month. I became angry with myself for losing patience and promised myself that I would be ready the next time he came.

I BEGAN TO go out after Tɔgā Pious's visit. I went to see my cousins in the early evenings when I knew Tɔgā Pious would be at a drinking spot or watching football with his raucous friends. I was happy to sit in a corner, away from the smoke of the coal pot, while *Daavi* Christy, Mawusi's mother, prepared the evening meal and regaled me with the latest family gossip. Tɔgã Pious was now allowing the family to use his flush toilet but was charging everyone a monthly fee, which *Daavi* Christy had so far refused to pay. She was certain that her defiance would soon lead to a fight with her husband and she was ready for it. She clenched her fists as she described the impending battle. One of my cousins had gained admission to nursing school and would soon be coming to see me with an appeal for funds. The neem tree a few houses away, which was older than everyone we knew and housed a god in the hollow of its trunk, had fallen after a heavy storm a few weeks ago and left gaping holes in several roofs. The god was angry, and a fetish priest, his job to mediate the falling out between the gods and mortals, had to be called to perform a pacification ceremony. Now the god, and the clay pot he lived in, was housed under a hastily planted shrub.

Each of my cousins had a theory about who had wronged the god, but none of them was certain. No one in our community had died since the tree fell. No one had even had an accident. As far as they were concerned, I was a more interesting topic of conversation. Each of them wanted to know about my life in Accra. Tɔgã Pious had come back with a description of my flat that defied the imagination of many; they all wanted to come and see it, and possibly live in it. I told them I would arrange visits. They no longer called me Afi, I was now Sister Afi, even to the cousins who were close to me in age. It was nice to sit on the bench in front of the house, after the afternoon's heat had subsided, and chat with passersby going about their day and with visitors who wanted to know what the rich woman from Accra had brought for them. Clara, one of Uncle Bright's daughters, had set up a sewing shop in a kiosk in front of the house. She had two apprentices, and also my old Singer sewing machine that my mother had given to her. She even had a ceiling fan installed. I sometimes sat in her kiosk to escape the heat and to hide from my uncles. The whir of the sewing machines, the soft squeak of scissors as they cut through fabric, and the smoke emitted by the charcoal pressing iron reminded me of my days as an apprentice in Sister Lizzie's shop. They also made me long for my life in Accra, Sarah's workshop, my air-conditioned flat, my husband. I wanted to go home.

ELI CAME FOR me eight days after I had packed my bags and returned to Ho. My mother and I were having a quiet supper when he appeared at the door. He greeted my mother and reluctantly accepted the glass of water she offered, but refused to sit as I hurriedly stuffed my clothes into my bags. When I came out, he was still standing beside the door. My poor mother was trying her best to make small talk despite his stony face. He was dressed in work clothes, neatly ironed black trousers and shirt sleeves rolled up to his elbow; he must have driven here from the office. I was so nervous that I didn't say a proper goodbye to my mother and I was in his car before I remembered that I had packed all of her boubous and brought them with me. I didn't dare ask him to turn around, not when he looked like he wanted to slap me. Even though this wasn't our first fight, I had never seen this side of him before: the clenched jaw, the flaring nostrils, the hand gripping the steering wheel so that his knuckles looked like they would pierce his skin, the eyes fixed on the road and the refusal to acknowledge me. All of this was new.

It was dark when we drove past the limits of Ho and I was glad for this. His anger was more bearable in the darkness; at least then I couldn't see his face. He ignored me when I asked him to stop at Kpong so that I could buy *abolo*, boiled shrimp, and fried one-man-thousand from the hawkers who mobbed any car that dared to slow down after crossing the bridge. I wanted to lash out at him more than anything, but my anxiety about what lay ahead kept me quiet. I somehow managed to doze off as we neared Asutsuare Junction but woke up before we reached the end of the Tema motorway. When we made the right off the highway and into East Legon, I sat up straight in my seat and gripped the soft, tan leather of the door handle; we were a short way away from both the flat and his house. What would I do if he took me back to the flat? I would refuse to enter! I would sit in his car and refuse to enter! If he tried to pull me out of the car I would resist, I would make a scene so that everyone in the building, at least those who had their balcony door open, would hear us, as would the security guards at the gate. I would hit and claw at him and curse the entire Ganyo family. Anything but go back into that flat. My heart continued to pound and my hand remained tight on the door handle as he drove straight, instead of making the left turn that would take us to the flat. About ten minutes later, he made a right turn, and we drove past a series of homes that were big enough to house multiple families. His was smaller and located between two of these mansions. He pulled up in front of the wrought-iron gate and honked. A moment later, a security guard rolled the gate open and we drove into the compound. Eli had brought me to our house.

TEN

It was a two-story house with five bedrooms, a lawn in the front, and a small pool and garden in the back. One bedroom was on the first floor and the other four were on the second. While the décor of the flat, my previous home, was modern with clean lines and sharp edges, the décor here was more classical. Each room was furnished in the style of Louis XIV. The sitting room was all polished brown wood and ornate blue and green upholstery. The headboard in the master bedroom was covered with a pink fabric layered with a gold motif, and the bedpost and two bedside tables had claw feet. White area rugs softened the marble floors and heavy curtains gave it a regal air. Crystal chandeliers added glitz to the sitting and dining rooms, as did paintings in gold frames. Even the kitchen had paintings! The wood of the kitchen cabinets matched that of the dining table, which seated ten people and shone so brightly that I wondered if it had ever been used. The gardener, who came every weekday, carefully tended roses and orchids that added color to an outside seating area near the pool, which was four feet at its deepest end. He was only one of many people who worked in the house; there were two guards at the gate, a cook and her assistant, two housekeepers, one groundskeeper, and one driver, who sometimes drove Eli to work and brought him home in the evenings. Most of them lived in a row of rooms at the bottom of the garden, and the security guards were supplied by the same company that employed my talkative friends back at King's Court.

A few days after Eli and I came back to Accra, Mensah had driven me to King's Court to pick up the rest of my things. Savior and Lucy, the most talkative of the lot, had insisted on helping load my bags into the car and hugged me goodbye. I could only imagine the stories that they were going to tell to anyone who stopped to talk to them. I went back to school the next day. Sarah had been very understanding, assuming my absence had something to do with my pregnancy. I was happy to be back at work and to be able to get out of the house where I rarely saw my husband. He left early in the morning, usually before I even came out of the shower, and often returned after I was in bed. I would hear him come up the stairs at night, enter the guestroom furthest away from the master bedroom, and shut the door. I'd been sleeping alone in the master bedroom since the first night. On that evening he'd asked one of the housekeepers, Hawa, to show me to the room; I had waited until three in the morning for him to join me in there. He didn't show up that night or any of the ones after. My attempts to talk to him went nowhere. He complained of fatigue when I met him at the top of the staircase and didn't respond when I knocked on the door of the guest bedroom. It was locked when I turned the handle. After the first week, I began waking up earlier than usual with the intent of making him breakfast, but the cook always beat me to it. The woman, Mrs. Adams, who was my mother's age but twice her size, had worked for Eli since he returned from Liberia and bristled at my presence in the kitchen.

"Please leave it, we'll do it," were her favorite words, which she usually uttered while hovering over me in the kitchen and trying to snatch some utensil or ingredient from my hand. I had never encountered anyone so desperate to get rid of me.

"I'll do it!" I finally snapped on the third day of our war. She froze. I guess she didn't realize that I had a mouth. I wasn't going to stand for this kind of treatment. This was my house, and it was my duty to take care of my husband. That morning, I beat her to the kitchen and was scrambling eggs in a bowl while she and her helper leaned against the marble island, glaring at me.

"Where is the salt?" I was sure that they had begun hiding utensils and ingredients from me; the salt wasn't in the cupboard where I had seen it yesterday.

"It's over there," she said, pointing to a cabinet above my head.

"It's not there."

"It's there."

"I said it's not there. Come and give it to me!" It took her almost thirty seconds to dislodge her feet from the floor.

I was fuming when I served Eli his breakfast, not that he noticed. His response to my greeting was curt and he asked how I was while looking at my stomach. He began to eat as soon as I placed the eggs, toast, and tea, before him.

"Is it okay?" I asked, nibbling on an almost-burnt piece of toast. I was sitting two chairs away from him at the huge dining table.

"It's eggs and bread, Afi."

"I know but is the salt . . ."

"It's fine," he said, cutting me off. He had a fork in one hand and a phone in the other and was scrolling through his emails and eating at the same time.

"What time will you be back this evening . . . so that I can have your dinner ready?"

"I have a dinner meeting so no need."

"Okay, what time do you think you will get back?"

He looked up from his phone and frowned. "Why are you asking?"

"It's nothing, I just wanted to wait up for you."

"Is something the matter?"

"No . . ."

"Then don't wait up for me."

I WAS DISTRACTED at school that day. My stitching on a skirt was so crooked that Sarah made me redo it. I never made mistakes like that, even when I was a fresh apprentice at Sister Lizzie's. When my mother called that evening, I convinced her that everything was fine. I told myself that I was lying because I didn't want to worry her any more than I already had. I had already strained her relationship with Aunty. She told me how the woman had remained cold to her since she went back to work. She stopped inviting my mother to her office to chat and one evening left her standing in a heavy downpour after work, whereas before, she would have offered to give my mother a lift home. I didn't want this treatment to get worse. Besides, I had gotten what I asked for: I was finally living in our home. Eli's anger was something that I would have to deal with by myself, without the involvement of my mother and the Ganyos. Mawusi agreed. "You can't go back and complain again," she said. We'd been on the phone for more than one hour and it was almost ten, yet Eli had not come back from the office.

"Are you sure he's at the office?" she said, expressing the thought that I had been too embarrassed to voice. Because what if he was with her now, as I lay alone in this ornate bed with this overheating cellphone pressed against my ear? Wouldn't I be the biggest fool on earth?

"He says he's at the office."

"Okay."

I tried to sleep after we hung up but I couldn't. My belly was getting bigger and now sleeping on my back was the only comfortable position. When I tired of tossing from my back to my side, I called him. He picked up on the second ring.

"What is it, Afi. Are you okay?"

"I'm fine. I just want to know when you will be home . . . where you are."

"I'm working, Afi. Is there something else?"

"No."

"Okay, goodnight."

"WE HAVE TO talk," I said as he ate breakfast the next morning. The meal was the same as what I'd served him yesterday but I had added pineapple and watermelon slices.

"It's too early, Afi, and I have to go to work."

"So when, then? Because when you get back it will be too late to talk."

He pushed his plate away, sat back in his chair, and folded his arms.

"I'm sorry about what happened, about Ho. It's just that I became . . . I was very upset, I was very emotional. I'm very sorry, darling." I was desperate enough to say anything that would get him to forgive me.

"Did I not ask you to be patient? But you refused to listen and preferred to force my hand." A vein pulsed in his neck; I'd never noticed it before.

"I'm sorry." I reached across and touched his arm. He glared at the offending hand but didn't pull away from me.

"What am I going to do with your sorry?"

"I know. Please forgive me. I miss you. Your son misses you." I stood beside him and placed his hand on my belly. I inhaled sharply at his touch through the thin fabric of my nightgown. How I missed him. How I wanted him. I was afraid that he would pull away but his hand remained still. Just when I thought we would stay frozen all day, he lightly pressed on the side of my stomach closest to him, as though he wanted to feel the baby inside me.

"He's not moving yet," I whispered as I placed my hand on his. He jerked his hand away. I wasn't forgiven yet.

"I have to go to work," he said, standing up.

"I will wait up for you tonight."

"Suit yourself."

I waited until two in the morning and finally succumbed to sleep. I woke up around 9:00 a.m. to the sound of laughter in the backyard. He was sitting in the garden with his brothers.

I QUICKLY GOT dressed and hurried down the spiral staircase. How could I be sleeping when his family was visiting! I should have been up early enough to welcome them and prepare breakfast for them. What kind of wife would they think I was? When I entered the kitchen, Mrs. Adams was bringing in a tray stacked with dirty plates from outside. Her smirk told me that she relished this victory. I would have to deal with this woman soon but now I politely replied "good morning" and exited through the back door into the garden. The sun was out but still covered by enough clouds that it was possible to sit outside without becoming shiny with sweat. The white and purple orchids had already opened up and the fragrance of the roses was in the air. Droplets of water dotted the leaves and petals but they would soon evaporate with the rising heat. Even though we were located on a busy artery, noise from the street barely reached the backyard. All I could hear was the sound of children playing behind the ten-foot fence of one of the neighboring houses.

Richard saw me first. "Mrs. Ganyo!" he said. I didn't know what to make of his words. He hadn't called me that before.

"Good morning," I said, my hand folded atop my belly. I could deal with any of the brothers alone, but the three of them together was overwhelming. I was suddenly shy.

"Good morning," the visiting brothers answered in unison. Eli said nothing. Fred stood up and gave me a side hug. "I heard you're putting my brother through hell," he said with a hearty laugh. Richard joined in while Eli looked on, his face devoid of expression. Fred pointed to an empty chair between him and Eli and I sat.

"Sorry I wasn't up to welcome you," I said. I didn't add that it was because Eli had not bothered to tell me they were coming and that he had made me wait up until the early hours of the morning.

"Don't worry, you need your sleep," Richard said before asking me how I was. I told him I was well, no need to bring up the swollen feet, nausea, and constipation.

"I heard you went to Ho and shook things up," Fred said, still mocking his brother. Or maybe he was mocking me.

"No," my smile quickly faded and I glanced at my husband from the corner of my eye. But Eli wasn't even looking at me.

"No? Well I heard differently," Fred persisted.

"I went to Ho but I didn't shake anything." I let out a half-laugh, half-snort that made me sound like a choking person.

"Don't be modest, you have done what Napoleon couldn't do," he said, before reaching over and patting me on the shoulder. Up close, he was a slightly older version of Eli, with a receding hairline. I hoped my husband's hair wouldn't follow suit.

"You're having too much fun with this," Eli said, mild irritation lacing his voice. He was drinking a cup of coffee in a gold-rimmed teacup that was too dainty for his hands. He turned and asked me if I had had breakfast and when I said no, told Mrs. Adams to make something for me. I left them outside talking business and went in to eat my almost-burnt toast with a light margarine spread. It was the only thing I could hold down in the mornings. The brothers left soon after, but not before Fred invited me to his house for a Christmas party next weekend.

"Make sure you come with Eli," he said as he slid into the leather seat of his Audi. Richard had already hugged me and driven out the gate. He appeared to be in a hurry.

"Make sure you bring her," he said to his brother who was standing behind me. I didn't hear him respond. Maybe he nodded. I waved until Fred's car was out of sight.

"What are you . . ." I began but when I turned there was no one behind me. Eli had already gone indoors. I went up to my bedroom to take a shower and put something pretty on. I had to talk to him today, to make him understand what I had done, to get him to forgive me so that we could move on with our life. I didn't plan to bring my child into an unhappy home. But Eli was nowhere to be found when I came out of the bathroom. One of the housekeepers was changing his bedsheets, and when I asked if she knew where he was she said he had gone to work.

"Work?"

"Yes, Madam."

"Oh yes, he told me he was going. I forgot," I said to the girl who wore glasses so thick that I could not see her eyes. It was bad enough that they all knew we didn't share a room; now they would know that he barely talked to me. I didn't even want to imagine the gossip that they were sending back home. I went back to my bedroom and called Mawusi, who was cooking on the small balcony of her shared room in the residence hall at the university in Côte d'Ivoire.

"You can't let things continue like this. You have to get him into your room, into your bed." I agreed with her; I remembered how our relationship had blossomed when he first began sleeping in the flat. I had to recreate that feeling of being a married couple.

MENSAH DROVE ME to the mall that afternoon and I shopped for maternity clothes and items for the baby. Quite some time later, I left with several large shopping bags and boxes full of clothing, accessories, and equipment, including a baby monitor set and a thermometer. I planned to come back with Eli to choose a bedroom set. We could turn one of the guest bedrooms into a nursery. I bought far fewer things for myself because I figured that it didn't make sense to spend a lot of money on clothes I would only wear for a few months. I settled into the backseat as Mensah loaded the bags and boxes into the trunk. My mother would collapse if she knew how much money I was spending. Eli was still giving me cash every month and most of it went into my bank account, which I had opened upon advice from Evelyn. I had sent a bit of money to my mother last week for the house. The contractors had completed most of the work and painting was the only major thing left to be done. She would be able to move out of Aunty's house and into our own in the new year. When we last spoke I got the sense that she was eager to do so. "A servant cannot be free while living in his master's house," was what she had said, to my surprise, when I asked her why she was in a hurry to move into the house when it hadn't been painted. My mother had always considered it an honor and blessing to be living in one of Aunty's houses, but obviously this was no longer the case.

I ARRIVED HOME to find two children, about ten years old, waiting for me in the sitting room. It took me a minute to recognize them. They were Uncle Pious's twins, Ata and Atafe, by his second wife. Mrs. Adams was standing in the kitchen doorway, watching as I gave each of them a cup of apple juice from the fridge.

"A driver brought them, with their suitcase," she told me as the children went outside to explore the backyard.

"A driver? Suitcase?"

"Yes. It's in the downstairs bedroom."

I went into the bedroom and let out a small scream when I opened the bulging suitcase; it even held the children's school uniform! I called Mawusi to ask if she knew what was happening, but her father hadn't told her that he was sending the twins to Accra. I called them indoors and sat them around the table in the kitchen.

"Why did you bring your uniforms?"

"Papa said we will go to school here."

"Here?"

"Yes."

I sent them back outside with a warning to stay away from the pool and called my uncle.

"Afi, have your brother and sister arrived?" were his first words.

"You didn't tell me you were sending them here, and to go to school."

"Yes, because if I had told you, you would have said no. They will help you around the house, especially in your condition."

"What condition?"

"Am I not your father, don't I know everything?"

"Tɔgã, please, I live in my husband's house. I can't just bring people to live here without telling him."

"Is it your brother and sister that you are calling 'people,' as if they are strangers off the street?"

"You know what I mean. I have to plan for these things. I have to talk to Eli first."

He laughed. "Afi, you're like your mother. This is the same thing she used to do when my brother was alive. But you are not your mother; she's an outsider. She could afford to say no because my children are not related to her by blood. But you cannot say no to your responsibilities. Why should your brother and sister be attending that government school when they have a big sister like you in Accra who can send them to an international school? Why should they be sleeping on a mat in my sitting room when you live in that big house with so many empty bedrooms? As soon as Mawusi finishes the university I will also send two to her. That is how it is done. It is your duty to care for them. If you don't do it, who will?"

At that moment, I hated my uncle more than I'd ever hated him in my life. What was I going to tell Eli? I set up a TV in the guestroom for the children and sent them in there after they had dinner and their bath. Eli was still not home when I went to bed. He was up and in the sitting room when I went downstairs the next morning. So were the children. He was listening to Ata, the boy, speak when I walked in.

"Good morning, Sister Afi," the children chorused.

"Good morning, how are you?"

"We are fine," they said, beaming. They were obviously happy to be in our house.

I sent them to the kitchen for breakfast and sat opposite Eli.

"What are they doing here?" he asked me. At least he didn't seem angry.

I explained what had happened. I didn't want my uncle to look bad, but I wasn't going to lie and say he had told me beforehand, especially when Eli and I were on such shaky ground.

"But is that how you send children to live with someone?"

"That's what I told him. And they are small, it's not like they can take care of themselves."

"That's not even the point. We have people here who can take care of them, but I don't like your uncle's behavior. My mother has already complained about him."

"I'm sorry."

"You can't just foist your children on people like this. Send them back. Today."

"What will I tell him?"

"Tell him your husband said he will not agree for them to stay because he wasn't first consulted. He needs to know that I'm very unhappy with what he's done. Allowing them to stay would be setting a very bad precedent. I'm not going to have people dictating how I live in my own house. I will not be disrespected like this. Get them ready so that Mensah can take them back. I will give him some money to give to your uncle."

"Okay."

To be honest, I was relieved. I had considered the possibility that Eli would allow them to stay. He *was* very kind so it was in the realm of possibility. But I was happy that he didn't yield because I didn't want that burden now, not when I was expecting a child and my marriage was balancing precariously on one leg. They could come back when I was more settled, even if only for the holidays. I told them this as they ate breakfast. Atafe began to sob and her brother refused to continue eating. They didn't want to go back to their father, they told me; they wanted to stay with me. Eli entered the kitchen and they became quiet. He sat at the table and told Atafe to stop crying.

"Why don't you want to go back?" he asked them.

They looked to me, unsure if they could speak to an adult, especially one who lived in this big house in Accra. I don't think anyone had ever bothered to ask them what they wanted before.

"Tell him," I encouraged Ata*f*e.

She wiped her face with the back of her hand, smearing snot and tears everywhere. Eli handed her a napkin to clean her hand and face. Then, she told us in a tiny voice that she didn't want to go back because her father often refused to pay her school fees and then she was embarrassed when she and her brother were kicked out of school by the headmaster in front of the other children.

"And he doesn't buy us books, and our uniforms are torn," her brother added.

"And he likes to shout at us and knock our heads," she continued. Now the complaints were rolling off their tongue and Ata*f*e's voice was no longer tiny.

"And he eats all the meat when our mother cooks," Ata said, while his sister nodded so hard I thought her head would detach from her neck.

"Even the fish, Uncle, he eats the fish. We only get *akple* and dry soup, no meat!" Ata*f*e added.

"And he doesn't give our mother money to cook," her brother continued.

"Okay, I will see what I can do," Eli said, cutting in before they could extend the list of complaints. "But you have to go home. I will make sure that you're not sacked from school and that you always get meat. And you can come and visit during the school holidays."

Their faces lit up and I could hear their cheery goodbyes even after the car was out of sight. I had sent them off with a bag of sweets. Eli had given an envelope of money to Mensah. "Give it to the mother, make sure their father doesn't see it," he warned the driver. "There's enough there for her to expand her trading," he told me as we walked inside on that Sunday. I thanked him with tears in my eyes. How many husbands would have done what he did? He went out soon after and I went back to bed.

A PHONE CALL from Evelyn woke me up from my nap. We hadn't spoken since I had returned to Accra. The last time I had heard from her, she sent me a picture from Dubai where she was on vacation with some of her girlfriends. It was a picture of her atop a camel, on a sand dune; she was on a desert safari.

"Why didn't you go with Richard?" I asked, happy to be talking to her again.

"I don't need Richard to have fun. Besides, I don't think he could have come anyway, not with this whole Muna, Eli, and you thing."

"You've heard?"

"Of course, I've heard. Richard was here all of yesterday. I had to kick him out today so that my vagina could get some rest."

"Ah, Evelyn, don't say such things," I said. Despite the many hours we spent talking, I was still not used to her openness. Mawusi would never say something like that.

"Why? It's the truth. My vagina is not made of iron."

"*Yoo*, it's okay; just tell me what Richard told you."

"You are the one who should be telling me what's going on. You're at the center of everything."

I told her about Ho, my talk with Aunty, and Eli coming to pick me up.

"Congratulations; I heard you made the old witch mad. Richard says that no one has stood up to her the way you did. Definitely not him or his brothers."

"Really?"

"Yes. Have I not already told you about that woman? I heard that when she realized you weren't joking, that you weren't going to move back into the flat, she called a family meeting with everyone, including the old uncles, and demanded that Eli take you to his house. I hear she told him that if he didn't do as she asked, he was forbidden to come to her funeral."

"What?"

"Yes, that's how far it went; he had no choice. The entire family was on his neck. Even his blind uncle who lives in Anfoega. They were all there. And it wasn't an empty threat; you know she has a serious heart condition."

"Eli has mentioned it."

"Ahn hahn."

"So that's why he came for me? Why he's so angry?"

"Of course. You really upset his mother and almost ruined their relationship. And you messed things up between him and Muna. I mean, he had to move her out of the house."

I inhaled sharply when I heard her name. "Where is she now?"

"Who?"

"That woman?"

"She's in one of their other houses, you know they own houses all around Accra."

"So he's still with her, still keeping her in his house?" I felt tears sting my eyes and my chest tighten.

"Look, Afi, it doesn't matter. Aren't you the one living in his house?"

"But what is the significance of being in this house when he has many houses around Accra and has put her up in another one? He couldn't even move her into a flat?" I yelled into the phone, enraged.

"Afi, calm down. The house you are in is Eli's main house. That is where he keeps his clothes, that is where he has his home office, that is where he entertains his guests, that is where his mother will stay when she comes to visit. You are in his house, so forget about Muna and where she is."

"It was never about the house. What I wanted was for him to leave her. I just wanted him to be with me. Only me." I was holding back tears.

"I know, and this is the first step. Does he not come home at night? His mother warned him not to sleep anywhere else."

"She did?"

"Yes, she laid down some serious rules, ehn. So it doesn't matter where Muna is, you're his wife and she isn't."

"Please stop saying her name."

"Sorry."

"Anyway, you would think that Aunty would be grateful for what I've done; if it wasn't for me, that woman would still be here. But she's so cold when I call to greet her."

"She's happy that the woman is gone, but she's angry that you disobeyed her. The fact that you didn't follow her plan is what is making her behave like that. She wants you to be like a sheep, following her blindly and not putting up any resistance. I know I told you not to leave the flat but I like what you achieved. You showed them that you're not some little girl they can just push around. Now let's see what Eli will do."

HE CAME HOME around midnight. I had turned off most of the lights and dozed off while seated upright on the couch; I was uncomfortable lying in it and putting my feet on the cushions. In fact, I felt uncomfortable doing so many things in the house, as if I was a visitor. Eli had on a pair of blue shorts, a white Lacoste T-shirt, and black leather sandals. I don't think he was coming from the office. He was surprised to see me in the dimly lit room and turned on the lamp closest to him.

I glared at the lamp and the crystals that fringed it. "Who decorated this room, this house?" I snapped.

"What are you talking about?"

"I said who did all of this?" I waved a hand around the room.

"That is none of your business."

"None of my business? Is this not my house?"

"Look, I don't have time for your irrational babbling. I already told you this morning that I will not be disrespected in my own house. Don't think you can talk to me this way just because I brought you here." He practically growled at me. I smelled alcohol on his breath.

"It is our house, our home, our son's home. It's not just yours and definitely does not belong to her. This is not her house and I shouldn't have to live with her pretentious furniture and these ugly paintings all over the place."

"You know your problem? You've grown wings. You must be insane if you think I'm going to redecorate this house because of you."

"Why, you want to keep it like this for when she comes back?"

"It's none of your business what I plan to do with my house."

"So you *are* keeping it intact for her? I know you're still seeing her. Isn't that where you go every night? Isn't that where you're coming from?"

"I don't care what you know; I owe you nothing more. You wanted to live in this house and I brought you in. You could have been patient like I told you to, but you refused."

"Patient? How long was I supposed to be patient, and what would have changed if I had been more patient? Would you have sacked her from here?"

He didn't say anything.

"Exactly, you were never going to ask her to leave this house, you were going to keep me in that flat forever."

"Well, now you're in the house so shut up and enjoy it."

I DIDN'T BOTHER making him breakfast on Monday. I could barely get myself out of bed and into the bathroom to throw up. Mensah was almost an hour late to pick me up for work. He had developed an attitude since we returned from Ho. Now he no longer offered to help me with my bag when I came out of the house in the morning and had the audacity to change the car radio station while I was listening to the news. He would turn down the temperature when I complained about being too cold and turn off the air conditioner and roll down the windows when I said it was hot. I had given him a strong warning on Friday when he answered the phone while driving and I guess this was his retaliation. I left school early that day and made him take me to a driving school a few minutes away from the house, where I registered to begin taking driving lessons the next day. I had spoken with Sarah and she agreed to let me out an hour early each day for the lessons. On Tuesday, I asked Mensah to drop me off at the driving school after work, instead of the house. I did the same on Wednesday and Thursday. I was surprised to find Eli working on his laptop in the dining room on Friday morning. He should have been on his way to the office.

"How are you?" he asked me. We hadn't spoken since the fight on Sunday night.

"I'm fine," I answered through clenched teeth. So now he cared about my well-being, when we had been together under the same roof for a week without his acknowledging me or asking about his son.

"I heard you're learning how to drive."

"Yes." I brushed bread crumbs off my new pair of maternity jeans. These days I always seemed to be covered in crumbs, even before I had breakfast.

"Is this the right time to be learning how to drive?"

"What do you mean?"

"I mean in your condition. Should you be learning in this condition?"

"My condition is not a problem." And it really wasn't. I'd already driven on a road, although it was a straight route and one with little traffic and the driving instructor was by my side with his set of controls. But it was still driving.

"Well, I think it's best to wait until you have the baby. It's safer."

"Pregnant women drive all the time. Besides, I can't wait when Mensah is misbehaving. Did he tell you that he was late picking me up on Monday and didn't offer an apology or explanation?"

"But that's nothing, Afi. That's not a reason to start driving yourself around."

"It's not the only thing he's done. I'm not going to sit down for everyone to disrespect me in this house. I also deserve respect."

"Look, I don't have the time to get into another argument with you. Just hold off on this driving business."

"I don't have the time either and I'm not holding off."

THE NEXT DAY was Fred's party. Eli knocked on my door after his breakfast but didn't enter when I asked him to. Instead he told me through the closed door that we would leave at three. Fred and his family lived at Cantonments, near the new international school. There were so many cars parked along his street that we had to walk about three minutes from our car to his house. I didn't mind the walk; I was just happy not to be sharing close quarters with Eli. Our ride over had been strained, with him looking straight ahead and me looking out my window. Thank God for the radio.

Fred and Cecelia welcomed us with hugs and big smiles. This was only my second time visiting their home.

"How come we never see you?" Cecelia chided me. She was holding my hand and leading me outside where their guests sat in thatched palaver huts that dotted the green of the backyard. The huts had been brought in specifically for the party.

"Eli is very busy," I told her.

"But you don't need Eli to bring you here; you have your own car, you can come on your own."

"I will try."

"You should, I want to see more of you."

We walked around and she introduced me to some of their friends. Somehow, I felt more at ease at this party than the one Yaya had taken me to. Not because the people here weren't sophisticated, but that they were subtler in their sophistication. In fact, most of them, both men and women, were dressed in shorts and sandals, and when they spoke, it was without a hint of American or English accents. I mentioned this to Cecelia, in the kitchen where she was checking on the caterer, and she laughed. "Yaya's friends are young and young people like to show off," she said. Laugh lines framed both corners of her mouth. She couldn't be more than forty years old.

"And you know how our dear sister-in-law is," she said with a wink. I smiled and nodded, not sure what to say. This was new terrain for me. I only ever discussed the Ganyos with my mother, Mawusi, and Evelyn, and as far as I was concerned, Cecelia was one of the Ganyos.

"You know she'll be here soon."

"Yaya?"

"Yes."

"She had to go to Ho to comfort her mother who is still recovering from your insubordination," Cecelia said again, and this time she chuckled. I tried to laugh but it came out sounding like a cough.

"Are you okay? Do you want some water?"

"No, I'm fine."

"Well, I want to congratulate you for what you did. It's about time that someone stood up to Aunty." She looked around after she said this, as though she expected one of her in-laws to be hiding nearby.

"I wasn't trying to pick a fight with Aunty. I just wanted them to do something about the woman. I didn't want to cause any trouble."

"And you were right. What they did to you wasn't fair. How could they deposit you in that barren flat and just leave you there like that? Are you not his wife?"

"Do you know the woman?"

"Which woman?"

"Muna," I let her name slip off of my tongue. I wanted to spit afterward.

"Not really. You know Fred has never approved of the relationship and she has never liked him either so we rarely went over. In fact, we only went there when the little girl was sick. Even Richard rarely went to that house. It's only because of you that they are now able to visit their brother's house freely. They should throw a party to thank you."

I'd never seen this side of her before. She had been kind but not this friendly during our first visit. It seemed like she had now decided that I was someone she could be more open with. But could I be open with her? I didn't have to answer that question because we soon heard Yaya's voice in the hallway and went out to greet her. She looked glamorous as always. She now had an afro that I thought was too thick to be natural, and she stood tall in a flower-patterned maxi dress and high-heeled sandals. She hugged me as if nothing was amiss and we ended up sitting at the same table in the backyard. Eli was chatting with a group of men close by. I expected Yaya to ask about Ho but she didn't. Instead she wanted to know how I was. I told her that I had been to the hospital last week for my prenatal checkup. We talked about my school and the fact that I would be graduating in under six months.

"What will you be doing after graduation?"

"I want to open a boutique."

"A boutique is an excellent idea," Yaya said. "Have you told *Fo* Eli?"

"We discussed it a while ago. He said I could open a boutique in the new mall. But it won't be completed for a while."

"Well, you should remind him. He also has shares in one of the luxury towers that just opened near the airport. That would be a prime location to set up shop as well. Anyone who's anyone is going to be shopping there so there will be no shortage of customers with money to spend."

I perked up at her response. She was right, owning a shop at that location would be perfect for business. Only rich people could afford the types of clothes I wanted to make.

"I will talk to Eli," I told her. I was already imagining what my boutique would look like, the displays, the mannequins. I would have a leather sofa, a white one, for customers to rest on, and would serve them champagne in flutes; I'd seen that at a boutique in Osu that Evelyn had taken me to. There would be freshly cut flowers in crystal vases and a uniformed doorman who let customers in and out.

"Yes, you should. And you should remember all that my mother has done for you."

"Pardon?" The colorful pictures in my head vanished.

"I said you should remember where you came from and all that we have done for you," she said in her perfect English. The sides of her mouth were turned up into a slight smile, as though the content of the conversation had not changed. "And like I said, your boutique is an excellent idea," she continued, as though she couldn't see the tightening of my lips. Aunty must have sent her to deliver this message.

I excused myself to go to the bathroom, afraid of what I would say if I stayed seated at the table. As I left the bathroom, still fuming, I bumped into someone. It took a moment for me to recognize the smiling, bald-headed figure. It was Abraham from the party Yaya had taken me to.

"How are you?" he asked, his eyes shining and his smile getting wider by the second.

"I'm fine, and you?"

"Perfect, now that I've seen you. You look great!" he said.

"Thank you."

"You look like a different person."

"I'm pregnant."

"Yes, but that's not it. You look incredible, like you've been spending a lot of time with your sister-in-law and her chic friends."

"I'm a designer myself," I said, irritated by the entire conversation. Why was he behaving as if I had looked like a maidservant the last time he saw me?

"So, I've heard."

"How was your trip?"

"It was good. I got back ages ago and wanted to reach out to you, but then I found out who your husband is. Only a fool would piss him off," he said and then laughed awkwardly.

"Well, it's nice to see you," I said, wanting the conversation to end.

"Yeah, you too. See you around."

ELI AND I fought again when we got home. That idiot Mensah had told him that I went to the driving school after he asked me to stop and now he wanted to know why I'd "disobeyed" him. Disobeyed! If it wasn't his sister, then it was him reminding me of my place.

"I went because I want to, Eli. It's what I want to do." We were standing at the bottom of the staircase.

"Stop being difficult. For once, just listen to what I'm saying."

"Why should I listen to you? Do you ever listen to me? You don't even talk to me. You don't treat me like your wife so why should I listen to you?"

"What do you mean I don't treat you like my wife? Are you not living in this house? Didn't I go to the party with you?"

"You think that's enough? Me living in this house and you taking me to a party?"

"What more do you want?"

"Oh, do you want a list? Because I can give you a list, a very long list. First of all, you haven't married me in a church."

"What are you even talking about now?"

"You know exactly what I'm talking about."

"Look, I don't have time for this. I do not want you back at that driving school and that's final."

"Okay, wait and see what happens on Monday," I said to him and began stomping up the stairs, my purse in one hand and one of the silver gift bags that Cecelia had given out at the end of the evening in another. Halfway to the top I missed a step, and because of the bags in my hand, couldn't grab the railing in time. I tried to break the fall with my hands but my stomach still hit the sharp edge of a step. The pain was so severe that my howl woke up the staff in their backyard quarters. Eli was on his knees beside me in a breath. He carried me down the stairs and, despite my protests, bundled me into the car and drove me to the clinic. The doctor wasn't even at the clinic and had to be called in from her home, which was a few kilometers away. After listening to the baby's heartbeat and doing a fetal scan, she assured us that everything was alright. Indeed, I felt fine. The pain had subsided by the time we had reached the main road, but Eli insisted we go to the clinic and now he was insisting that they keep me overnight for observation. It was clear that the poor doctor wanted to go home and to bed, but she wasn't going to argue with Eli so they both slept in chairs by my bedside. She conducted another scan before we left the clinic that morning. At the house, Mrs. Adams had breakfast waiting and Eli brought it up to me in bed. This was the first time he had been in the master bedroom since I moved in. He sat on the edge of the mattress and waited quietly as I ate my burnt toast.

"More?" he asked when I was finished. I shook my head. I just wanted to take a bath and get back into bed.

"No, I'm fine. I want to take a bath."

He took the tray off my lap, set it on the bedside table, and stretched out a hand to me. I took it and he helped me to my feet and led me into the bathroom. I thought he would leave me alone in there but he stayed. I looked at him, seeking an explanation but he said nothing. Instead he came closer and began to undo the top button on my dress.

"Eli?"

"Let me help you."

I stood quietly, barely breathing as he undid the buttons. I felt my skin jump every time his hands brushed against me. I covered my chest and belly with my hands when my dress came off. I gasped when his fingers touched my back, he was undoing the clasp on my bra, and I shuddered when he began to pull down my panties.

"Eli?"

"Yes?"

I wanted him. I was naked and he was fully clothed staring at my body as if it was his first time seeing me like this. He reached out and spread his hands against my stomach, as though trying to envelop our baby.

"Does it hurt?" He was touching the red bruise on my belly where I had hit the step.

"No."

His hand fell away and I climbed into the bathtub and sank into the warm water. He knelt beside me and began to wash me with the loofah. When I flinched, he switched to using the face towel. I closed my eyes and gripped the curved rim of the bathtub when he began to soap my breasts and then I felt his lips pressed against mine. I kissed him back, maybe a little too hungrily, but it had been so long. I took the towel from him, dropped it into the water, and guided his hands between my legs. I cried out when he touched me and shook so much that I splashed him with water. In the bedroom, he joined me in bed, but despite being pressed against my back and cradling my breasts, refused to unzip his trousers. He stilled my hand when I reached out to do it myself.

"What's wrong?" I knew he wanted me, I could feel him.

"The baby."

"It's fine. The doctor said it's fine."

"But that was before you fell. Let's wait for a few days."

"No, no, please, no."

I turned to face him. "I need you. Please. You only need to be gentle." A small, exhilarated cry escaped my lips when he reached down to unzip his trousers.

MY MOTHER CAME to visit for Christmas and stayed after the holidays. Eli and I visited Ho on Boxing Day to give gifts to our families. Mawusi had come to Accra to help me shop; I was determined not to forget any of my cousins. We spent days in the malls, looking for something for each of them, even though Eli begged me to stay off my feet. Mawusi carried a list and crossed out a name after each purchase. We bought mostly clothing but a few of the older cousins got electronics. Shopping with Mawusi and handing out the gifts made me happy. My father was the one who used to buy Christmas presents for everyone, so while the older cousins remembered the gesture, the younger ones were in awe, never having received gifts wrapped in sparkling paper before. They carefully unwrapped the presents, saving the boxes and paper they came in. I knew they would all be reused. Of course, I had to give money and foodstuffs to the older people who only wanted a gift box if it contained cash. Tɔgã Pious was furious when I gave him the same amount as his wives, but this time I didn't give in. I was getting used to his anger. He had been angry for weeks after I sent the twins back and had taken to calling and delivering tirades. Now, I rarely answered when he called. He frowned for the rest of my visit and refused to wave as Eli and I drove away but I didn't care.

We went to inspect my house after this. The painting of the exterior was completed; all that was left was to paint the interior. My mother would be able to move in by the end of January. Eli suggested we erect a stand for a water tank behind the house and that we raise the fence a few inches. He promised to send people over to do these things. My mother thanked him but he only complimented me on putting up the house, as though it wasn't his money that had made it all possible.

"I should thank you," I said to him. We were in the kitchen and I was leaning against him, my feet already tired.

"Why?"

"I wouldn't have been able to do it without you."

"I don't believe that. I think you would have built this house, even if you had never met me."

I beamed at the praise and his generosity and hugged him.

AFTER THE HOUSE, we had lunch at Aunty's and then Eli gave her his gift, two new vans to transport goods from the factories in Tema to her depot. He told her it was from us, but when she said "thank you," it was only to him. I wasn't surprised; she knew it was his money that bought the vans and she had still not forgiven me for leaving her son and refusing to return when she ordered me to. She had never been a warm person, but now when she spoke, I sensed a sharp undertone. My mother and I avoided her for most of the visit, instead sitting in her garden and exploring the parts of the huge house we were allowed to enter. It was dark and I was asleep when we arrived back in Accra.

I returned to school in the new year. Most weeks I attended at least three out of five days and sometimes I drove myself. But it was becoming harder to do either. My feet swelled so much that I took to wearing my soft bedroom slippers to school, and there were many days when I didn't even make it down the stairs. Mrs. Adams prepared my meals under my mother's supervision; she'd come to Accra laden with all kinds of herbs and with a gallon of palm oil. I don't think I'd ever seen so much oil floating on soup before. Ma insisted that I needed the extra fat for the baby. If you asked me, the baby didn't need any more fat, not when my stomach looked like I was carrying twins. In addition to feeding me oil, she rubbed unprocessed cocoa butter on my stomach twice a day to help with the stretch marks.

"It worked for me," she said, when I protested the amount of butter she used. My bedsheets were always stained dark with oil spots. I had Hawa change them every day. I didn't mind sleeping on those sheets so much but I couldn't let Eli sleep on them.

He had moved into the master bedroom after I fell, and he took over the cocoa butter-rubbing duties on the days that he got home early enough. He made it home for supper most evenings and I tried to be in the kitchen when Mrs. Adams prepared the evening meal. It was the least I could do. I faced no more resistance from her, not since Eli sat her down and gave her a good talking to. Eli replaced Mensah with a new driver in January; Yeboah was an older man who knew to follow my instructions and not give me attitude. Eli and I also went baby-furniture shopping in January. After the frenzy of the Christmas shopping period, the stores were almost empty.

"People have spent all their money," Eli joked when we drove into the almost deserted parking lot of the furniture store.

He did most of the work setting up the nursery. Yaya, excited about having a new nephew, also helped by ordering personalized wallpaper for the room. My mother stood with her mouth agape in the doorway when she first saw the room. She'd never seen a nursery before and hadn't even known that there was such a thing, that parents could dedicate an entire room to their newborn child. I had shared a room with her and my father until he died. She was equally in shock when I took her to see the boutique I was going to open and broke into tears more than once as I showed her around. I had settled on a ground floor location in the tower near the airport, between a luxury watch store and a perfumery. I began setting up the boutique in January, even though my graduation from Sarah's fashion school was not until

April, four months away. Eli hired workers to build shelves and
to install clothes racks. I was now looking for tailors to hire.
They would work out of a nearby house, owned by Richard. I
would pay him a monthly rent. But I wasn't paying rent on the
boutique. Eli said we could talk about rent later, when business
picked up.

He was very supportive and caring. We hadn't had any fights
since I fell and had returned to talking and laughing with each
other since he moved into the bedroom. And until recently, we'd
been having a lot of sex, but now I couldn't bear to have him
touch me. I pushed him away when he crossed the invisible line
I created to divide the bed. We started going out again and spent
a weekend in the riverfront resort at Kpong, this time without
any of his friends. But we spent most evenings in bed, him on
his computer or phone while I read a novel or went over plans
for the boutique. My mother took his place in bed when he traveled or was late coming home. He once came to find her asleep
on his side of the bed, but he didn't seem to mind. Beyond the
usual greetings and short conversations about the baby, he didn't
say much to my mother, which was fine because she was still in
awe of him and was uncomfortable in his presence. But he was
kind to her and constantly asked me if she was happy and if she
had everything she needed. I assured him that she was fine. I
knew that she was happy to be with me. She had confided that
she didn't intend to go back to Aunty's store after the baby was
born. She would stay with me as long as I wanted and would
start a small business when she went back to Ho. She wanted to
go back to baking cakes and pies, this time in the kitchen of our
new house. She felt that the relationship between her and Aunty
had soured so much that she no longer wanted to work with the

woman. Before she left for Accra, Aunty had begun berating her in front of other workers and had once prevented her from joining a Women's Guild meeting because she was late in coming, that lateness caused by Aunty who had increased her workload. Surprisingly, my mother didn't blame me for any of this. Instead, she had come to realize that our benefactor was no saint.

Aunty came to visit at the beginning of March, my eighth month. She had recently had a minor stroke and Eli wanted her close by, but she was eager to get back to work. She only stayed for four days but it felt like four years. Luckily, I had my swollen belly and feet as excuses for staying in bed and out of her way. Of course, that didn't mean she couldn't find me. The evening before she went back to Ho, she came into the room and sat on the bed beside me. We talked a bit about my health, the clinic where I would give birth, and the boutique. Even though I was no longer afraid of her, I could not relax in her presence. My back was so stiff that I feared I would have spasms.

"And your mother has moved," she said, when I thought there was nothing more to talk about. My mother had returned to Ho for a few weeks to move her things out of Aunty's house and into ours.

"Yes. She likes the new house."

"I know, I went to see it. I hope she has thanked Eli for it and all he has done for you. And you too. I hope you're showing him your gratitude."

I didn't say anything to that. Nothing. I just glared at her. Eli had never once made me feel like I owed him anything for the house. In fact, he had made it clear that it was my house, that he had no claim to it. It was the only thing I owned, the only thing of value that truly belonged to me. Even though I shared this house in Accra with him, I was aware that it was his. My name was not on a single document in Accra, not for a house, or a plot of land, or the boutique, or a car, nothing. That three-bedroom house in Ho with a pawpaw tree shading the front porch was the only thing I owned and this woman could not even let me enjoy that fact. I locked myself in the bathroom and refused to come out to say bye to her. My mother and I were glum for the rest of that week.

I WENT INTO labor two weeks early, on the day of my graduation from Sarah's. I hadn't intended to attend the ceremony so the unexpected labor did not scuttle my plans. Eli was not home so Yeboah, the new driver, took me to the hospital. My mother sat beside me in the back seat, panting more than I did. Eli met us at the hospital about an hour later and our son was born soon after that.

ELEVEN

I was grateful for my mother's help after Selorm's birth. Even though he was almost one year old now, I was still more comfortable having her look after my son than someone we hired. I had heard so many stories of maids abusing children that I couldn't bear the thought of leaving my child with one of them. Every day like clockwork, I would hear him on the baby monitor while we were still in the throes of sleep. My mother had her own monitor and would quickly go to the nursery to pick him up so that Eli and I wouldn't be disturbed by his cries. She had asked me more than once to switch my monitor off but I refused. I liked to know what was happening in the nursery even if I wasn't the one responding to his cries. On the days that she was in church or traveled to Ho, Eli or I would go for him when he cried. We would pass him back and forth as we showered and dressed for work, and I usually prepared his breakfast porridge, which was a mixture of rice or corn and dried fish high in protein. My mother said it's what she had fed me and it's why I was known as Afi Fatty until I turned five. On days when I was in a hurry, he ate the purees that we bought in jars. Eli usually fed him in the highchair that we had set up in the kitchen. It was best to keep him out of the dining room because he enjoyed projectile spitting his food.

After breakfast on days my mother was away, I would take him with me to work, either to the workshop or the boutique, although I usually went back and forth between the two. The shop girls helped me tend to him during the day by carrying him on their back or playing with him while I tried to get some work done. Thankfully, my mother was rarely away from the house. She relished the time spent with him and was often reluctant to hand him over to me when I came home in the evening. I complained that she was spoiling him but she wouldn't listen. He only had to sniffle and she would come running to pick him up. I had told her that it was okay to let him cry every once in a while, but she didn't want to hear that. Now he expected to be carried around throughout the day and would begin wailing as soon as his chubby feet touched the ground.

Eli was almost as bad as my mother. As far as he was concerned, we had to indulge Selorm to no end. Many mornings, he would give the squealing baby a piggyback ride while already dressed for work. My mother never ceased to be amazed at the sight, to see someone so big become so small. He also had no problem giving his phones to Selorm to play with. Now Selorm seemed to enjoy nothing more than pushing the buttons on his father's phones and listening to the sounds this made. I had bought him two toy phones, much bigger and more colorful than his father's, but he loved the real thing. He had already plunked one into the guest toilet downstairs and cracked the screen on another, but Eli kept giving them to him whenever he stretched out his hand. He was incapable of saying no to his son. He had started taking Selorm to work with him around his seventh month. I worried that he would be too disruptive and make work impossible but Eli said he had been easy to manage. His assistant, Joanna, had helped, and Selorm had charmed everyone in the office with his cheeks that got rounder as he got older and a laugh that triggered laughter in everyone around him.

Yaya also adored him and came by quite regularly to play and bring him toys, which were rapidly accumulating in his room. There were so many that I wondered if I should turn one of the guest bedrooms into a playroom. My mother had scoffed at the idea, even she who adored him to no end thought this was too much. It was one thing to strap him to her back all day, another to devote a room to his playthings, especially when there were children in our family whose only toys were empty milk tins, sticks, and old tires.

Aunty also visited several times. She had suffered a second stroke but was determined to keep moving. Even she seemed to be captivated by Selorm. I had been amazed the first time I saw her chasing after him as he crawled on the back porch. Somehow, he could not tire her out despite how energetic he was and how frail she was becoming. Indeed, it was only with him that I saw her let her guard down. I heard her burst into laughter more than once, and when I poked my head into the room to investigate, I found her alone with Selorm, holding him or running behind him. She wasn't this affectionate with Fred's teenage daughters, though she might have been when they were younger.

"Finally, a grandson. Well done, Afi," she had said on her last visit. We were on the back porch watching as Selorm pounded the keys on a colorful, miniature keyboard that Yaya had brought for him. I knew that it would soon be discarded onto the toy heap in his nursery and he would move on to something else. Before I would have been happy about Aunty's comment, happy that I had pleased her and met her approval. But now her words irritated me. I hadn't given birth to my son to fulfill her desires. I knew she was now more content than ever before, Selorm had righted my every wrong, and her affection for him seemed to have caused her to forget my insubordination. In fact, she hadn't reminded me or my mother of the gratitude we owed her and her family since he was born.

She was now free to come and go as she pleased, unlike when the other woman had occupied the house. She and Eli's relationship had long recovered from the quarrel I started with my ultimatum in Ho; he was now welcome at her funeral. He visited Ho regularly, more than he had when he lived with the woman, sometimes with me by his side. Aunty waited on him hand and foot during those visits and he loved it: what do you want to eat, is it too warm, is it too cold? None of her househelps were allowed to cook for him; she did all of it herself no matter how many times he begged her to stay out of the kitchen. And during the meal she would sit at the table, ready to dish more food onto his plate at the slightest sign. She seemed to forget that I was there, which was fine by me. I usually ate at the other end of the table, in silence, while she mounted this performance of motherly love. I would have preferred to stay at my mother's house but Eli insisted we stay together. After two such visits, I concluded that she loved him more than her other children. Even Yaya, her only daughter and youngest child, did not receive a fraction of the affection that Eli received. Luckily, this didn't seem to affect his relationship with his siblings.

Eli's siblings spent a lot of time in our house. In fact, they too came and went as they pleased. On more than one occasion, I had returned from work to find Yaya barefoot on the sofa in the sitting room, working on her computer, or Richard and Fred in the dining room, eating a meal they had asked Mrs. Adams to prepare. Fred's two secondary school–aged daughters came by almost daily during their vacation to use the pool and they slept over when they felt too tired to go home. No one ever asked me before doing any of these things, which I accepted. And I knew that Eli also paid similar visits to their homes. He had returned home on several occasions with plates of food for me, sent by Cecelia, and he told me that he sometimes napped in Richard's house, which was less than five minutes away from their office.

"That's just how it is," my mother had said. We were watching Fred's girls, still in their wet bathing suits, walking back and forth in the kitchen. Those children could open and close the fridge more than a hundred times in the course of one visit. Only God knows what they were looking for! That day I instructed my driver, Yeboah, to take them home even though they wanted to sleep over. I needed a break. Besides, their grandmother would be arriving the next day to cook for her son with ingredients that she carted all the way from Ho. "He needs home-cooked meals," she had the audacity to tell me over the phone. Now all she had to do was spoon-feed him. I would have been more bothered by this intrusion if I didn't have work to do.

The boutique was thriving. Despite Eli's objections, I started working six weeks after Selorm was born. Knowing that every day I stayed at home the shop was empty pushed me out of the house. With Sarah's help, I was able to hire five tailors; three of them were Togolese men. One of the women had graduated from Sarah's school before me but hadn't made it on her own, and the second woman was the product of a rival design school. I also employed three young people to assist the tailors with the ironing and to clean and organize. Nancy, my overly serious cousin and Tɔgā Pious's daughter, oversaw production and kept everyone in line in my absence. I had brought her from Ho to help me set up and manage the workshop. She had been selling tomatoes in the big market and had been happy to leave that job behind.

At my workshop, a three-bedroom house I rented from Richard, I tried to maintain everything I had learned at Sarah's. We began work at eight and closed at five, both at the workshop and the boutique. I usually arrived at the workshop around the same time as Nancy and the assistants to ensure that everything was in order before the tailors arrived and production began. That meant assigning bundles of pre-cut fabric to each tailor for the day, recording the previous day's expenses and production, and topping up the fuel in the generator in preparation for power outages, among other tasks. When I was satisfied that all was in order, I drove to the boutique, which was thirty minutes away in bad traffic. Ellen, the boutique manager, and her two assistants usually opened before I arrived. The boutique was everything I had wanted. The interior was white with bright paintings and colorful ornaments; it looked just like the ones I used to watch on the style channel. We had the white leather couch and served champagne, fruit juices, and cupcakes to our regulars. And in addition to the clothes, we sold handbags and jewelry. I designed and produced some of the handbags, including the ones made of raffia, but I bought most of them from artisans around the country. The beads were authentic Krobo ones; Yaya had introduced me to the guy who made them because she bought her beads from him as well. They were some of the most popular items in the store. Our customers couldn't get enough of the brightly colored glass bead necklaces, earrings, and bracelets and didn't seem to mind that they were sometimes as expensive as gold. I had to call the beadmaker every week for a new consignment and I think that's why he recently informed me that he was raising his prices. I would need to find another supplier soon.

But Yaya was right when she said I would attract the right kind of customers in the tower. Sales had been slow in the beginning because people were still figuring out who we were, but now our clothes flew off the racks. In fact, we had several items on back order and my tailors had to come in on more than one Saturday. Within a few months, all of the fashionistas in Accra knew of my brand and my trademark mixing of feathers, lace, beads, and leather in the garments I produced. Seamstresses had even begun copying my designs around Accra. Less than a month ago, I saw a woman climbing into a *trotro* with a half-beaded skirt that looked exactly like mine but couldn't be mine because I didn't recognize the beads and no one who shopped in my boutique traveled in *trotros*. But I wasn't worried about the copycats because people still wanted the originals. I had already lost count of the number of celebrities who had worn my custom designs. I attracted more customers by pricing my ready-to-wear pieces just below my competitors, who believed that they should charge Versace prices. It was three months before I was able to pay rent to Richard but I hadn't missed a payment since I started. I still wasn't paying for the boutique space yet though. The location cost several thousand dollars more than I had left over every month after paying my employees, paying the utility bills in the workshop, buying supplies, and paying rent to Richard. I would either have to sell much more or drastically raise my prices but none of this seemed feasible now. I brought it up with Eli but he thought I should first focus on building my brand. With a strong brand, I could sell more and raise my prices if I wanted. He asked Richard to help me mount an advertising campaign and Richard eventually handed me over to Evelyn and her firm. So I was getting to see a lot of my next-door neighbor and friend again.

She and Richard were still together in a way that I didn't quite understand. Richard had recently begun a relationship with a young woman from Anfoega. He had met her at church of all places; I didn't even know that Richard attended church. She was an anesthesiologist at the Korle Bu Teaching Hospital. Most importantly, Aunty knew her family well and approved of her. She and Richard had already visited Aunty in Ho and had been warmly received, according to Cecelia, who told me this one day when she came to pick up the girls from the pool. In fact, the Ganyos were already talking about the knocking ceremony when they would visit her family to ask for her hand in marriage. All of this while Richard still spent nights in Evelyn's flat.

"But how can you bear this?" I asked her. She had come to the boutique to discuss some concepts for the ad campaign. She had on a fitted gray suit and electric-blue pencil heels that made her tower above me.

"I told you a long time ago that Richard and I will not be going anywhere as long as Aunty is alive. This is not unexpected. He has his doctor and I have my lawyer," she said and laughed, throwing her head back. We were seated on my white leather couch sipping fruit juices in flutes. Neither of us could stand champagne in the morning; I don't know how my customers did it.

"Lawyer?"

"Yes, lawyer! Do you think I'm sitting in that flat waiting for Richard to stand up to his mother? Please. And the best part of it is that this one's mother is dead," she said and laughed some more, almost spilling her drink.

"How can you say that?"

"What? I didn't kill the woman. She was dead before I met her son. And he doesn't have any sisters, only one brother who lives in the UK. You have no idea how easy my life is. I don't have an entire clan breathing down my neck over one man."

"Does he know about Richard?"

"He knows that Richard is my ex and that the flat I live in is his flat."

"And does Richard know about him?"

She laughed again. "It's none of Richard's business. You know, Richard is one of those men who doesn't want to be serious with you but also doesn't want anyone else to have you. All I can say is that I like living in his flat and I will stay there for as long as I can. When the time comes to move out, I'll move out. The Ganyos are not the only ones who have put mortar between cement blocks in Accra. In the meantime, he and his mother can parade their doctor around as much as they want."

"But don't you love him?"

"Yes, but I love him with my head. I'm not going to waste my life on a man who lets his mother tell him who to marry. A grown man with a pot belly and receding hairline who is afraid to tell his mother what he wants. I deserve better than that. By the way, how are things with you and Eli?"

I looked around to make sure that none of the workers were in earshot. "It's fine," I told her. Eli and I had settled into a comfortable truce since I fell and hit my belly on the steps. He was affectionate. We had been socializing more since Selorm's birth. Last week we were at a reception at the American ambassador's house; Eli was friends with the woman. The week before that, we saw a play at the Conference Centre. There were fewer late nights and he worked from home some weekends. When at home, he enjoyed playing with Selorm. He had begun teaching him how to swim, much to my alarm. Two weeks ago, my mother and I had stood at the edge of the pool, clutching each other in terror, as Eli submerged Selorm in the water. Selorm had cried out the first couple of times but after had moved his arms and legs as if he'd been swimming his whole life and Eli had laughed at my distress.

We didn't talk about the woman. I knew that he still saw her. He had to rush out of the house more than once because of an emergency with Ivy, and I understood that. He had to spend time with his daughter. In fact, he usually told me when he went to see her and I greatly appreciated that. I had asked him several times to bring her over to spend time with Selorm. I wanted them to get to know each other; they were brother and sister after all. Eli had promised that he would talk to the woman about it but nothing had happened yet. I suspected that the woman was being difficult, punishing the child to spite Eli and me. I planned to ask him again. It was Selorm's birthday in a week and the whole family was coming, I wanted Ivy to be there. I knew he would agree with me; he was being very reasonable. He had agreed for the entire house to be redecorated. The ornate furniture, paintings of people, none of them black, on horseback and in various uncomfortable poses and the heavy damask curtains were gone, replaced by a modern look. At least now it looked like we lived in a house in Ghana and not in a palace in England. And the sex was better than it had ever been.

"You actually did it," Evelyn said after I told her all of this.

"Did what?"

"Got the man."

I smiled. I had long ago stopped thinking about this as some kind of task or challenge and had embraced it as my life. I didn't get the man. I was with my husband and son in our home.

"Congratulations!" We clinked our champagne flutes and laughed. But the irony of the situation was not lost on me. In her story, I was the doctor, the one Aunty approved of, and she was the other woman. But I didn't dwell too much on Evelyn's relationship. I had a party to plan. And hopefully, I would soon meet my stepdaughter, and Selorm, his sister.

TWELVE

I would have been happy with a small party. A birthday cake, homemade food, some games for the children in our backyard, but Eli wanted a big party. He wanted an event planner, a caterer, a photographer, a DJ, a live band, a clown, a petting zoo, everything. He wanted to rent out the entire Efua Sutherland Children's Park but I talked him out of it. We settled on Fred's and Cecelia's backyard, which was much bigger than ours.

"I can only imagine what you people will do when he turns ten," my mother said as she watched the organizers lug in the poles that would hold up the white canopies. She, Mawusi, Nancy, and I had arrived at Fred's house at seven that Saturday morning to oversee the setup, although I quickly realized we didn't have to do anything. The event planner, Grace, had arrived before we did and by ten had completed the entire setup. The canopies were up, the tables were set, a kiddie pool complete with fake palm trees was in place, and an ice cream stand was in one corner of the yard, while bouncy castles, a slide, two swing sets, and a jungle gym were installed in the other corner. A small fenced-in area with rabbits, tortoises, and two lambs was beside the playground. Only among rich people in Accra would rabbits and sheep be considered a novelty! There was a machine that dispensed toys to the children and a sandbox with treasures hidden in it. The chef and his servers arrived soon after and set up in the kitchen. There were four different birthday cakes and an assortment of food for the children and adults. There was a bar and a grill station. Yaya had brought one of her South African friends to man the grill.

"They grill a lot, all kinds of meat," she explained to me when I asked why we had to bring him instead of using the chef.

"Are you paying him?" I asked her.

"No! He's a bank executive. He just likes to grill," she said that morning, and sure enough he showed up in his chauffeured car, grilling tool set in hand. I'd never had a white person do anything for me before. What a day.

Yaya wasn't the only Ganyo on site. Cecelia and Fred were there, making sure things were running smoothly, and I suspected also keeping an eye on everyone who came into their beautiful house. Their daughters were also there, playing with Selorm in the sandbox. I worried that they would find and open all of the hidden treasures before the other children arrived but Eli wouldn't let me take him out of the sandbox.

"He's enjoying himself, leave him there," he said, tickled at his son's antics. I left Selorm with Mawusi and Nancy and went inside. Aunty was in the kitchen with the catering team; she had come the day before and slept at Fred's. When I entered, she was trying to tell the chef that the rice was undercooked but he was ignoring her, much to my delight. The man was chef at a five-star restaurant for goodness sake, but this woman wanted to teach him how to boil rice! She was now walking with a cane but could still make her children jump when she wanted. At least she was in the kitchen and not outside where the rest of us were. I went back outside.

At about eleven, Eli and Richard were inspecting what the organizers had done and asking for some things to be moved around. They wanted the petting zoo farther away from the food. Yaya was with them for a while but then left to make sure that the DJ wasn't going to block foot traffic into the house with his huge speakers, and Fred was out front making sure the extra security people who had been brought in knew where to direct guests to park and also to ensure that only people with invitations were allowed in.

There wasn't anything for me to do so I went upstairs to get Selorm dressed; we had asked people to come at noon.

"Which one is he going to wear?" my mother asked. We were in one of the guest rooms and I had six outfits laid out on the bed. Mawusi and Nancy were already dressed and were outside with some of my relatives who had come from Ho. Tɔgã Pious was at the enstoolment of a new chief in Vakpo and couldn't make it, thankfully.

"Probably all of them. You know he will be dirty in thirty minutes and I will have to come and change him."

We agreed on blue shorts, blue shoes, and a white T-shirt to begin. I also added a gold chain and bracelet that Eli had had made for him the week before. Once he was dressed, my mother took him downstairs while I showered and changed into a white knee-length dress with a boat neckline and short sleeves. It was simple but lovely, a gift from Evelyn. Unfortunately, she wouldn't be at the party; Richard had come with the doctor who I had spoken to briefly when I went into the kitchen. She was really sticking to Aunty's side; she had obviously figured out that that was the only way she would end up with a ring on her finger.

Evelyn laughed when I told her this over the phone. I was dressed and sitting on the bed.

"I don't care," she said.

"That's good," I told her, even though the dip in her voice told me that she did care. That she wanted to be here with Richard. But she was too proud to admit that to me.

"Take lots of pictures—I want to see everything."

"Don't worry, there's a professional photographer and she has about five assistants, all taking pictures and shooting videos. You won't have time to look through all of the pictures."

"Okay, good. And enjoy yourself. Remember that this is also your day, you are also celebrating you. You have gone through so much. Think about where you were two years ago, and where you are now. You've come so far; you came and showed these rich people that you're not to be messed with and you have your husband and a happy home. How many women can say the same?"

"I know, I'm blessed."

"Is Ivy coming?"

"I don't think so. Eli went to pick her up this morning but came back without her. He said we would talk about it later. I was really hoping that she would be here. I really want her and Selorm to get to know each other. Imagine if she could spend some weekends and vacations with us, then Eli wouldn't have to be running back and forth between two homes. Even Aunty said this when she last visited. I think the whole family wants to have her near. You know the woman won't even let them visit now. At least when she was in the house, she allowed them in every once in a while to see Ivy, but now Eli is the only one who sees her. It shouldn't be that way."

"It's a shame but I also don't blame her. I mean, they did kick her out of the house and she hated them before all of this even happened. Can you imagine how she feels now?"

"You're right. But the child shouldn't suffer because of it."

"Look, forget about this for now, go out there and have a good time. Today is your day!"

And I did have a good time.

THERE WERE SO many people, some of whom I had never met before. Chris and Ade even flew in from Nigeria. There were way more adults than children, and without the decorations and play stuff one would have thought it was an adult's party. Even the First Lady was there, invited by Fred. They had become good friends while on the campaign trail together. The gift table soon became the gift room; even people who had never met Selorm before came with gifts. I suspect that many were trying to curry favor with Eli and his brothers. The children also had fun. There was so much screaming and running around that it was a miracle no one got hurt. I left my mother to run after Selorm and took a seat at a table with Sarah, Mawusi, and some of my other cousins from Ho. I had barely begun to eat before Cecelia walked over to the table with the First Lady.

"This is Eli's wife, the mother of the celebrant," Cecelia said as she introduced me.

The First Lady shook my hand and we chatted for a few minutes. I mentioned that I owned a boutique in the tower.

"Yes, I know it. My assistant has shopped there for me before and I just love the things you make. Your bags are exquisite," she said.

"Thank you."

"No, thank you for such excellent work. I'm always happy to see young women doing so well, and all while balancing a home and children. Your husband must be proud."

"He is," Cecelia said. "We all are."

I beamed. The First Lady promised to be in touch; she wanted to order some dresses for an official trip she would soon be making. I gave her my card.

"The student has passed the teacher," Sarah said when I sat down.

"Oh, please, you started sewing for important people before I even knew how to sew," I told her and we both laughed. I think she was happy for me.

After eating, Mawusi and I walked to the ice cream stand.

"Can you believe all of this?" I whispered to her, even though it was so loud around us that no one else could have overheard our conversation. We were standing beside the ice cream stand. Aunty, my mother, and a couple of women from the Women's Guild were hovering over Selorm, ready to pick him up if he even wobbled. Eli, Richard, Chris, and others were sitting around a table, deep in conversation; I knew they were talking about work. Yaya was dancing with her nieces, Fred's daughters, and

Fred and Cecelia were seated at a table with the First Lady and some big people from the government.

"Can you believe this?" I said again to Mawusi.

"Yes, I can. If anyone could do this, it was you. But let me confess that there were times when I thought you wouldn't make it. Remember when you first moved to Accra and he wasn't coming to see you, and then you moved back to Ho. Those were times when I thought everything was going to come to an end, that you were going to lose him."

"But you didn't tell me."

"Of course not! What good would it have done to tell you these things, as if you weren't worried enough? But what is important is that you made it through. Now they are all benefiting because of you. Free to come into your house, to see Eli whenever they want. Look at how many times he has visited Ho this year alone. Remember they said he stopped coming because of the woman?"

"Hmmm."

"In fact, they should throw a separate party for you, to thank you for saving their family."

"I agree," I said and laughed. "Have you and Yao decided on the wedding date?"

Yao's family had performed the knocking ceremony in January and they were trying to decide on the date for the wedding.

"I want to do it around Christmas."

"Why Christmas?"

"You know I love Christmastime. And by then I will have graduated and hopefully begun working." Yao already had a job with one of the telecommunications companies. Eli had helped him get it.

"A Christmas wedding would be nice."

"But when are *you* having your wedding?"

"My wedding?"

"Yes, your church wedding."

"Ah, I haven't thought about that in a long time. And who has the time for a wedding now? Between work and Selorm, I have no time for myself, and you know we're expanding the business."

"But it doesn't have to be a big wedding. You can just have a simple ceremony and have lunch with a few relatives and friends after. A lot of people are doing that now, mainly to save money, but it also makes sense for someone like you. It's really just a formality, but it's important."

"I remember you thinking that this wasn't a big deal before. What's happened?"

"Nothing really. It's just that I've been thinking a lot about my own wedding and the importance of formalizing things and of having the proper paperwork for everything. And with the church wedding, there can be only one official wife. All the traditional marriage does is recognize you as the first wife, but not the only wife."

"But what stops a man from marrying a second woman traditionally even if he already has done the church thing?"

"Ah! You can't marry someone in church and then go and marry another person outside. It's not done! I don't think you have anything to worry about with Eli, but still, why not go ahead and do it? You have nothing to lose."

"That's true, even though I haven't thought much about this recently."

"Because things are going so well?"

"Yes. But you're right, I should make it official. I will discuss this with Eli."

"Good."

THE PARTY WENT on until midnight. Some guests took their children home and came back. My mother went home with Selorm, and Aunty retired upstairs. Those who had come from Ho reluctantly boarded the bus that Eli had hired to bring them; they were the last to leave.

"Did you enjoy yourself?" he asked me as we drove home. I could barely keep my eyes open.

"I did. Thank you."

"For what?"

"For organizing everything."

"I didn't do anything," he said and reached for my hand.

At that moment, I felt my heart would burst with joy.

THIRTEEN

Eli and I were scheduled to travel to Paris in two weeks. Joanna, his assistant, had braved the chaos, inefficiency, and corruption at the passport office to get my first passport about a year before. Getting a French visa had been easy; all I had to do was attach bank statements from one of Eli's accounts to my application. We had done all of this while I was pregnant, but of course traveling during that time was out of the question. Not when I could barely make it down the stairs on most days. And after Selorm was born, I couldn't bear the thought of leaving him for more than a day and was too busy getting the boutique ready for our grand opening to travel for leisure. But now that Selorm was a bit older and I could depend on Ellen and Nancy to manage the boutique and workshop while I was away, Eli and I had agreed to take a one-week vacation to Paris.

I would be a liar if I said I wasn't excited. It would be my first time on a plane and we would be going to Paris of all places. I'd seen movies set in Paris, the glamorous people and the fabulous clothes. I planned to visit as many boutiques as I could to see how mine compared and what new ideas I could get. Joanna had booked a suite in a small hotel close to the Louvre and in addition to visiting boutiques in the shopping districts, we were going to see all of the sites that I'd only ever before read about and seen on TV.

More importantly I planned to propose to Eli on the trip. Mawusi burst into laughter when I told her this.

"Propose?"

"Yes. I'll surprise him."

"You're mad," she said, still laughing.

"What's wrong with it? I'm just having fun and I think he will like it."

"So you will do the whole going down on bended knee thing?"

"Yes, I might even give him a rose," I said, joining her in laughing.

"How about a ring?"

"He already wears a ring, we both wear our rings from the traditional ceremony. Or do you think I should get new ones?"

"No, the ones you have are already very nice. Didn't Richard buy them?"

"Yes, and they're proper gold, ehn, and mine has a diamond in it."

"Then just use that. I still think you're crazy though."

"It's ok to be a bit crazy and to have a bit of fun."

"That's true, and it's romantic."

"Right? A Parisian proposal," I practically squealed. My mother would take care of Selorm while we were gone. But before we left, Eli had to make a three-day visit to Nigeria where he had meetings with Chris and Ade. He would be gone from Thursday to Sunday and I also had to be away at work for most of that Saturday.

Evelyn called at the last minute to say that she had scheduled a fashion shoot at a beach house in Ada for our second ad campaign. The first had been a hit and really put us on the map. But this Saturday shoot was totally unexpected. We had agreed to do the shoot after I returned from France, but another client had booked a shoot and then cancelled at the last minute so that Evelyn's agency now had a location, photographer, hairstylist, make-up artist, models, and caterer, but no products. I didn't want to take Selorm with me because I knew I would be running around the entire day but I had no choice. My mother couldn't get to Accra until much later on Saturday because she had an order for pies, the largest she had gotten since she started baking again. She would leave Ho around noon and would be in Accra in about three hours but I couldn't wait for her; the shoot was scheduled to start early Saturday morning. But at least she would be at home to take Selorm off my hands after the shoot and would stay until Eli and I returned from our vacation.

Nancy and I spent all of Friday in the workshop, getting the tailors to finish our latest designs. In fact, I found myself behind a sewing machine for the first time in months to help them. We worked past midnight but weren't able to complete

254 • PEACE ADZO MEDIE

everything. Some of the outfits would have to be pinned onto the models. Nancy and I loaded the racks of clothes into a van that I borrowed from Richard and we were ready to leave on Saturday morning. Richard lent us a driver, who drove the van while Yeboah drove my car with Selorm, Nancy, and me in it to the location, which was about a hundred kilometers outside of Accra.

THE SHOOT WAS in someone's house in a gated beachside community. I was amazed when we parked and got out of the van. The beach was pristine and the water clear. The trash that littered some of the beaches in Accra hadn't made it this far. Houses with large windows and sliding glass doors lined the beachfront. Children with colorful plastic spades and buckets dug into the sand in front of the house nearest to us. I would have taken Selorm over to play with them if he was a bit older. Evelyn helped Nancy and me unload the clothes onto the front porch. Today she wore striped shorts and a T-shirt. I had on an A-line dress that fell slightly above my knee. We both wore flip flops. We had barely finished when the photographer, make-up artist, hairstylist, and models pulled up in a minibus, speakers blaring. Evelyn ran up to the bus and yelled at them to turn the music down.

"Bush people," she muttered when she returned to my side. This was not the kind of place to blare music. People moved to places like this to run away from loud music and noise. I gave Selorm to her and went inside to check on Nancy.

The only person yet to arrive was the caterer who had been hired to feed us, but we weren't going to wait for him. The hair and makeup people began working on the models while we began fitting them into the clothes. Evelyn reminded me that these things could drag on for hours so we had to move quickly. She had a date with her lawyer that evening and Selorm would start to get fussy soon. I set up a play area for him in the room where we had the clothes and made sure that either Nancy, Evelyn, or myself was in there to keep an eye on him at all times. While we got the models ready, the photographer and his assistant set up his equipment outside. The first model, who looked like she was no more than sixteen, had closely cropped hair and freckles everywhere. We put her in a white linen shift that had strips of color at the bottom. It was a perfect look for the beach. The photographer began snapping as soon as she came out of the house. I stood on the balcony for a moment and looked on, pleased. I could use that shot for a full-page ad in one of the glossy magazines that I saw when I visited the hairdresser's. Luckily, the children had disappeared so there was nothing but sand and water in the shot. I went back inside to help Nancy get the other models ready. The hairdresser and makeup artists worked alongside us, teasing hair into every imaginable style and using combinations of color that I would never try on my face. The girls looked like beautiful works of art. I was sad to see them wipe off one look for another when they changed outfits. It was soon midday and everyone was hungry. The caterer had come about thirty minutes before and set up a table outside but the wind and the sand it carried sent all of us scurrying into the beautiful house. I had already fed Selorm who was now becoming clingy and wouldn't let Nancy touch him. I knew that sleep was not far behind. He sat on my lap as I ate.

"Shoes off. Don't touch anything; don't spill anything. I'm paying serious money for this house," Evelyn warned everyone. Every five minutes or so she would walk around and inspect to make sure that no one had pawed the white walls or spilled food on the cream-colored shag rug. When the shoot restarted, I heard a child crying. Evelyn was on the phone in the bedroom with her lawyer friend so I went outside to find out what was happening. Selorm was balanced on my hip and falling asleep. There, I saw a woman holding a little girl's hand and walking away.

"What happened?" I asked the photographer.

"Oh madam, don't mind that woman. My boy just shouted at her daughter and she got angry," the man said. He was shirtless and appeared to be under the illusion that he was the subject of the photographs.

"He hit the girl," the young model with the freckles said. "How can you just hit someone's child?"

"I didn't hit her; I just touched her head like this," the photographer's assistant said while tapping his own head to show me what he had done.

"But why would you do that?" I asked him, enraged. I would fight anyone, man or woman, who touched my son.

"Madam, the children were ruining the shots. I was trying to get rid of them."

"So you had to hit the child?" I asked him.

"He didn't hit the child; you people are talking like he beat her," the photographer, his hands on his hips, told us. I had a sudden urge to grab his oddly big nipples and twist them until he fell to the sand in pain.

"What do you mean? Do you think that this is your village where you can just go around disciplining other people's children? Look at where we are. Do you know the kind of people who live in these houses? Do you think that this is the kind of place where you can come and hit children? What if they call the estate manager and kick us out? Or call the police?"

The photographer rubbed his head and laughed nervously while his assistant looked on with a clown-like smile on his face. They obviously hadn't thought that far. I decided to go over to apologize to the woman.

THE HOUSE NEXT door was a replica of the one we had rented. My arms were aching by the time I got there. Selorm, now asleep, was heavy, his head on my shoulder. The glass door was open and Highlife music played in the background. The woman met me at the door.

"Hello," she said, looking puzzled. I figured strangers didn't come to her door often.

"Hi," I responded, staring at her. I don't think I'd ever seen a more beautiful woman in my life. Not in person, anyway. She had the darkest skin I'd ever seen, but it glowed. I imagined that is what gold would look like if it were black. She had a heart-shaped face and high cheekbones and was slim and much taller than I was. Her limbs made me think of the ballet dancers I glimpsed on TV as I clicked through channels. I imagined that she did everything gracefully. A flowing, ocean-blue, halter-neck dress billowed around her in the sea breeze and she was barefoot. I could build my entire ad-campaign around her. It would be unfair to place any other models beside her in a shoot. Behind her, four children were bent over a large jigsaw puzzle on the floor. I immediately knew which one was hers.

"I'm from next door, I came to see if your daughter is okay," I said while doing my best not to gawk. She took a step back into the house and I realized that my staring was making her uncomfortable. I too took a step back.

"She's okay. Thanks for coming. There was no reason for him to touch her; she would have moved if he had asked. I don't know why people behave like this." She didn't sound Ghanaian.

"That's what I told him. I'm so sorry."

"I appreciate . . ." she began but was interrupted by someone inside the house. "Babe, who is it?"

"It's someone from next door," she yelled back. Even her yell was graceful, smooth like a musical note.

"Who?" he asked, walking out of the kitchen. He stopped when he saw me.

"Afi?"

"Eli?"

I'd often fantasized about what I would do when I met the woman. These fantasies varied depending on my mood. I would slap her and walk away without saying a word. Or I would give her a vicious tongue-lashing that would leave her sobbing and begging my forgiveness. I would call her a shameless husband-snatcher and a home-wrecker. I would ululate so that everyone around would gather as she huddled on the ground in a public place and join me in humiliating her. I would punish her for all the heartache she had caused me, for the sleepless nights and the tears. But now I just stood there staring at Eli and the only thing that I could think was that the Ganyos had lied to me. They had told me she was ugly. But there she was, the most beautiful woman I had ever seen.

We were motionless, except for Selorm, who lifted his head off my shoulder. I don't know if it was because he sensed something was wrong or if he had heard his father's voice. But when he turned his head, Ivy shouted his name and came running onto the porch. Her mother held her shoulders and stopped her before she could reach me. To my surprise, Selorm stretched out both hands to the woman. I took a step back and held him closer to me.

"Afi, let's go." It was Evelyn, I hadn't heard her come up behind me. Despite her words, I couldn't get myself to move, I couldn't take my eyes off Eli. He was shirtless and wearing swim shorts. He held a dishtowel in his hand. He was staring at me, confusion and guilt mingled on his face. I felt a grip on my arm. Evelyn tugged until I began to move and then she guided me off the porch and into the sand. As we walked away, Selorm fidgeting and still trying to get away from me, I turned to look back. Eli and the woman were still standing where I'd left them. They were looking at me but he didn't come after me.

WE ENDED THE shoot. The models, photographer, hairdresser, and makeup artist drove away. They were followed by Yeboah, who would drop Nancy off at the workshop before continuing home. I would ride back with Evelyn.

"Are you okay?" she asked me. We'd been driving for about five minutes. Selorm was asleep in the car seat.

"You knew, didn't you?" I asked in anger.

"I knew? That he was there with her? Why would I take you there if I knew, Afi?"

My jaw was clenched and I was breathing very fast but I wasn't crying. I wasn't going to cry.

"But you knew he's been with her this whole time. That he's been taking my son to see her."

"Of course not! I would have told you. Didn't I tell you before when I knew he was hiding things from you? I swear to God, I had no idea. I mean, we all know he goes to the house to see Ivy but that's it."

"And the Ganyos know?"

"I don't think so. I can't remember the last time Richard mentioned her and even when he has, it has been to rejoice that she's no longer in their lives. I think Eli convinced all of them that he was no longer with her."

I fell silent. I rolled down the window, even though the air conditioner was on, and let the wind pound my face. Evelyn, who drove like a race-car driver, passed every other vehicle on the road. I willed her to go even faster. I wished I could feel the wind on my entire body. I relaxed in my seat and rolled up the window when my neck began to hurt.

"They said she was ugly."

"Hmmm?"

"They said she looked like a man."

"They said many things about her that are not true. I was also shocked when I first met her, after everything that Richard had told me."

"Why?"

"Why was I shocked?"

"No, why did they say things that are not true?"

"Because Aunty doesn't like her. The brothers don't like her. Yaya doesn't like her. She does as she pleases and doesn't care what they want. She doesn't follow their rules, she doesn't care about our traditions. She did not let the family outdoor her daughter. She has no problem refusing to visit Ho, even on important occasions. You won't see her in Ho every weekend at a funeral or at some other event. When she was in that house in East Legon, they couldn't come and go as they pleased. They had to first call and say they were coming, and as soon as they arrived, they had to tell her when they planned to leave; even Aunty, who now prances in and out of your house as she pleases. They couldn't just walk into the house and start taking food out of the fridge or ordering the cook around. That has been the problem from the beginning, from the first time that Richard met her in Liberia, and that is why they tried so hard to separate them even then. But you've seen the woman; she's not the kind of woman that a man just walks away from, even a man like Eli whose love for his mother has become folklore in Ho. The only thing Aunty could do was forbid Eli from marrying her and to get the old uncles to back her. And we both know there's no way he can marry a woman without his family's blessing. I know one guy from university who did that and he hasn't been able to visit his hometown since. Can you believe it? It's been more than ten years and he hasn't been able to go home! Muna is too proud to give in to Aunty, and Eli will do what he can to please his mother . . . while she's alive."

"And when she's dead?"

"Well, she's the ringleader in this whole thing. Once she's out of the picture, well . . ."

MY MOTHER WAS in the house when I arrived but I didn't tell her what had happened. Instead, I locked myself in our bedroom. I was feeling a mix of sadness and fury, but the latter seemed to be gaining the upper hand. About an hour after I arrived, I heard Eli trying to get into the bedroom. He knocked a few times and called my name but I refused to unlock the door. A few minutes later I heard another knock.

"What do you want?" I shouted.

"Selorm is crying for you. His father has tried to calm him but he won't stop." It was my mother.

I could hear my son crying on the other side of the heavy wooden door. I opened it and took Selorm out of her arms but blocked her path when she tried to follow me into the room. I knew she wanted to find out what was going on and I wasn't in the mood to explain anything to her or to hear what she had to say. I placed Selorm on the bed. He had already stopped crying and was punching the buttons on one of Eli's phones. I hadn't even realized he was holding it. Eli must have given it to him downstairs. I pried the phone away from his surprisingly tight grip and gave him mine when he began crying in protest. Eli's phone was unlocked. I scrolled through his call log. He hadn't made any calls in about three hours. I switched to his text messages. About half of them were to his brothers and business partners. A few were to Yaya. The others were to M. It had to be her. I began reading the messages. Many of them were about Ivy. But many more were also just about the woman. He missed her smile and her body. He wished she was in his arms. He couldn't wait to see her, to hold her. He adored her, felt blessed to have her, loved her. I felt tears run down my face. Most of the messages were from this month. He had sent her seventy-four messages in that week alone, and while some were sent when he was at work, most of them were sent from home. In fact, I noticed that he mostly called her during the day and texted in the night. The time stamp also showed that many of those texts were sent when we were together in bed. He had texted her while we were in bed on Wednesday night, discussing our Paris trip. I had gotten used to him being glued to his many phones and the tap tap tap as he sent messages. I'd been so foolish as to believe that those messages were for work. I picked Selorm up and we went downstairs. My mother was in the sitting room watching a Nigerian film. I handed Selorm back to her.

"Where's Eli?"

"He's outside. Afi, what is happening?"

"Nothing."

I passed Mrs. Adams in the kitchen and went into the backyard where Eli was seated, an expression akin to fear on his face. I sat across from him and placed his phone on the table. He picked it up. A look of renewed panic came on his face as he realized that it was unlocked.

"I'm sorry. I never wanted this to happen; I'm sorry," he said. His voice was low and he was not making eye contact.

"What am I going to do with your sorry, Eli?"

"We can make this work."

"Are you ever going to leave her?"

"Afi, let's not do this . . ."

"Ok, marry me," I said, desperation causing my words to come out in a rush.

"What?"

"I said marry me. Let's go to the church on Monday and get married. Father Wisdom can arrange everything and we can be married in less than thirty minutes."

"What are you talking about? We're traveling on Monday."

"There's a flight to Paris every day and the airline won't charge you a fee for changing the dates because of your frequent flier status; you told me that yourself. Not that it would matter if they charged you. So let's leave on Tuesday. But on Monday, let's go to Ho and get married."

"Afi . . .why . . .this is not the time."

"This is the time. Now. If you love me, let's get married in church."

"Afi, you know . . ."

"Stop. Just stop. I don't want to hear about you sorting things out. I don't want to hear any of that. Just be honest with me. Will you marry me or not? Just for once, Eli, tell me the truth."

He sighed and leaned back in the wrought-iron garden chair. His weight pushed the legs deeper into the soil. He looked down at the phone, which he'd placed on his lap, and then looked back up at me. "I can't do that, Afi, I can't marry you. I'm sorry." His voice shook.

"Because you want to marry her? You want to marry her when your mother dies. You want to marry her and you want her to be equal to me and you know that we both can't have a church wedding. So if we both can't have a church wedding then neither of us will have it."

He didn't say a word.

"Was there ever, ever a moment in this marriage when you thought of me as the only one, when you wanted only me?"

He didn't answer me.

"Why do you love her so much? Why am I not enough for you?" I said, my voice breaking.

"Afi, you know I love you."

"But you love her more than me. Don't you?"

"What kind of question is that, Afi?"

"It's a very simple question. Yes or no. Do you love her more than me?"

"I love you both."

"Do you love her more?"

"I love you both."

"You love us both so you will marry us both, because you're special and deserve to have everything you want. Everything! But I don't deserve to have what I want, what I've suffered for."

"You will still be my wife, my first wife. It won't be any different from the arrangement we have now."

"We both know you plan to go back to how things were. To sleeping in two homes and driving around Accra with a traveling bag in the trunk of your car. It's only a matter of time; this show that you're putting on for your mother is not going to last forever. I'm not ready to go back to that. I won't go back to lying in bed alone and crying for you. Crying for you while you take my son to live in another woman's house."

"Afi . . ."

"Don't say my name. And don't you dare call our marriage an arrangement. We don't have an arrangement, I'm your wife! Your family married me for you. All of our relatives were there. Father Wisdom was there. I'm your wife!"

"That doesn't mean I can't have a second wife. Please be reasonable, Afi."

"Reasonable? You are wicked. You are a liar."

"I never lied to you. I never told you I was going to leave her. Never."

He slept in the guestroom that night, and the next day I told him I wanted a divorce. We were standing on opposite sides of the kitchen, our backs against the countertop. Sensing the mood, Mrs. Adams and her helper had made themselves scarce. It was a Sunday and my mother had taken Selorm to church with her. I was considerably calmer than the day before. Probably because I was exhausted after having stayed up all night, thinking about what I would do and what my decision would mean for me and Selorm. No matter how hard I tried, my spirit continued to rebel at the idea of me as one of Eli's wives. Just the thought of him sharing a home with her left me feeling hot, as though the air conditioner had been turned off, and caused a dull ache to take over one side of my head. By the time the first sunlight filtered through my curtains, I was certain that I would rather live without him than share him with her. "I want a divorce," I said quietly.

"Divorce? You can't be serious, Afi. Because of this?" His incredulity surprised and angered me. So he really expected me to sit quietly and accept whatever he threw at me?

"Yes, because of this. Because you've been cheating on me and lying to me. Because I don't want another woman in our marriage."

"Stop being unreasonable," he said, a cup of coffee in hand. He had been holding it without touching it to his lips since he came into the kitchen.

"I really hate it when you say that!" I said, glaring at him.

"Say what?"

"When you dismiss my pain and suffering as unreasonable. When you refuse even for a minute to empathize with me. How would you feel if I cheated on you? If I told you I wanted to be with another man while married to you?"

He put his coffee mug down and scoffed. "That's different, Afi. You know it's not the same thing."

"It's the same thing, but you would never agree to it. So why should I agree to this, to you being with her?"

He took a step forward and I scooted sideways. I didn't want him to touch me. A pained look settled on his face. "Okay, fine," he said very slowly, locking eyes with me. "Let's not waste our time on hypotheticals. I'm sorry about everything, I'm sorry I hurt you. I know that this is very difficult for you; it is difficult for me too. I love you and I love the life we have together. I don't want to lose this, to lose you."

"You love me, but not enough to leave her and be with me?"

"Darling, I can do anything for you, but not that. She's my family too, I can't leave her. Just like I would never leave you."

"Then stay with her, I will go," my voice caught in my throat as I realized that we were nearing the end, that he would not change his mind.

"Please don't say this, Afi."

"I wish you had told me all of this before I fell in love with you."

"I never meant to hurt you."

"But you have and I can't be with you anymore."

"Afi, don't do this. Think about Selorm, think about our baby, don't do this to him."

"I'm not the one doing anything to him, it's you. You are the one breaking apart our family because of another woman. You should at least take responsibility for that."

He begged me to reconsider but I refused. It was either the woman or me; he couldn't have both of us. He grabbed my hand when I tried to walk out of the kitchen and I jerked it away from him. I saw tears in his eyes as I turned to walk away but I steeled myself. My mother also began to cry when I told her but I think she already knew that there was nothing she could do. Mawusi, on the other hand, tried much harder to get me to change my mind. She was determined to salvage the fairytale.

"Afi, he's a good man. Apart from this thing, he's a good man. You have to remember that. And what he's proposing is not ideal and it's not common like before, but people still do it. I even know women with university degrees, doctors and lawyers, big, big, women, who are co-wives. It's manageable as long as the man is not like my father who'll make all of the women stay in the same house and refuse to take care of his children." She was sitting with me in my bedroom. My mother had called her to come over as soon as I announced my decision.

"Mawusi, you don't know what it feels like, how it hurts. He wants to marry her. I cannot live with that, I cannot live with that woman in our marriage."

"He said he loves you both."

"Ah! Even parents do not love their children equally; how much more a man and his wives? If he really loved me, he would have left her a long time ago. But I'm obviously not enough for him. After all this time, after all I've done, after Selorm, and I'm still not enough for him. How would you feel if Yao did this to you?"

"This is different."

"Because he's rich?"

"No, because you can still have what you've always dreamed of. A good life with a man who loves you, and is kind, and takes care of you."

"I want more than that. I want him to be mine only. Is that too much to ask? I'm sorry that I'm not like other wives who are able to happily share their husbands with co-wives and mistresses and girlfriends. That's just not me. I'm not built like that. Look at what happened when I was pregnant. I can't live the rest of my life with that kind of heartache."

"It will get better with time."

"How do you know? The last time it got worse. I used to lie in bed pregnant and convinced that the sadness would strangle me. The longer I stay in this marriage, the longer it will hurt. It will either drive me insane or leave me permanently depressed, and that's not the life I want for myself or my son."

She sighed heavily. "Afi, you know that people will talk."

"Let them talk. Am I the first woman to ask for a divorce in this country? Women do it all the time and their lives don't come to an end. They continue to breathe and work and some of them even manage to find love again. Why should I be any different? I'm still young, my business is doing well, I will work and take care of myself and my son. Even if Eli decides not to give me one cedi after today, we will still be fine."

"Hmmm. Where are you going to find a man like Elikem Ganyo to marry you again? Especially now that you have a child?"

"I don't want to marry a man like him again."

MAWUSI HAD BARELY left before Richard and Yaya came. It couldn't have been a coincidence; their brother must have called them. I was sitting on the back porch, getting some air and.watching Selorm try to kick a ball in the grass. My mother was taking a nap after complaining about a headache and Eli was upstairs. His brother and sister came outside to talk to me.

"Eli told us what happened," Richard said quietly, his hands folded in his lap. I don't think I had ever seen him so serious. They were seated across from me. For the first time since I had known her, Yaya was dressed in jeans and a T-shirt, her hair in a bun, slides on her feet, and no makeup on her face. She looked like she had rushed out of her house.

"Hmmm," was all I said before looking past them to see what Selorm was doing.

"Remember, I told you that this woman did something to my brother, this is not the Eli we know. The woman is evil, pure evil, she ∴ . ."

"Please, just stop there," I said, cutting him off. "She hasn't done anything to your brother. Eli just wants to have his cake and eat it. He thinks he should be free to accumulate as many cars and houses and women as he wants. He never intended to leave that woman and you all knew it, but you led me to believe that it was just a matter of time." Richard appeared shocked at my words, his eyebrows climbing his forehead. He obviously still thought that I was the same girl he sat on my mother's verandah with, spinning tales about the Liberian woman.

"Be careful what you say, Afi. Don't insult us," Yaya said, a forefinger and her voice raised in warning to me.

How dare her, after all they had put me through. I had had enough of her, and her mother, and her brothers. "Don't tell me to be careful! Didn't you people tell me that he was going to leave her? And now two years later you are back, telling me it's spiritual, that she has scrambled his brains so that he can no longer think straight. Why can't you just admit that your brother was with a woman that none of you liked and so you tried to use me to get him to leave her. Just admit that she's not crazy, or manly, or suicidal, or an alcoholic, or a chain-smoker, or a bad mother. There's nothing wrong with her! She's a woman who you don't like because she does as she pleases and doesn't dance to your tune. You shouldn't have dragged me into this. You should have fixed it without involving me. Or better still, you should have just let your brother be with whomever he chose." I was enraged and saying everything I had thought about last night as I paced my bedroom, fearing that the pain ripping through my chest would never stop.

"Haha," Yaya said drily, rolling her eyes and clapping slowly. "Dragged you? You, Afi, who was stitching rags together and calling yourself a seamstress in Ho. Dragged you? You should be grateful that we rescued you from that miserable existence and gave you the life you have now." Her eyes flashed as she spoke and for the first time, I noticed that she closely resembled her mother.

"Yaya," Richard said and touched his sister's shoulder but she shrugged his hand off and rose to her feet. I stood up too. My words had pushed her buttons and caused her to show me her true colors.

"You want the truth? This is the truth: We picked you from the gutter and gave you a life that you would not have had in a thousand years. There are countless women in this country with pretty faces and fat asses—you are not special. We could have chosen any one of them for my brother. How far do you think that face and body would have taken you? Where would your high school degree have taken you in this country where even university graduates can't make it? You were nothing and you are still nothing. Think about that before saying that you are divorcing him and allowing that woman to come back into this house."

"Get out," I said, nose to nose with her. Her words stung.

"Me get out? Is this your house? Did you buy this house? You are only here because we have allowed you to be here."

"Okay then, watch me leave." I scooped up Selorm and took him inside, leaving them on the porch.

"Ah, Yaya. Why?" I heard Richard say in exasperation as I walked away.

NEITHER MY MOTHER nor I bothered to tell Aunty what was happening in Accra. That was her son's job. Instead I called Tɔgã Pious and told him to return the schnapps to the Ganyos.

"What are you saying, Afi?" He had only recently begun to talk to me again after the issue with the money I gave him at Christmas.

"I'm saying I don't want to be in this marriage anymore so please return their drinks so it can be over."

"What happened? Come home and let us talk about it. There has to be a way to solve this."

"There's no way; please return the drinks."

"Afi, you can't just leave your husband like that. And what are we supposed to tell the family when we go? You have to at least come home first."

I WENT TO Ho with my mother and Selorm on Monday morning and bought two bottles of schnapps on the way, the same brand that Richard had given to my uncle at the wedding. In Ho, my uncles and Aunty Sylvia, who had come from Togo that dawn, tried to change my mind. Tɔgã Pious begged me more than Eli had; you would have thought he was begging for his life. We were in his sitting room, the same room in which I had waited on the day of my marriage to Eli. The louvre blades were shut because they didn't want a word of this to get out.

"What will people say about us?" Uncle Bright asked.

"Uncle, I don't care what people say."

"Of course it's easy for you not to care. You live in Accra. We are the ones who live in Ho and have to face our neighbors every day. Will we even be able to go to the depot to buy things after this? You know my wife buys flour from there and Aunty allows her to buy on credit. She only pays after she has sold the bread. So stop thinking only about yourself and think of us," Uncle Excellent said.

"If you refuse to go to Aunty's house, I will return the drinks myself," I told them.

"Heeeeeeeeey," Aunty Sylvia shouted in shock and folded her hands on top of her head as if she had just received news of a death in the family.

"Olivia, what is wrong with your daughter, what kind of new madness is this? Have you heard of a woman returning her drinks before? Do you not have people?" Tɔgã Pious said. He was now on his feet and pacing the small room. My mother ignored him and fanned Selorm with a newspaper. He had been fretting in the heat.

"I'm saying that if you refuse to take it back, I will."

"You'll not rest until you shame all of us, until we all become outcasts in this town. I thank God my brother Illustrious is not here to see what you're doing."

"I wouldn't have married Eli if my father was alive. He would never have agreed to this marriage."

THEY SAID AUNTY smashed one bottle of schnapps against a wall when they went to her house to return the drinks. This was after she told them she wouldn't accept that I was leaving her son. She cursed me and my mother and threatened to deal with me severely. Aunty Sylvia said spittle had begun to bubble in the corners of the old woman's mouth as she spoke, like some kind of rabid animal. Halfway through her rant, she had had to pause and gulp air like a dying fish. I just shook my head when Aunty Sylvia told me this. I was no longer afraid of Aunty.

Evelyn was silent for a while when I recounted all of this to her. She was visiting me in the workshop. I had converted one of the rooms back into a bedroom, which I shared with Selorm. My mother slept in the second room.

"I don't really know what to say," she finally said.

"You want to say that I should have learned to enjoy the money and ignore his faults."

She chuckled. "Yes, that's true. But also that you should be happy—most importantly, that you should be happy. That you should have your peace of mind. That marriage shouldn't be a never-ending competition where you spend your life fighting to be seen and chosen. That all the money in the world is not worth the pain and tears and sleepless nights. So you did good and you will be fine. You are smart and you are not afraid of hard work; you will be fine."

"Eli said he will give me money for Selorm every month. And he said I can keep the car and driver and have one of the houses."

"But of course, that's the least he can do."

"But I've had enough of living in other people's houses, I want my own. I . . ."

"Let me stop you right there. You had better accept that car and house and even ask him to add a flat and another car to it. Think of it as payment for what he put you through. It is not other people's house; it is your house! Just make sure that he puts your name on the title. In fact, make sure your name is on every piece of paper, for the house, the car, everything. I know a lawyer that can fast-track it; I will take you there myself. As long as your name is on the title, Small Aunty will not be able to open her big mouth to tell you nonsense. You have to be tough, Afi. Make sure your name is on every document, make sure Selorm's name is on every document, so that tomorrow if something happens to Eli, you will get what you are entitled to."

I smiled knowingly.

"Why are you smiling? I'm serious."

"I know and I will think about it."

"There's nothing to think about, just do it."

"You know, I wish I was strong like you. Then I would have been able to accept him being with another woman, then I would still have him. I mean, a lot of women are co-wives and they are happy."

"Afi, you are not weak, there is nothing weak about you. Do you hear me? Don't even think that. It takes strength to walk away from someone you love. You were brave to say that you didn't want to be miserable, to have your heart break every time he walks out the door. I know I said to love with your head but I'm also the first person to tell you that it is hard to live like that. It is brutal and it eats at you every day and leaves you empty. Don't beat yourself up for not choosing that life; you did the right thing. You deserve to be happy, to be with a man who wants to be only yours."

I nodded as my friend spoke. Deep inside, I knew she was right. But my heart still needed to be persuaded.

IT'S BEEN FIVE weeks since I moved out of Eli's house and into my workshop. I had to fight with him over my decision. He didn't want Selorm living in the workshop, he wanted us to move into one of his houses, but I wasn't willing to go back to that. I wanted to live in a house where my name was on the title or where I paid rent, even if my landlord was his brother. While we went back and forth about this, we reached a compromise on where Selorm and I would live in the interim; he brought in workers to extend the boys' quarters behind the workshop so that all of the production moved there. Mawusi helped me shop for furniture for the house while Nancy and my mother did most of the setting up. It doesn't seem like my mother will be going back to Ho for a while. She recently joined the Women's Guild here and has started baking pastries, which I serve in the boutique alongside the fruit juices. Customers have even begun buying them to take away. I'm opening up a second boutique in

Cantonments, a few minutes away from Fred's house. I plan to slowly transition from the tower to this second boutique because the rent is more affordable. I want to clear out of the tower and give the space back to Eli. Evelyn's ad campaign generated so much business that I'm confident I will be able to expand to a third location soon, and maybe overseas. I'm thinking about a branch in Lagos. I'm also thinking seriously about opening an accessories-only store. I now have more than three people supplying me with all variety of beads and there isn't enough space for all of the trendy bags and shoes that artisans are making and trying to get me to stock in the boutiques. I even have a few of Sarah's bags on display. We still talk every once in a while, although I'm sure Yaya doesn't know this. In fact, we've never brought up my ex-sister-in-law in our conversations. Richard has been to the house a few times, always on landlord business. I was nervous the first time he came but I was relieved to see that he didn't treat me differently. But he didn't bring up his brother either. Evelyn asked me last week if I'm angry with Richard and I told her no. Yes, he lied to me about the woman, but I no longer have regrets, not when I have Selorm.

Eli comes by several times a week. I haven't tried to stop him from seeing Selorm; we've agreed that he can come by as often as he wants, he just has to tell me beforehand. I've also asked that he keep my son away from his woman. I heard from Evelyn that she has not moved back into the house. But how can she, when Aunty has instructed Yaya to move in and take care of her brother, as though the houseful of servants is not enough, as though Eli is a baby who can't take care of himself. He usually doesn't stay long when he comes here and he's mostly in the bedroom with Selorm or in the front yard. I try to stay away from the house when he gives me enough warning of his visits. I have to do this because my heart still beats wildly when I see him. I still wish that he had been at our wedding, that he, instead of Richard, had given me the ring and the Bible, that he had married me, that he'd wanted me to be his wife, his only wife.

ACKNOWLEDGMENTS

Chuck Adams, for being a thoughtful editor, and the entire team at Algonquin for giving Afi a chance.

Kiele Raymond, my agent—for believing and sharing my vision for Afi.

Kuukuwa, Nana Ama, and Teki—hype women extraordinaire.

Adobia—for the support, for always listening.

Erica, my first reader—for giving me hope, for laughing with me.

This book is dedicated to my grandmother, who created a space where I could write.

Akpe na mi.

9/21 - 4 (2/21)
5/24 - 5 (12/21)